DRIFT

RACHEL HATCH BOOK ONE

LT RYAN

with
BRIAN SHEA

LIQUID MIND MEDIA

THE RACHEL HATCH SERIES

Drift

Downburst

Fever Burn

Smoke Signal

Firewalk

Whitewater

Aftershock

Whirlwind

Tsunami

Fastrope (Coming Soon)

RACHEL HATCH SHORT STORIES

Fractured

Proving Ground

The Gauntlet

1

THE SMALL FORD FIESTA HAD BEEN PARKED BETWEEN THE LARGE Blue Spruce and massive boulder since nightfall. It was their spot, secluded and hidden from the main road. They'd used it many times before and had grown confident few ventured to this remote section of the lake. Which was why they'd selected it many months back. The smell shrouding the air around them was an obnoxious chemical odor that could burn the lining in your nose. A byproduct of their chosen career path. The openness of their locale managed to mitigate some of the stench, but not all. Even in the rural areas, neighbors took notice of such things. And it was for this reason they'd been careful in their scouting.

The two men sat on a rock looking out at the lake. The stillness of the water gave a glass-like quality to the surface, serving to bounce the moon's glow up onto the surrounding hills. More light to work by, but that also meant more light to be spotted by a curious hiker or fisherman.

Steve Swanson worked a lump of tobacco from the left to the right side of his mouth. "How long we been goin' at it?"

"Do I look like a damn clock to you?" Barry Munson shook his head. He was the older of the two by four years, and had somehow become the de facto leader of their operation. A clout he used with increasing frequency to verbally abuse the younger man. "It was dark when we started. Darker now. If you're so damned concerned about the time, get a watch. If you had one, then you wouldn't have to ask me every time we took a break."

Swanson pulled off his red paisley bandana. Even in the crisp, cool autumn night air, sweat had pooled around the undercarriage of his nostrils. Making the devil's brew, as he called it, was hard work. His wire-thin mustache was moistened, glimmering like morning dew on a wheat field. He wiped at it absently, transferring the glisten to his forearm as he sought to find a comeback to Munson's latest taunt. Nothing witty came to him. Nothing ever did. If he was ever to work up the nerve to talk back, it would most likely end with him catching a beating from the bigger man.

"Just feels like we've been burping that last batch forever," Swanson said.

"This is the best run we've had in a few weeks. Gonna make some good money on this." Munson thumbed back toward the various pots and glass beakers on the flat rock behind them.

Tendrils of noxious gas snaked into the air as the pots cooled. The chemical's reaction peak had fallen off. Once it stopped altogether, they'd dump it and run a new batch. Swanson had learned how to cook meth using a cheap and easy system called the one-pot method. It was a dangerous technique in which all the ingredients were put into the bottom of a big-mouthed bottle of soda. Swanson's bottle of choice was the one-liter Mountain Dew. The heavy plastic worked well to prevent breakdown during the volatile reaction of lithium and water.

During the reactive process, a good cook must learn to feel the pressure within by gently squeezing. Like a good chef can press a steak on a grill and know whether it's medium or well-done, a meth cook needs to have the same ability and know when to "burp" the bottle by opening the cap at the proper interval to release the gas. Swanson's inability to master this technique is what had indirectly brought Munson and him together.

About a year ago, Swanson had been doing the one-pot in the woods behind the town's post office when the bottle he was using exploded. The lithium infused water burned the left side of Swanson's face and hand. When he woke in the hospital several hours later, he was shocked to find he'd been handcuffed to the metal arm of a medical bed. Apparently, the local deputies didn't take pity on the burned man. They'd found his stash of finished product and charged him with operating a drug factory. Hard to make the argument the drugs weren't his when Swanson's face bore the evidence.

It was during his stint in the county lockup subsequent to his failed entrepreneurship that Swanson and Munson first met. Much of their time was spent talking women and drugs. Not much else to do when you're cut off from the outside world. Bonding over their mutual love of crystal methamphetamine, the two would spend hours discussing the best methods for cooking. Comparing epic highs was another pastime, as each tried to outdo the other's story of drug-induced euphoria. Swanson got out a few weeks earlier than Munson, but the two promised to keep in touch. Swanson kept his word, and when Munson was released, he was there to pick him up. The two had been collaborating in the hopes of expanding their production efforts ever since.

"Wanna give it a little taste?" Munson asked. Only three teeth were visibly present in the man's gapped smile.

If Swanson's weakness was his cooking technique, then Munson's was that he couldn't stop himself from using the product they created. It was a big hiccup in their *Breaking Bad* scheme to get rich selling crystal. They ended up smoking most of the fruits of their hours of toil, forcing them to resort to their old habits of stealing the necessary ingredients.

Swanson couldn't resist the temptation when presented and readily agreed to sample the goods.

Munson disappeared to the flat rock they'd affectionately named "the lab." It was a naturally formed, perfectly flat surface they used to set up their homemade chemistry laboratory. The rock's surface now bore the scars of their work in the stained dye from the Sudafed they used as their source for ephedrine, a key ingredient in their formula.

Swanson watched as his partner hustled back with a small clear plastic bag in hand, the contents of which looked like broken bits of glass or rock candy. The crystallization process had been completed from the night's earliest batch and was now ready for consumption. Munson eagerly fished out the glass pipe and lighter from the front pocket of his tattered jeans. The jeans were baggy and hung loose from his diminishing body composition.

He sat and gently tapped out the small opaque pieces into the base of the pipe's bowl. The new shards clinked quietly as they landed, coming to rest on the burnt residue. A clear indication of the pipe's numerous previous uses.

"We'll get straight after a couple hits of this, and then get on the next batch." Munson smiled, exposing missing and cracked teeth, rotten from years of abuse. His lips were chapped, with cottony remnants of dried spit caked into the corners.

Swanson edged closer like Gollum drawn to his Precious. "Sounds like a plan. Fire it up."

Munson rolled his callous-burnt thumb across the lighter's flint wheel. A spark flickered, illuminating his face and casting it in a yellowish orange. The butane was low, and the flame didn't hold. Munson cursed and slapped the bottom of the metal zippo against the palm of his hand.

Staring out at the lake, Swanson impatiently waited for the familiar crackle and pop of the heated meth. It was a Pavlovian response and music to his ears. Absentmindedly rubbing the scar tissue on the side of his face, he stared out at the lake. The water's flatness was shattered as something broke through the surface, sending out concentric ripples from its epicenter.

"The hell's that?"

Munson continued his efforts to light the glass pipe, shooting an angry glance in Swanson's direction, obviously annoyed by the interruption. He huffed and looked out at the water. "Don't know. Probably just a log."

Swanson squinted, trying to make out the dark shape. "I don't think so."

"What the hell are you talking about now?"

"I ain't never seen no log wearing a dress."

Swanson stood and looked back at Munson, who was still troubleshooting the lighter, intent on firing up the glass. Swanson didn't wait for his partner's approval and began making his way down the uneven terrain toward the lake's shore, where the body appeared to be drifting.

It didn't take long to traverse the distance to the dirt-lined shore. Swanson's initial interest was driven by a sense of humane purpose, but he found himself stricken by an intangible fear.

Munson ambled up beside him, wheezing his exertion. "You're a dumb son of a bitch, you know that?"

Swanson ignored the comment and the two idled in silence for a pensive moment. The only sound came as the body bobbed, sending minuscule waves that lapped at the shoreline.

"What's the plan, hero?" Munson asked.

"Not sure."

The body was drifting on a slow collision course with shore, in a direct line to where the two men now stood. Their worn sneakers sank into the muck.

"Maybe she'll sink back under and we can forget we ever saw her."

"What?" Swanson knew the older meth addict had spent much of his adult life in and out of correctional facilities from Arizona to Colorado, but hearing his lack of concern for the dead woman shocked him.

"I'm just saying. Cops and I don't see eye to eye on too many things. And with my track record, there's a good chance they'll assume we had something to do with it." Munson's eyes widened and his hand trembled ever so slightly. "I ain't goin' to jail on no dead body case!"

Swanson broke his stare away from the woman and side-eyed his partner. "You really think they'll pin it on us if we call it in?"

"You tell me. How'd you like waking up in the hospital to find the police put those charges on you? Did they give you much of a chance to explain yourself?"

Swanson felt the truth in those words. "Well... then what do we do?"

Munson played with the lighter still in his hand. He flicked the lid open and closed. The clicking seemed to be a countdown to his decision. It stopped and he spoke. "How about we get a stick and push her back out and away from shore. Maybe she'll just sink."

"I can't do that."

"If you've got a better idea, I'd be happy to hear it."

"We'll block our number and call the police. Then we'll get the hell out of Dodge before they get here."

Munson took a moment before answering. "Okay. You're really trying hard to get your junior detective badge out here today, aren't you, Nancy Drew? Maybe that's what I'll call you from now on. Nancy has a nice ring to it."

Ignoring the older man, Swanson continued to watch the body. It had edged closer during their debate and was now only a few feet away from shore. The lapping sound grew louder as the splashing became more pronounced. Swanson grabbed a large branch from nearby and walked to the edge of the water.

"Don't go touching it. Those cops will sure as shit put this case on you if you do. They'll have your DNA and you'll never see the light of day again. Lock you up and throw away the key. Probably make up some story how you killed her 'cause of your messed-up face."

"I'm not going to touch her. Just gonna make sure she's out of the damn water before we jet. It's the right thing to do." Swanson lunged outward with the branch, snagging a bit of the shoulder strap of the woman's dress. He tugged hard. The woman moved across the remaining three feet of water more rapidly with Swanson's assistance.

She was face down. Her wet hair enveloped her head, completely masking her face from view. As the body came to shore, she got stuck in the shallow water.

Swanson turned to the man behind him. "We gotta pull her out."

"We ain't got to do nothing! I already told you—if you touch her, you might as well have killed her yourself. Do you want to do life in prison for this woman?"

Swanson thought hard about the question. He looked back at the woman in the water and gave one final effort with the stick. She barely moved.

"The bloat is gonna hold her. She ain't goin' nowhere."

Swanson tossed the stick as far from her as he could and

looked back at his friend. Munson was already moving and had begun his trek back up the hill toward their lab.

Swanson gave a last look at the woman. Her skin was a milky white and looked more so in the moon's glow. He likened it to the porcelain dolls his mother collected. His current life choices had estranged her from him, especially when he pawned several pieces of her jewelry and a few of those dolls to get enough money for a fix.

In this surreal moment with the porcelain woman, he oddly wondered if his mother still missed him.

He then looked away from the drowned woman and wondered if anybody would miss her.

2

SHE WATCHED THE MAN, JUST AS SHE'D DONE FOR THE PAST HOUR. He'd been fueling himself with Crown Royal and Coke since she'd arrived. He reeked of it when she entered the bar. Even from where she sat now, it was all she could smell. And he was starting to show the ill effects of his relentless consumption. His glassy eyes bore the signs of intoxication. The man was large, bigger than she'd expected. But that was of limited concern. She'd seen men of his kind many times before. A body built through an intense steroid-backed fitness regimen in his younger days had given way to sloth in his later years. The result was a mass of bulk, made up of more fat than muscle, but the sheer girth would make him a powerful contender.

Rachel Hatch knew better than to underestimate any opponent, regardless of outward appearance. Threats came in all shapes and sizes. Take her, for example. As a woman, most had concluded she was no danger. Overlooking her proved to be an advantage more often than not. An advantage she would capitalize on tonight.

The big man's name was Randy Bosley. She knew this because her neighbor at the motel had told her. Monica was an eighteen-year-old stripper who'd somehow managed to end up in Killeen, Texas, after running away from Montana. Abuse had pushed the girl to leave her home. Sadly, where she ended up hadn't turned out to be much better.

She'd met the girl while staying at the Wayside Motel outside of Fort Hood. Ever since leaving the military, Hatch had been on the move, looking for some way to find the point and purpose to life outside the Army. Drifting around the country, she always found comfort in being close to a military installation. The familiarity of the people and places that sprouted around bases reminded her of a time when she belonged. Her most recent trek had brought her to Texas. With winter soon approaching, it seemed like a reasonable place to spend a few weeks or months, depending on how things went. Her last stop had been Fort Benning, Georgia, home of the Army's Infantry. Hatch only managed to stay a week before a series of unforeseen events caused her to make a hasty departure.

She'd been staying at the Wayside for nearly ten days when she'd bumped into Monica. The girl was leaning against an out-of-order vending machine and crying hysterically when Hatch walked up. At first Hatch had considered ignoring the girl and continuing on to her room, leaving the girl to sort out whatever life crisis was causing her the emotional breakdown. But when she saw the broken nose and busted lip, Hatch stopped in her tracks.

Monica was standoffish at first, not accustomed to the helpful offerings of others. Based on what Hatch later learned about her life up to that point, she couldn't blame her. After some gentle prodding, the girl agreed to let Hatch take a look at the injuries.

By no means was Hatch an expert at wound care, but she'd had enough field experience to help the girl. The break along the

bridge of her nose was relatively straight and, in time, would probably heal with minimal cosmetic change. The girl's bottom lip was
split and two of her teeth were chipped. Hatch tended to the girl,
packing the nose and stopping the bleeding. Then, she helped
clean up some of the dried blood from her face.

Monica spent the night in Hatch's room. There were two twin
beds, and Hatch hadn't had any real social interaction since
arriving in Texas and didn't mind the company. During her stay,
Monica told Hatch about her rough upbringing and the reasons
for leaving home. Hatch understood, having left home at an early
age herself, albeit for different reasons. After listening to the girl's
tragic story, Hatch was glad she'd found her own way in the Army.

Hatch was a little baffled as to why or how the girl ended up in
a trashy strip club outside of Fort Hood. Monica relayed she'd
been trying to get over to her half-brother who lived in Baton
Rouge, Louisiana. She'd run out of funds and thought she could
make a quick buck. It was her second night at the club when she'd
bumped into Randy.

He offered her extra money if she went with him to his apartment for a private dance. Monica made him promise the two
hundred dollars were for a dance only. She was scared, but it
would've been enough cash to get her back on her way again and
figured it was worth the risk. Monica broke down again during
this point in her retelling. The anguish of the moments inside
Randy Bosley's apartment would leave a permanent emotional
scar, long after the physical ones healed. And for all she'd
endured, the large man paid her absolutely nothing. The last
words he said to her as he put her out on the street were, "Go
ahead and tell somebody what happened. Good luck getting
anyone to believe your trashy ass."

Hatch replayed the girl's story as she sat across from the man
who'd brutalized her the previous night. He had an air of indiffer-

ence. Being in the same room with him made her pulse quicken and she fought to control any emotional response. Effectiveness came in the cold, calculated control she'd learned through years of combat experience.

She picked up her drink, a seltzer with lime. To the average bar goer, the drink would look like a Seagram's and Seven. This was done so with purpose. Just as the intentional wobble she added to her walk. The unevenness of her steps added to her projected image. A girl out on the town who'd had far too much to drink.

Hatch walked by Randy and stumbled. Bumping into him, she clutched her free hand on his thick shoulder. "I'm sorry." Her words slurred for added effect.

Randy Bosley turned and eyed her. At first, there was anger at the jostled interruption, but as he took a closer look at Hatch's tall, slender physique, he softened. "No problem at all, sweet thing."

Hatch smiled coyly and gave an extra squeeze to the man's shoulder. "You're a big guy."

"You got no idea." A cocky smile stretched across his face. "You wanna find out?"

Under any normal context, Hatch would've laid the man out right then and there. But she needed a few minutes alone with the overly-confident woman abuser and decided to lower the bait instead. "Maybe I do."

"I got a place not too far from here."

Hatch knew this. Monica had told her where he lived when she was going through the details of her encounter. It's how Hatch knew what bar to find him at. She'd been camped out near the man's apartment this evening and had followed him there.

"How about you drive. I'm a little too drunk."

The big man's eyes lit up at the comment, and he shoved back from the bar, emptying the last of his Crown and coke as he stood. He gave a knowing smile and wink to the bartender, who returned the gesture with a thumbs up. Hatch stifled her indignation and followed Bosley as he strode toward the door.

Hatch knew the man lived within walking distance of the bar but didn't divulge that information. If he made a move in the car, she'd react, but deep down she hoped for the privacy the vehicle would offer.

Bosley walked to a faded blue Nissan and pressed the unlock button on his key fob. "Your chariot awaits."

Hatch sat in the passenger seat. The car smelled of stale beer and corn chips. Whatever someone would consider an aromatic aphrodisiac, this was its opposite. Bosley looked over at her longingly, in the way a lion looks at its next meal. She prepared herself as he moved. But he didn't touch her, only slipped the keys in the ignition and started the car. Dropping it in drive, he accelerated away from the bar.

He pulled out a small bag of white powder from his pocket and dangled it in front of her. "Hope you like to party."

"I think you're in for a real treat."

The distance from the bar to the apartment complex was less than a mile and it only took a few minutes to arrive at their destination. Bosley pulled into a spot covered by a beige canopy. He exited the vehicle without saying anything. Hatch got out and followed him.

They walked up a zigzagged staircase to his second-floor apartment. The keys jingled in his hand as he finagled the lock. Opening the door, Hatch caught a whiff of an indiscernible sour odor, making the car's stench seem fragrant in comparison. Hadn't this guy figured out how to use soap and water?

Bosley waited with the door held open and ushered Hatch in with a push that was less gentle than it should've been.

Stepping inside, Hatch scanned the one-bedroom accommodation. Old food containers were left on top of a circular table in the small kitchen area. The two-burner stove was stacked with discarded pizza boxes, indicating its lack of use. The living room area looked as though burglars had raided it and the television had been left on, blaring some mindless action flick.

Neighbors must absolutely love this guy, Hatch thought.

She turned to face the man as he closed the door, locking it behind him. Hatch was caught off guard to see Bosley was already working the zipper on his pants.

"You don't waste any time." Hatch dropped the fake slur, but the man didn't seem to notice. He was now interested in only one thing.

"I'm gonna rock your world." With that, the man's pants dropped to his ankles.

Hatch smiled at Bosley's state of undress. Not because she was remotely interested, but because the big man had removed two potential weapons from his defense by shackling his ankles with his jeans. "Funny you should say that because I was just thinking the same thing."

She moved a step closer, bringing the man's boxy chin into range. Bosley lowered his hands to the elastic band of his maroon boxer-briefs.

Hatch struck out with her left fist, striking hard against his lower lip. She felt his tooth sink into the skin of her knuckle. The force of the blow rocked Bosley's head backward and his body followed. Tripping over his pants, he lost his balance. Hatch was already moving in, wasting no time on the follow-up. She swung her right elbow in a downward arc, crunching the bridge of his nose and driving the big man flat onto his back.

Shocked and devastated by her vicious attack, Bosley screamed and wriggled backwards, bringing himself into a partially-seated position against his front door.

He spit a bloody tooth into his hand and looked up at her with a crazed look. "What the hell is wrong with you—you crazy bitch?"

Hatch stood over him. "You like to hurt girls, Randy. And I've got a real problem with that."

Bosley cowered. "The hell are you talking about? Thought you said you like to party?"

"Party? Is that what you call it? Beating and raping is partying to you?"

And with that he put two and two together. "That little bitch put you up to this?"

"Sounds like your mother never taught you how to treat a lady. Please let this be a crash course on the subject matter."

Bosley's face reddened to a point of explosion. He pushed down on the floor, trying desperately to rise and face his adversary. The effort was pointless. His pants continued to hinder his legs and the dizzying blows coupled with his intoxication left the man off balance. Seizing his weakness as opportunity, Hatch stepped forward, slamming her knee into his forehead. The bone on bone contact sent his head back, and the base of his skull struck the stainless-steel doorknob with a loud thud.

The man's body went limp, and he slid down the door, flattening himself back onto the floor. He lay unmoving on the dirty linoleum as blood continued to ooze from his nose and mouth. Hatch evaluated her work. The physical damage was comparable to what he'd done to Monica.

He remained still, and, for a brief moment, she wasn't sure if the doorknob to the back of his head had killed him. The thought was cast aside as she registered the shallow rise and fall of his chest. Although she firmly believed he deserved to meet his end, a dead body created a series of complications Hatch preferred to avoid.

Grabbing the man by his ankles, she pulled him into the living room area and away from the doorway. She strained her taut muscles moving the dead weight. He had to be on the upper side of two-hundred-fifty pounds. Not sure how long the man's impact-induced slumber would last, Hatch unplugged a lamp on a nearby end table and tightly wrapped the cord around his wrists. The knot was simple but would hold.

Hatch pulled a wallet free from his pants. In it she found four hundred dollars in cash. Twice the amount he'd offered Monica. Pocketing it, she stood and headed toward the door.

As she turned the knob to leave, the man coughed and groaned loudly. "I'll have your ass arrested."

Hatch turned. "Good luck getting anyone to believe you."

His eyes went wide as she shut the door.

HATCH TAPPED the door with her knuckles. She heard the soft shuffle of footsteps and saw a shadow momentarily block the light. The girl had listened to her when she told her to never open the door without checking who it was first. The chain lock unlatched, rattling against the door as it opened.

Monica stood there, offering a weak smile, her lip still sensitive from the recent tear along the bottom. Swelling had set in, and the girl's face bulged and was discolored in several places. Ice and rest had helped reduce some of the fallout, but it would take a week or two before the evidence of violence would totally dissipate. "Where've you been? I was worried you'd gone."

"Not yet. Needed to take care of a few things first."

Hatch reached into her pocket and pulled out a wad of cash. The girl gave her a confused look. "I—I can't take your money."

She pressed the money into the Monica's. "It's not my money. It's yours. Plus, a little interest."

Now the girl looked even more confused. "I'm not sure I understand."

"Let's just say, Randy had a change of heart."

The girl looked at her. Hatch had blood spatter from the big man covering her knee and the sleeve of her shirt. Her left hand was red along the two big knuckles with a small cut where Bosley's tooth stuck before being knocked out of his mouth.

"You did that to him? For me? I don't know what to say."

"Nothing to say. You're a good person and you needed help. I was in a position to do it, and so I did. Simple logic really."

"Not so simple. Nobody's ever stuck their neck out for me like that before."

"There's five hundred there." Hatch didn't feel it necessary to tell the girl she'd thrown in an extra hundred of her own. "Should be enough to get you where you need to go."

Monica's eyes welled with tears as she gave Hatch a big hug.

Hatch's phone vibrated. She separated from the embrace and pulled it out of her pocket. Flipping it open, she looked down at the message. Hatch was shocked to see who it was from, and more so at the message itself.

Closing it, she turned to leave. "You take care of yourself, Monica. I hope you find what you're looking for in Baton Rouge."

"You can come with me if you want. I'm sure my brother wouldn't mind."

Hatch shook her head. "Thanks for the offer, but I've got somewhere else I need to be."

"Where?"

She stuck the phone back in her pocket. "Looks like I'm going home."

3

"How long do we need to wait?"

Sheriff Dalton Savage's eyes widened at the rookie deputy's question. "What are you talking about? Wait? Please don't tell me you're asking me how long we have to wait to list someone as a missing person?"

"Well, I remember something about it at the academy, but it's a little foggy." Deputy Kevin Littleton retreated behind his desk.

Savage sighed and refrained from berating the eager new addition to his small department. Littleton had arrived at the Hawk's Landing County Sheriff's Office at the same time as Savage. The difference was Littleton had come with six months of basic recruit academy training under his belt while Savage had fifteen years of experience with the City of Denver, the last ten spent with Homicide.

The smaller department appealed to him for a multitude of reasons. He made his bid for Sheriff, winning the election by a narrow margin. The incumbent's history of misappropriation of funds and allegations of embezzlement proved to be the tipping point in the electoral decision. Even with the negative exposure, the vote in favor of Savage was narrow. To say he wasn't welcomed with open arms would've been an understatement.

The new job took some adjusting. Being a department of only three plus Savage, it was smaller than his Cold Case unit in Denver.

He quickly found he would be wearing a variety of hats in the understaffed and minimally trained agency. Savage had to be trainer, investigator, and leader all rolled into one.

As Hawk's Landing's only experienced investigator, Savage took the initial reins of most of the investigative cases and used them as teachable moments for the other deputies. He took it upon himself to provide guidance anywhere he could. And the most recent case that had fallen into his lap came in early this morning and would require his entire unit to rise to the next level. At the moment, and with Littleton's question, it appeared this would be an uphill battle.

Savage addressed Littleton with the same fervor of a dad teaching his son to catch a baseball for the first time. "There is no time limit before we can label a person as missing. If someone is late for dinner, then we can enter them into the system. In this case, we've already lost a piece of the timeline because it wasn't reported right away."

Littleton nodded his understanding.

"She probably had gone off with some friends to get high at the basin, slipped and fell in," Donald Cramer chimed in, exiting the hallway bathroom. "Wouldn't be the first drunk or stoner to drown out there. Won't be the last." Cramer swung the local paper back and forth behind him, fanning off the odorous trail that followed. His pistol belt was slung over his shoulder, as if he'd just won a title fight.

Savage eyed Cramer hard. "Number one, how many times

have I told you not to use this bathroom for your post coffee regimen? There is a perfectly good bathroom in the back by the interview rooms that doesn't fill the main lobby with your all too familiar scent. Number two, don't apply a half-assed theory to a case before you've looked at the facts."

"As you command, my liege." Cramer gave an exaggerated salute followed by a curtsy.

Cramer had been a deputy with the sheriff's office for just over ten years. Based on what Savage had initially observed of his ability, his time had done little to amount for anything in the way of experience. Ten times zero was still zero. Cramer also carried an allegiance to Savage's predecessor, resenting the change of command at a personal level. Savage hadn't fully fleshed out the reasons why, but presumed it was because the former sheriff turned a blind eye to the deputy's lazy efforts. In a department consisting of four sworn personnel and a few civilians, it was critical everyone pulled their weight, otherwise the workload, albeit limited in this small town, would quickly become burdensome.

"You and I need to sit down soon to get some things straightened out," Savage said quietly enough for only Cramer to hear. There was an intensity to his words, but Cramer seemed oblivious or flat out just didn't care. The portly deputy continued walking toward the small break room without saying a word.

Cramer stood in front of the vending machine, obviously looking to refill the void created by his recent bathroom exploits. Savage watched the man ponder the choices of junk food and was convinced this would be the most difficult decision he'd make in the course of his eight-hour shift.

Savage rubbed the short salt and pepper hair along his temples, trying to alleviate the budding roots of a tension headache. In the three weeks since he'd assumed the role as

Sheriff of Hawk's Landing, Donald Cramer had already managed to make his shit list. A hard thing to do by Savage's own account.

"So, where do we start?" Littleton asked, interrupting Savage's thoughts.

"Well, we've got the body of a woman in the morgue and a grieving parent in the lobby. Let's deal with the human element and talk to the mother first. Remember, approach each investigation with an open mind." He shot a glance at Cramer, who was still pondering the conundrum of honey bun or cupcakes. "And listen to what she has to say. Things that seem innocuous at first may be the detail that later breaks a case wide open."

"You're going to let me interview her?" Littleton's eagerness was contagious and contrasted Cramer's demonstrated laziness. Like a cosmic yin and yang.

"How are you ever going to learn if you never do it? And no better way than drinking straight from the firehose."

In the bigger departments, Littleton would be assigned a Field Training Officer, typically several if manpower allowed, who would spend the better part of the four months following the completion of basic academy training teaching him the ropes.

These programs were structured around the crawl, walk, and run approach in which a boot rookie, like Littleton, would be given more of the day-to-day patrol responsibilities until he reached a base level of competence prior to being set free to save the world all on his own. Everybody's experience was different. Some saw more, did more, depending on the criminal element of a respective city or town. Savage's first day on the job as a new probationary police officer had skipped the crawl and walk phase, plunging him into the front row of police work like few experienced during a career of law enforcement, let alone the first eight hours.

While he and his field training officer, Clinton Briggs, were finishing their pre-shift vehicle inspection, a Code 10 call had come across the radio. Savage knew this was a request for an immediate lights and sirens response for all dispatched units, and in this case, it was for an active shooter situation. A beer bottling company reported that a recently fired employee had returned and was shooting up the management office. Savage remembered the look on Briggs' face. He hadn't understood it at the time, having never seen a person channel the energy it took to head toward a life and death situation. Steely-eyed focus. Savage knew he didn't have it then but did his best to hide the panic.

The Noble Creek Bottling Company was set in an industrial complex not far from Denver PD's main headquarters. Briggs pushed the cruiser hard, the other motorists a blur as they zipped past. Briggs and Savage were the first on scene as they entered the lot.

People streamed out of the building. The blood-covered shirts of the employees and the desperation in their eyes was something he would never forget. It was the reason he'd taken the job. To help people when they needed it most.

Briggs' words stuck with him to this day. "Fate picked us today. Let's not let her down." And then the wiry veteran patrolman did something Savage didn't expect. He smiled. Gunshots rang out from inside the building, and Briggs took off running in the direction of the noise. Savage didn't hesitate, keeping step with the man.

Other units were filling the lot, sirens and squealing tires announcing their arrival. Briggs didn't look back and neither did Savage. The gunfire ahead of them continued. Screams followed. They climbed a short stairwell to an employee entrance as the door burst open, slamming wide as a horde of workers spilled out. They nearly knocked Savage backward over the railing.

Savage followed Briggs, cutting a path through the traumatized victims. Once inside, he could hear people calling out from various points in the building. Desperate and wounded, these employees were not lucky enough to make their escape. The gunfire had momentarily stopped, and now they had the dangerous task of playing hide and seek with a deranged gunman.

Briggs silently gestured with his hands, showing Savage the direction to go. They were staged behind a walled partition that divided the management floor into two separate hallways, each lined with offices. Briggs would go left. Savage right. A 50/50 split. An even share of the danger. Fate chose us today, he remembered thinking as he stepped to the edge of the wall. A local paper later referred to his actions, saying he was fearless in the face of danger. The reporter's description couldn't have been further from the truth. Savage had never been more scared in his entire life and he fought to control the shaking of his entire body.

Savage looked back over his shoulder toward Briggs, seeing the man disappear from sight as he moved forward. He took this as his cue and stepped out into the hallway.

His department-issued Glock 22 pressed out in front of him as he stared down the long corridor. Savage desperately tried to remember his weeks of firearm training from the academy, recalling the importance of taking in quick, controlled breaths. Stepping forward, he saw an open door to an office less than ten feet away. On the floor, poking out, was a hand. A pool of blood formed an ever-expanding oval. The darkness of the liquid reflected the ceiling light's glow.

Savage moved forward. And then among the moans and cries for help he heard a sound that sent shivers down his spine. The familiar click of a magazine being seated. The bolt release was loud. Apparently, the gunman didn't worry about noise discipline in his deranged state. Even worse, he was looking for a fight.

Savage keyed his radio. In a hushed whisper, he transmitted, "Briggs, he's on my side."

A static return. Savage didn't know if his message was received. Some building's atmospherics interfered with radio communication.

Halfway to the open door, Savage stopped. The bloody pool changed. The reflected light was obscured and replaced by a muddled figure. Savage had a choice. Wait for the gunman to enter the hallway. Or close the distance and take the fight to him.

Split second decisions don't always lend themselves to reason. Of the two choices, Savage made his.

Rushing forward, he closed the gap in a few steps. Stepping wide, he straddled the pool of blood with his gun pressed out at chest level. Standing before him was a short, middle-aged man with a receding hairline and wire-rim glasses. If it wasn't for the assault rifle in his hands, he could've been mistaken for a banker. The gunman had the stock tucked into the pocket of his right shoulder and was looking through his sights at the man on the floor.

The gunman, surprised by Savage, seemed torn between pulling the trigger on the wounded man on the floor or redirecting his aim toward the new threat. This dilemma, taking place in a fraction of a second, gave Savage the advantage.

Savage would forever remember the first time the gun kicked. It was unlike any other time before. No amount of range training could equal the uniqueness of firing in a real-world situation. He didn't know how many times he'd pulled the trigger but was told later after the scene was processed. Four shots, dead center, had ended the man's life. An act of violence to end a continued act of violence.

Four civilians were killed by the gunman before he and Briggs had arrived on scene. The man on the office floor was not one of the casualties. Because of Savage's decision to press forward, the man lived. *Fate chose him that day.* And he answered.

Through the fog of the past, Savage stared at Littleton and wondered how he would have fared under those circumstances. Hard to tell just by looking at a person. The true measure of a person's mettle can't be qualified on the outside. They need to be thrown into the fire.

There would not be a field training officer like Briggs to show Littleton the ropes. Staffing levels and agency size meant the young deputy had been released upon the citizenry without any hands-on practical experience, and it would be up to Savage to guide him.

"MRS. HATCH?" Littleton asked, awkwardly entering the quiet of the main lobby.

The only woman sitting in the room stood up from a wooden bench. She was disheveled and looked as though she'd slept in her clothes. Based on the lines of worry stretched across her face, it was probably a reasonable assessment.

Littleton approached and shook the woman's hand. Savage watched the exchange and focused his attention on the mother's physical state. She appeared younger than her age. She carried herself with a gentleness, but grief surrounded her like a shawl.

"Call me Jasmine." She ran her hands through her platinum hair repeatedly while speaking with Littleton, and it was clear to Savage she was devastated by the news of her daughter's passing. By those subtle observations, Savage deemed her a caring mother. The importance of such details is paramount when beginning any death investigation.

"Okay, Jasmine."

Littleton seemed a bit uncomfortable in calling an elder by their first name. To Savage, it was a sign of a good upbringing. The rookie just scored a point in his book.

"When was the last time you saw your daughter?" Littleton asked.

"Yesterday morning. Olivia lives with me. Along with her son and daughter. She has since her husband died in a construction accident a few years back. She works late sometimes, and I take care of her children while she's away. Normally she calls, but sometimes she gets busy and forgets. I just assumed it was one of those times." Jasmine Hatch broke into tears. "My God. Her poor babies!"

Littleton was in a state of total unease now. He rocked back and forth on the heels of his boots and fidgeted with the pen in his hand. Then he made an awkward gesture to console her, placing his hand on the woman's shoulder. Savage knew it was done with good intentions, but the timing was off, and she reeled back and flinched at the contact.

Jasmine reached into her purse and pulled open her cell phone. She scrolled the text messages, opening the most recent one. "See? Just this message. Nothing else after."

See you later for Nakatomi Night! The date time stamp put the message sent time at three-thirteen P.M.

Jasmine stared down at the message. Savage recognized the desperation in the bereaved woman's eyes. He'd seen parents of the deceased cling to the last item their dead child touched as if it were a direct connection to their soul. Savage recalled one distraught mother who'd vacuum-sealed the crust from the last slice of pizza her son had eaten before he'd been gunned down on their front porch. Over his tenure in Homicide, Savage had learned never to judge the grieving and had come to the conclusion each does it in their own unique way. Just as he'd done in his own life.

And was still doing.

"If you don't mind me asking, what's Nakatomi Night mean?" Savage asked, injecting himself into the conversation.

Jasmine smiled weakly and looked past Littleton, making eye contact with Savage for the first time. "Olivia and I always watch *Die Hard* between Thanksgiving and Christmas. It was a tradition we started when she was a teenager and it just stuck. We were supposed to watch it last night."

Savage returned her smile. "The best traditions seem to be the unforeseen ones."

Littleton stepped back.

"Mrs. Hatch, where does your daughter work?" Savage assumed control of the interview, as he sensed the seriousness of the situation was beyond the young deputy's ability.

"Nighthawk Engineering. She's an administrative assistant for them. She's been working there for several years now. She started when she was pregnant with Jake. They needed the extra income. She's been there ever since."

"And you said it's not unusual for her to work late?"

"That's right." Jasmine Hatch's eyes watered.

"Why did you wait until this morning to report her missing?" Littleton asked. His pen at the ready to log what he deemed a pertinent question.

Savage shot the younger deputy a contemptuous glance. The words used and the tone of their delivery sometimes meant the difference in a victim or witnesses' level of cooperation. Littleton's question, although appropriate, carried a hint of judgment. Savage knew this registered with the woman. He watched as she broke eye contact and looked down at the floor. The non-verbal communication was as loud as a scream to Savage, but Littleton seemed not to notice and stood ready to jot down her response.

"I just thought—hoped she'd maybe met someone. She's been so lonely since her husband's death." She looked down at the floor. "I ended up falling asleep earlier than usual last night, but when I got up this morning and saw she hadn't messaged me, I got concerned. That's when I called—"

"You've already answered my next question," Savage said. "Olivia's husband passed, and you said she doesn't have a boyfriend?"

"No. She's never even gone on a date in the years since he died. At least not that I know of. She barely has any friends left at all. All she does is work and spend time with the kids."

"Does she have a cellphone?" Savage asked.

"Yes, an iPhone. I tried calling when I first woke up and it goes straight to voicemail. I'm guessing it's either off or the battery is dead."

"Do you have her password?" Littleton asked. "Can you access her account?"

"Yes. I can get that—I think. We have a family plan. I'm not very tech savvy. Her son, Jake, would probably be able to help me."

"Okay, we'll need you to get that info for us." Savage knew this information would be helpful, but more importantly, it gave Jasmine Hatch an opportunity to assist in the investigation. Even the most menial tasks provided a desperate parent with a modicum of relief and sense of purpose.

Savage shook the grieving mother's hand before turning to return to the office. "I think we have enough to get started. We'll be in touch later today once we do a little digging around." He paused for a second and waited for her to look him in the eye. "I'm truly sorry for your loss."

Jasmine Hatch said nothing. The tears began to fall freely now.

"And don't worry, ma'am, we'll figure out what happened to your daughter," Littleton said, falling in step behind Savage.

The Sheriff and his deputy entered the secure office space, which consisted of six desks with low partitions separating each workspace. Apparently, there had at one time been hope the department might add to the staffing levels, but budgeting had not allowed for it. Two of the desks became dumping grounds for unfiled paperwork. Reorganizing the space was one of many things on Savage's ever-growing to do list. He turned to face Littleton, who had plopped his lanky frame into the swivel chair at his desk.

"We never do that." Savage gave the young man a stern look.

Littleton looked up from his notepad. "Do what?"

"Give them false hope."

"False hope?"

It was apparent by the flush of his cheeks; Littleton was worried he'd failed his first attempt at real police work. Savage softened his tone slightly to accommodate this teachable moment. "We never tell a parent or loved one we're going to find the person responsible or solve the crime."

"Why?"

"Because sometimes we don't."

4

THE BUMP AND SKIP OF THE WHEELS AGAINST THE CRACKED concrete of the tarmac shook the plane's cabin, violently stirring her from a poor attempt at something resembling sleep. Her stomach wretched as the momentum of the small puddle-jumper came to an abrupt stop. Rachel Hatch surveyed the older man slumped in the seat next to her. The jerky landing didn't wake him, and his labored breathing rang out his contentedness. Hatch was jealous. Sleep, the truly deep and uninterrupted kind, had eluded her for years.

"Thanks for taking the hop from Denver to Durango-La Plata Airport. If you're visiting the Four Corners area for the first time, please enjoy all the scenic beauty. If this is your final destination, then welcome home." The pilot's words were barely audible over the whir of the propellers as they strained to slow their spin.

Home? She hadn't thought of it in those terms since leaving almost fifteen years ago. The Army had been her home. And now she was, by her own choosing, homeless.

Hatch bent to retrieve the camouflage backpack resting at her feet. One of the few items she'd carried with her since leaving the service. All the rest, the variety of skills, lay dormant in the recesses of her mind. But they were always with her. She'd unpacked those items on occasion as situations dictated. Each time, the consequences were dire. And the last time nearly cost her life.

She returned the seat upright and rested the sack on her lap. The man seated next to her was now awake, but just barely. He gave her an easy smile. She made a meager attempt at returning his gesture before turning her attention back to the bag. She unzipped one of the side compartments and snaked her scarred hand into the recess of its interior. Her fingers moved through the odds and ends until finding the cell phone. She never wanted one, but after much peer pressure, she caved, though she held her ground in not getting the latest smartphone. Instead, she opted for a flip phone with buttons she could feel. A small notch on the five-button meant she didn't have to look at the thing to dial a number. Hatch rarely used it and had never once bothered to send a text message even though she'd received a few. Friends trying to reconnect after her discharge. None of consequence until recently.

She felt the hard plastic of the compact phone and retrieved it. Flipping it open, she looked at the message.

Rachel, come home. Olivia's dead.

Her mother was a woman of few words. It proved to be one of the many challenges of their relationship. Not the biggest, but definitely one that left any potential mending unfulfilled. Hatch wasn't much better. Maybe their parallels were the wedge continually driving them apart like magnets of similar polarity, pushing them farther away from each other. Her dad's death was the final nail in their dying relationship after which Hatch deemed it a lost cause and had written off the urge to mend their rift. It had been years since she'd heard her mother's voice, and she wondered what impact it would have to see the woman again after so long. The many life miles between them would be hard to bridge.

The man sitting next to her had eyed the phone's message and the damaged knuckle in the hand in which she held it. She wasn't in the habit of exposing any personal details about her life, especially to strangers. She folded the phone and tucked it into the front pocket of her jeans. He cleared his throat to speak. Hatch turned away and looked out the window. A silent rejection of his offering of condolence or whatever awkward conversation he planned to initiate. He must've taken the hint because he never spoke.

In a few minutes, they'd never see each other again. Most of the people in her life were in and out. A passenger on a plane or bus. A nearby patron seated at a diner counter or bar stool. Minimal connections. In her disconnect, she felt more balanced. After leaving the Army, moving forward was the only way Hatch was able to keep herself from looking back.

Hatch reached into the seat pocket in front of her and removed a water bottle. The crinkled cheap plastic crackled as she swirled its remnants. Already dehydrated from the recycled air of the plane, she knew the high altitude and dry climate that she was about to set foot in would only serve to exacerbate the feeling. Drill sergeants and black hats always pushed water. Cut your arm. *Drink water.* Broken nose. *Drink water.* In battle, she pulled a piece of shrapnel from under her eye after returning a volley of gunfire. Hatch drank water.

Movement in the cabin around her snapped her back, and she adjusted her body, angling her knees to the aisle. Hatch stood, bending to adjust for the low ceiling. At 5'10", she was taller than most women. Her wire-tight sinewy frame gave her the appearance of being even taller. Most presumed her to be six feet, and because of this, she was used to the looks others gave her. In her constant battle for anonymity, her body drew unwanted attention. Where it came to her advantage was when she took on her male counterparts in all things physical. Although many had tried, few could best her.

She slipped the straps of the backpack over her shoulder and then resumed waiting in a hunched position for the wave of passengers to make their single file exit.

Hatch held the empty water bottle in her hand and moved into the aisle. The bobbled walk of people after airplane confinement always reminded her of a group of penguins marching to the sea. She shuffled along and paused momentarily upon reaching the door. The sun was strong, causing her to squint as the beams of light blinded her when she looked out onto the airport. She almost lost her footing on the narrow stairway extending down from the hatch door. Grabbing the railing, one grip stronger than the other, she traversed the steps to the hard tarmac. The smell of jet fuel permeated the air and she was grateful for a passing breeze.

Her olive drab duffle bag stamped with bold black lettering "U.S." was waiting for her among the others. It stood out against the brightly colored hard plastic name-brand travel gear of the other passengers. She felt the eyes of a few of them looking at her as she hoisted the bag up onto her right shoulder.

Hatch moved quickly toward the airport's main terminal building, striding by some of the slower moving travelers. She reached the door and stopped, knowing that crossing through would bring her back to the world she'd left behind. She inhaled deeply and released a long slow exhale. She pulled the door open and entered.

HATCH MOVED through the arterial expanse of the terminal toward the main exit as the conversations from other travelers blurred into one indecipherable droning hum. A passerby bumped her, causing the heavy duffle's weight to shift. It slid down her right arm to the elbow. The canvas strap scraped across the old scar tissue, sending an uncomfortable tingle up her arm into her shoulder. Hoisting the sack back to its original position, the sensation faded along with the memory of the moment that had caused the damage.

Hatch saw them in the crowd before they noticed her. Her heartrate accelerated, and her cheeks warmed. She knew the pale skin of her face had taken on a blotchy tinge. Her face did little in the way of hiding any emotion, whether it be happy, angry or sad. Or in the case of this moment – absolute dread.

Taking two quick combat breaths did little to calm the nerves prickling at the surface like a thousand mosquito bites simultaneously screaming out to be scratched. Hatch knew she'd only have a second or two left before they'd see her. A woman comfortable with bullets snapping around her head was now in a state of total dread. She tried to push away this anxiety or, at the very least, mask its outward signs.

"Auntie Rachel!" Daphne squealed.

The six-year-old's long curly brown hair bounced wildly as she zigzagged through the maze of people, her head disappearing and reappearing amid the bodies and bags of other travelers. Each time her face came into view, so did her toothy smile.

Rachel let the duffle bag slip from her shoulder and drop to the ground. She took a knee and steadied herself for the impact of the approaching child, now accelerating at full speed through a clearing of people. Daphne was airborne, launching her petite frame as if shot from a cannon. Rachel caught her in mid-air and was immediately sucked in by her small arms. With her sister's youngest child's arms constricting tightly around her neck, Hatch tried to return the embrace. It felt awkward. The girl's outpouring of unbridled love for an aunt she'd never met was dizzying. Hatch wanted to reciprocate, but her effort fell short. She hated herself for being emotionally numb to the moment. Hatch closed her eyes tightly, willing her mind to hold on to this one.

Her eyes opened and she saw Jacob peering out from behind the floral pattern of grandmother's hand-stitched long dress. On making eye contact, her sister's eight-year-old son disappeared from view. Whatever feeling Daphne's embrace gave was washed away and replaced by the emptiness created at the obvious distrust from her nephew.

She eyed her mother. Jasmine Hatch threw her hands up and cocked her head as if to say she was helpless in fixing this rift. Hatch's face flushed again, betraying the anger bubbling inside her. She knew without a doubt her mother had filled the boy with stories of how she'd abandoned the family to join the Army.

Daphne peppered Hatch with a barrage of rapid-fire kisses and giggled with delight before releasing her hug. Hatch shouldered the military-issued duffle as she stood. Daphne gripped her hand. The two walked hand-in-hand over to Jacob.

"Hi, Jacob. I'm your Aunt Rachel," Hatch said.

"It's Jake. I don't like Jacob. I go by Jake."

"Okay, Jake. Nice to meet you." Hatch bent slightly, lowering herself to the boy's eye level. She extended her hand. Jake took it and gave a hesitant shake.

The boy then shielded himself, disappearing behind the hemp dress once again.

"Mom." Rachel stood facing the woman.

"Rachel." Her mother sized her up and down slowly with the contemptuous eyes of judgment. "You look different."

"It's been nearly fifteen years."

"I guess it has. A lot can happen in fifteen years."

"You have no idea."

Jasmine Hatch was a woman of rare beauty and seemed to only get more beautiful as she aged. Her long silver hair, teal eyes, and sun-kissed skin were a stark contrast to Rachel's short-cropped black hair, hazel eyes, and pale complexion. The two stood locked in a visual standoff, holding their contempt for one another just beneath the surface. No words were exchanged, but the silence spoke louder than any poorly aimed attempt at small talk.

Jasmine spun, flaring the skirt of her dress, and headed out of the airport's exit into the daylight with Jacob in tow. Hatch followed and Daphne resumed her grip, intertwining her little fingers around Rachel's pinky. The sensation in her hand had long been deadened after a roadside IED's detonation over two years ago. Daphne skipped alongside, and the slap of her sneakers on the sidewalk caused Hatch to break into the slightest of smiles.

THE OLDER MODEL Chevy Astro van pulled away from the airport, and it wasn't long before the scenic highlands buried the industrial airport complex from view. Hatch half-listened as Daphne began reciting a song learned in her music class. Jake pressed his face against the window and blankly stared out at the passing landscape. She felt his intentional avoidance of her presence. She understood it on many levels. Hatch and Olivia were twins. Seeing her must be difficult for the boy's mind to process. It took Hatch time to warm up to people too. Maybe her nephew suffered from the same social affliction. Maybe they were more alike than they realized.

Rachel turned her attention to her mother, who was

pretending to be more focused on the road ahead than was partic-
ularly necessary. Hands at ten and two. The whites of her knuckles
bore evidence of her excessive grip.

"Your message didn't have much in the way of details," Rachel
said. "When's the service?"

"We'll bury Olivia tomorrow." Her mother choked slightly on
the words.

"Jesus Christ! What if I'd been delayed?"

"It's not like you've been a part of this family in a very long
time. To be honest, I didn't think you'd even show."

"She's my sister. Time and distance don't change that."

"Family is more than blood. Family means being around.
Taking care of each other during the good and the bad."

"I was in the Army. And I was deployed—a lot."

"Sounds like you're still making excuses. Justifying your
actions yet again."

Rachel recognized the patronizing tone she'd heard a thousand times before during her adolescence. Anything coming out
of the woman's mouth was a verbal slap in the face. She also knew,
without a doubt, her mother never would have rescheduled the
funeral on her behalf. It would've been the ultimate win in the
constant battle waged between the two stubborn women. Rachel
decided not to engage her any further and turned away.

She now took a similar position to Jake's, pressing her temple
against the cool glass of the window. Her eyes traced the rise and
fall of the landscape and lulled her into a trance-like state as she
tried to put the thought of her dead sister out of her mind.

THE ROCKS CRACKLED and popped under the van's weight as it left
the paved road, beginning the long wind up toward the secluded

house of Hatch's childhood. Trees blocked the home from view. There was no mailbox denoting the dirt path even led to a house. The large boulder at the base of the driveway still held two handprints. One was Rachel's. The other belonged to Olivia. They'd left their mark on the stone when the girls were five. Faded and barely visible, Rachel could still see the remnants of orange and blue. The polar opposite colors of the color wheel were indicative of the disparity in the two girls' personalities.

A divot in the road jostled the van, jarring Hatch and slamming her right elbow into the armrest. A pulsing heat rippled down her forearm, tingling her scarred fingers.

"I'm going to see Olivia."

Her mother cast a glance at the children in the rearview mirror and whispered, "Do you really think that's necessary? The funeral's tomorrow. We'll have a small service beforehand where you can pay your respects."

"I'm going."

"You just got here. Don't you want to settle in?"

"I haven't been here in fifteen years. Do you really think any amount of time is going to help me settle?"

Jasmine Hatch bit the bottom of her lip but offered no retort.

"Where is she being kept?"

"You'll have to talk to the police. They were conducting an investigation. They told me that when they were done, they'd release her to the funeral home. I haven't heard anything yet. So, I'd assume she's still in their care."

"I guess that'll be my first stop then. Is the truck still running?"

"That old thing? Not sure. It's been forever since anyone's driven it." Jasmine paused and hesitantly offered, "You can always drive the van if necessary."

Just then, the bend in the road gave way to the sight of the angled rise of the wood-shingled roof. The years of shade from the tall surrounding pines and heavy snow of past winters had left patches of molded green moss in the corners. The dry mountain air countered some of the caustic effects. Had her father still been alive, all of the damage would have been immediately addressed. The house, built by her father's hand, was his pride and joy.

Seeing it again after so many years away caught Hatch off guard as a tidal wave of memories came crashing back. Some good. Some not so good. But all were the foundation of the woman she was today.

The van stopped and a whirl of red dirt floated by the windows. The kids unlatched their seatbelts and made quick work of their escape from the van, disappearing into the house.

Hatch stepped out onto the familiar grounds. Her mother offered to help with her bags, but they were already shouldered.

Neither spoke. Hatch had envisioned crossing the threshold of this doorway again many times in the years since her departure. From outward appearances, nothing looked too different. But Hatch knew better. With Olivia dead, nothing would ever be the same.

5

"MAY I HELP YOU, MISS?" THE WOMAN BEHIND THE PLEXIGLAS window asked.

"I'm here to speak with whoever's handling the investigation into my sister's death."

The woman unsnapped her purple framed glasses at the bridge and refastened them around her neck. She leaned in, squinting her eyes up at Hatch. Recognition flashed across her face. Her eyes widened at the sight of Hatch. "Oh my, I'm sorry I didn't see the resemblance before. My eyes aren't what they used to be. You're her spitting image. An absolute tragedy."

Hatch wanted to comment about the woman removing her glasses to conduct a more thorough examination but thought better of it.

"Twins."

"You don't say?" Her face warmed. "I'm so sorry for your loss. You must be devastated."

"Could I speak with the detective?"

"Of course. Well, he's not a detective. We don't have those out here. The Sheriff is handling things. Detective. You must be from the city?"

"Actually grew up here. But I've been away for a while."

"Sheriff Savage is out of the office right now. I can have him call you when he gets back in. He's in charge of things, and it'd probably be best if you speak to him."

"I really just need to see my sister's body."

The woman's eyes widened. She cleared her throat. "Um—the identification was made last week by your mother."

"I know. I just want to see my sister. Can you point me in the right direction?"

"Not sure you want to do that right now."

"Why's that?"

"Because she's undergoing an autopsy as we speak. That's actually where the Sheriff is at this very moment."

"Then that's where I need to be."

"Not sure an autopsy is something you want to see."

"Fifteen years in the Army. Military Police. I've seen my share of things people don't want to see. Most of which I wished I could unsee. But what we want and what we get aren't always the same thing."

"Well, I'll give you the address for the Coroner's Office. Not sure you'll be allowed to enter while the procedure is taking place, but I'll leave that for the Sheriff to decide."

The woman returned the glasses to her face and scribbled down the address on a slip of paper. "Not too far from here."

"Thank you."

"Not sure if I've been much help, but I sure hope you find whatever it is you're looking for."

Me too, Hatch thought as she turned and exited.

ALTHOUGH THE SUN WAS OUT, the temperature had already begun its rapid descent as Hatch stood outside the tinted glass door of the building. The place containing the dead body of her sister. She stepped inside the main lobby of the Coroner's Office. Had the stenciled letters on the front door not identified it as such, the interior could have been mistaken for the waiting area of any hometown doctor's office. There was sterility to the air. A distinct medicinal odor lingered.

Hatch approached the receptionist. The man smiled expectantly. She assumed the older woman manning the front desk at the police station must have called ahead to alert them of Hatch's impending arrival.

"Miss Hatch, I presume?"

"Yes. Is Sheriff Savage available?"

"He's indisposed at the moment. If you wait over there, I'll let him know you're here." He motioned to a row of cushioned chairs along the wall. "When he's freed up, I'm sure he'd be willing to speak with you."

"I'm sure he's already been made aware that I was coming. You were."

The man took an audible gulp. "Not sure wha—"

"Look, either go back and get him or I will."

Hatch looked hard at the man. She could tell he was unaccustomed to confrontation. His face blotched and she could see his breathing rate had increased exponentially since the conversation began. She then looked to the only door beyond the man's desk. It was off to the right and was marked with a sign, *Official Use Only*.

She smiled and purposefully walked toward the door.

"Miss, you can't—"

Hatch dismissed the man's feeble attempt at stopping her, turning the unlocked knob and opening the door to a short hallway. Moving briskly, she passed an office and a bathroom. Further down on the left she saw the closed door marked Laboratory. Pressing down on the latch as she heard the footsteps of the receptionist close behind, she opened the door.

Her entrance caused the two people standing by the aluminum table to turn and face her. Their positions blocked Hatch's view. And she was grateful for the additional moment's pause before she would lay eyes upon her sister's dead body.

The pathologist was in full garb, and his eyes widened at her interruption. The other man was dressed in a button-down cream-colored shirt and jeans, a badge and gun clipped to his right hip. Savage. He had a similarly perplexed look. Hatch was accustomed to the double take she and her sister were given throughout their childhood. The current circumstances caused the additional shock value. And it was apparent to Hatch, when informed the victim's sister was on the way, that neither man knew she was a twin.

Just as Rachel was about to break the awkward silence, the thin receptionist skidded into the room. "Doctor Tyrell, I'm so sorry. I tried to stop her."

"It's okay, Gerry." He gave the exasperated assistant a reassuring look. "We'll take it from here."

The receptionist departed as the Sheriff approached Hatch. "I'm Dalton Savage. I'm the Sheriff of Hawk's Landing."

Hatch nodded.

"Miss Hatch, I understand you've just arrived in town, and you must be extremely upset. But I don't think this is something you want to see."

The man's breath had the overwhelming odor of black licorice. "It's Rachel, but people just call me Hatch. And yes, I do want to see."

"An autopsy isn't something even most cops want to witness. Actually, most never do."

The man, who was a few inches taller, intentionally blocked her view while talking. "Listen, I'm not your typical person. Cop or otherwise. So, yes, I want to see. More importantly—I need to see."

Savage shot a glance back at the medical examiner, who shrugged his indifference. "Okay. But you're observing and that's it. I don't want you touching anything."

"I know the rules. This isn't my first rodeo."

Savage gave no further protest and turned. Hatch followed him back to the table. The chemical smell combined with the pungent emanation from her sister's body to create a unique blend of awfulness.

Seeing her sister on the table, with her chest cavity opened and internal organs exposed, gave her pause. Hatch had seen some horrific scenes during her time in the military, and she'd overseen numerous autopsies, but this time was different. Her knees buckled slightly and she felt warm. Hatch fought back against her body's involuntary response, willing the return of her control in two deep breaths. Exhaling, composure regained, she took up a position alongside Savage.

The doctor continued his summation, logging the procedure into a digital recorder. "The organs have been removed and weighed. No abnormalities noted in the heart or lungs."

"What about water?" Hatch interrupted.

"Excuse me? I think you were asked to remain as a silent observer during this procedure."

Hatch eyed Savage. "I didn't hear anything about remaining silent. And back to my question—if she'd drowned, then there'd be water in the lungs."

"True."

"So, was there any water in my sister's lungs?"

"No."

Savage held out his notepad so Hatch could see. He tapped his pen against a notation with an asterisk, *no water in lungs*. "Not my first rodeo either."

Hatch smirked. "Fair enough."

———

THE AUTOPSY PROCEDURE was nearly complete by the time Hatch barged in. The doctor continued his verbal notes and then placed all of the removed organs into a thick plastic bag. He then stuffed them back inside her sister's open chest cavity and sewed the signature Y, closing it. The cold hard reality of a death investigation.

"To officially determine cause of death, we'll need to wait until I get the toxicology reports back from the lab. I've sent the bloodwork off to the state for analysis, and I'll let you know as soon as I have them in hand, Sheriff. Should be a couple of days."

"Thanks." Savage turned his attention to Hatch. "We've finished up the autopsy if you'd like to take a moment alone with your sister."

"Thank you."

The two men exited, leaving her alone with her sister's body. The only sound was the whir of the vent fan above, failing to rid the stench from the room.

Hatch leaned in, hovering over her sister's face. Death steals the humanity and leaves behind a shadow of the person. Olivia was gone. And in the isolation of the cold, uncaring surroundings, Hatch gave in. Lowering her guard, she absorbed the pain of her sister's death.

Laying a kiss on her icy forehead, Hatch sealed her vow. To find out what happened to her. To make sure that whoever was responsible would pay. It was a promise she was more than capable of carrying out.

———————

HATCH EXITED THE ROOM. The doctor slipped by, returning to the lab and closing the door behind him, leaving her in the hallway with the Sheriff.

"You okay?"

"As good as can be expected."

"Didn't seem fazed by the autopsy process."

Hatch shrugged indifference.

Savage cocked an eyebrow. "Are you a cop?"

"Used to be."

"Where at?"

"Everywhere and nowhere."

"What's that supposed to mean?"

"I was a warrant officer with the Army. Spent my last eleven years with the Military Police's Criminal Investigation Division. So, I've worked cases pretty much everywhere in the world including the most remote parts of nowhere. Everywhere and nowhere. Something we used to say in my unit."

"Hmm. Are you still in?"

"No."

"Why'd you get out?"

Hatch rubbed at the rippled scar tissue under her sleeve. She eyed the tall investigator warily. "It's a long story. And as I see it, you've got a case to be working on."

Savaged nodded and fiddled with his notepad. "I guess we should get going then."

The two proceeded back along the short hallway, through the door, and into the lobby. The receptionist looked up. He nodded warmly at Savage but averted his eyes in a snooty protest to Hatch. She threw up her hands in an apologetic gesture and followed Savage out of the building.

"What's next for you?" Savage asked.

"Burying my sister. After that, I'll be looking into figuring out who's responsible."

"I understand you're upset, but it's best you let me and my deputies sort this out. I hate to break it to you, but you're not an investigator anymore. And even if you were—you'd have no juris-dictional powers here."

"Maybe it's better that way. I don't have to play by all your rules."

"Please do me a favor and let me do my job. As I said, this isn't my first rodeo either."

"You get a lot of bodies up this way, Sheriff?"

"I spent ten years working Denver Homicide before coming out this way."

"Why the change?"

Savage shook his head. "I guess we both have a long story to tell. But like you said, I've got a case I should be working on."

6

HATCH HAD BEEN AWAKE FOR CLOSE TO TWO HOURS. SLEEPING IN HER old room, now converted into a study, left her back sore from the leather couch she'd bedded down on. She decided not to linger about the house until the others awoke and quietly made her exit. It had been a long time since she'd run the hilly terrain, but her feet navigated the uneven ground with ease. Memories of long runs with her father flooded back as she crashed through the tree line.

Running was their thing. The early bond solidified on the Colorado trails. He'd gotten her into it when she was young. A Vietnam-era green beret, he'd taught her the value of being able to move her body over long distances, always pushing Hatch beyond her limitations. He'd taught her other skills, too. Ones that aided in her survival overseas. But like running, all skills were perishable if not practiced. Although it had been a year since her separation from military service, Hatch was as sharp today as she'd ever been.

Hatch ran for several miles before coming to a stop near a small brook. She stopped to stretch by a large boulder. Placing her hands on the cool stone, she alternated flexing her ankles in an effort to loosen her calves. The altitude, combined with the dry thin mountain air, caused them to cramp, and it felt good to take a momentary rest.

This rest spot wasn't chosen by accident. It was the same place where she'd found her father's body twenty-one years ago. One bullet had penetrated his heart, killing him instantly.

His body had been cold by the time she'd discovered him. The darkened dirt surrounding his lifeless form was an image that surfaced in her nightmares. Being here now brought the surreal imagery back to the forefront of her mind. At twelve, she didn't know much about rendering first aid. But she knew enough to check for a pulse. Hatch knelt by her father and found no sign of life. She lay upon his chest and wept. His blood covered her clothes and no amount of washing ever seemed to remove the stain of it from her skin.

His death was deemed a hunting accident by authorities, even though the hunter responsible was never located. At age twelve, Rachel Hatch learned a hard reality. *Sometimes bad things happen to good people.* And sometimes the people responsible for those bad deeds go unpunished. Both became guideposts of her life. Her calling was forged in the blood-soaked dirt by the brook.

Help good people and punish those who hurt others.

Since leaving the Army, her ability to find a way to honor that code had been more difficult. And she'd spent most of her time during the last year adrift.

She hoisted herself up on the rock, letting her body cool against its surface. Hatch felt this to be as good a place as any to start the day of her sister's funeral.

As dawn broke with the brightness peeking through the tall pines, she stared at the ground where her father had drawn his last breath.

AN HOUR LATER, Hatch crested the path's rise to the clearing behind her childhood home. Slowing to a walk, steam rose from her body as she approached the back porch. The swing where she and her father would sit and watch fireflies in the summer nights swung gently from the strength of a passing breeze. She could see inside the windows, and the heads of her niece and nephew bobbed along to the kitchen area.

She entered, half expecting to hear the chaotic ramblings of children, and was caught off guard by the silence. There was only an occasional ding of a spoon against a porcelain bowl as Daphne methodically scooped her cereal, head down in a trance-like state. Jake munched on a Pop-Tart. Each bite sent down a cascade of chocolate rain onto the plate and table below. Hatch's mother, seated at the head, sipped slowly from her coffee. Her eyes were red, but her tears had been wiped from her face. Hatch knew the woman well enough to know she was doing her best to shield the children from her pain. Hatch had seen this before during her own childhood.

"I see you were up early," her mother said, not looking up from her cup.

"Couldn't sleep. Went for a run."

"Some things never change."

"Some things do. Since when do you allow sugar cereal and Pop-Tarts? I'm pretty sure I wasn't allowed to eat anything you didn't grow yourself or buy direct from Hoskin's farmer's market."

Hatch's mother offered a weak smile and shrugged. "Special occasion."

Daphne pushed her chair back. She crossed the wood floor toward Hatch with a pitter-patter of bare feet and walked right into Hatch's side, locking her arms around her waist in a tight embrace. This kid was definitely a hugger.

Hatch felt out of her element. She gently patted the young girl's head. Daphne gave a whimper and her body trembled. Convulsive vibrations resonated with increased intensity as the sad reality of the day gripped her niece.

Hatch knew the child felt her mom in Rachel's form. The similarity must've given Daphne equal parts pain and comfort. Hatch peeled the child's arms free. Holding the six-year-old by the hands, she took a knee, coming to eye level. Daphne's dirty blonde hair hung in lazy curls around her face.

"I know this day is going to be hard for you. My dad, your grandfather, always used to say to me, the hard times define us and how we use the memory of it defines our future."

Daphne cocked her head. Eyes still moist, she asked, "What's that supposed to mean?"

"I guess it means we stay strong even when we don't want to. Use your sadness as a reminder, but never let it hold you back."

Daphne nodded, but Hatch still wasn't convinced the little girl even remotely understood what she was trying to say. She was used to motivating soldiers on a battlefield. Deploying similar tactics with a child was uncharted territory.

"Let's not go spouting your father's wisdom today," her mom said. "The kids need to process this in their own way."

Hatch stood. She looked at her mother, the perennial hippie. To this day Hatch never understood how her parents had been so happy together. Jasmine a flower child, and her father, a warrior. Maybe in those polar differences came an unlikely balance.

Hatch walked into the kitchen without furthering the confrontation and poured herself a cup of coffee from the percolator. If there was one thing the two agreed on, it was that her mother could make one hell of a cup of coffee. Whether it was the beans, the grind, or the percolator itself, Hatch didn't know, but she'd never found a better cup in her life's travels.

Taking her mug in hand, she left the three to return to their silent breakfast and went upstairs to wash off the caked sweat of her early morning jaunt.

And to prepare for her sister's funeral.

"THANK YOU ALL FOR COMING. Olivia was loved by all. She was a sweet child, always looking out for the well-being of others. She instilled those same values in her own children. And so, in many ways, Olivia will live on. I'm not much for speeches. But I will share one story I think exemplifies the beautiful spirit of my daughter.

"When Olivia was ten, she found a baby bird that had fallen from a tree in our yard. I remember her coming to me with the bird cupped gently in her hands. The little goldfinch had fallen from its nest and injured its wing. Olivia spent the day making a splint. She then spent several days nursing it until finally taking the bird to the animal rescue where it made a full recovery. I asked her why she cared so much for the bird. And she answered in the simple phrasing of a ten-year-old: because it needed me. Olivia lived her life the same way. Giving to anybody who needed her help. She had a big heart and the world is a darker place without her light."

Hatch watched her mother's poise and grace in the delivery of the speech. For the first time in a long time, she found herself looking at her mother with something she'd thought she had long since lost. Respect. Something she didn't think was possible. Not after what she did after her father's death.

Her mother's brief but powerful eulogy concluded. Daphne

walked over and placed a hand drawn picture, depicting her and her mother holding hands in a bright green field, on top of the casket. Jake stood silently by, battling with his emotions bubbling inside. Hatch remained stoic as she stared at the box containing her sister's body, having already said her goodbyes.

People meandered in the grassy field near the upturned earth where Olivia was soon to be interred. Several attendees, some of whom were old friends, eyed Hatch hard. She couldn't tell if it was because of the resemblance to her sister or the hateful distrust of outsiders to the tight-knit community. Even though she'd been born and raised there, departing was frowned upon. To them, she was now an outsider. Returning only to attend a funeral was seen as an insult and, by the judging eyes of a few, meant she was no longer welcome to the town's embrace.

But one face stood out from the crowd. Cole Jenson, who apparently hadn't aged a day since she'd left, pushed his way through the other attendees and approached. "Rachel."

"Cole."

"How long has it been?"

"Fifteen years."

"Fifteen? Man—feels like forever." Cole leaned in closer and gave an awkward hug. The air around him held a hint of mint and leather. A fitting scent for the ruggedly handsome man. "I'm so sorry about your sister. I can't believe she drowned."

"Not so sure she did."

Cole released his hold and stepped back. "What are you implying?"

"Nothing. Just waiting to see what the sheriff's office investigation turns up."

"Last I heard you were in the Army. A cop or something?"

"Yeah. Something like that."

"What happened?"

"Nothing worth talking about." The truth was, Hatch didn't want to talk about her past with Cole Jenson, or anyone else from Hawk's Landing for that matter.

"I'd love to catch up sometime. Maybe you'd be interested in meeting me for a beer at Miller's Walk?"

Hatch looked over at her sister's children. Their faces were stuck in various states of distress. Jake was fighting to mask his pain, which resulted in a contortion of his cheeks, causing his ears to turn fire engine red. Daphne was a waterfall of emotion, having crumpled to the ground holding her teddy bear. "Now's not really the time. My family needs me."

"Seems like they got along fine without you for a while."

Hatch flinched as if ducking a blow. A flash of anger came over her. The words struck a chord because deep down she knew the truth behind them. "What's that supposed to mean?"

"Sorry. I didn't mean anything by it. Just saying—you've been gone a while."

Hatch folded her arms. "I had my reasons. Remember?"

"Listen, I didn't come over here to upset you or bring up the past. I really just wanted to see if you were doing okay." He scribbled onto the back of a business card. "Here's my number. I wrote my cell on the back. Give me a call later if you want to meet up."

Hatch looked at the number and then flipped the card over. Executive of Operations, Nighthawk Engineering. "You worked for the same company as Olivia?"

"Pretty much everybody in town does. It's been great for the local economy. But to answer your question, yeah, we worked together. She was my administrative assistant. I saw her every day." He looked over at the casket. "I really can't believe she's gone."

Hatch pocketed the card and sighed, realizing Cole might be able to shed some light on Olivia's work life. As painful as the thought was, she conceded. "I'll see you tonight."

"Really?"

"How's eight sound?"

Cole smiled. "Perfect. I can pick you up if you want?"

"No thanks. I'll find my way there."

Hatch walked away and back toward her sister's grieving children, hoping she'd be able to deliver some level of comfort. If by no other means than her mere presence.

7

"What's that you're holding?"

"Just the information the Sheriff was asking for." Her mother held the slip of paper in her hand, guarding it from view. "He needed the password for Olivia's phone."

Hatch's arm outstretched. "Let me take a look at it."

"Not sure what you plan on doing with it, but I need to get this over to Sheriff Savage. He told me to bring it by the station. I meant to do it before but got sidetracked preparing for Olivia's service."

"No need for you to bother. You stay here with the kids. I'll run it over to him. I wanted to follow up with how things were progressing with the investigation anyway."

Her mother looked down at the paper in her hand, and then over at Daphne and Jake. She let out a sigh of resignation, placing it in Hatch's open palm. "It's important he gets that."

"I understand."

Hatch turned to leave. Daphne looked up from the couch where she and her brother were sitting. "Can I come?"

"Not today. I'll be back soon."

Daphne turned her attention to the television without saying a word. She folded her arms in silent frustration.

Jake's despondency was painted across his stoic face. He was lost. She knew the feeling. Hatch had been there herself and had faith he'd bounce back. She did. He played a game on his iPad, his padded headphones blocking out the world around him.

Hatch tapped the boy on the shoulder. Startled from his trance, he looked up at her. He slid one earphone off.

"Jake, you look pretty handy around a computer. Do you think you can help me with something?"

He gave a weak shrug. "Guess so."

Hatch held out the piece of paper. "Can you log into your mother's account?"

Jake looked over his shoulder, back in the direction of his grandmother, looking for approval. But she'd already returned to the kitchen and was busy stowing prepared meals given by well-meaning family friends.

"Don't worry, you won't get in any trouble. I'm just trying to figure some things out so I can help the sheriff." It wasn't a complete lie. She was trying to answer some questions. Whether it would help the sheriff or her was still up for debate.

Jake took the slip of paper, minimizing the screen he was playing on. He accessed the Find My Phone application, and after entering the info Hatch had provided, a map popped up with a small dark green dot surrounded by a larger circle of light green. Hatch knew the general area of the phone's last location. There was one road leading to the dot.

"Can you zoom in?"

Jake pressed his fingers on the screen and separated them. The map's details came into focus. Hatch realized the road was a long private drive that dead ended near the spot of her sister's last known location. Familiar with maps and how to read terrain features, Hatch committed the image to memory.

Jake must have noticed her studying the map because he asked, "Do you want me to just text you a screenshot of it?"

Hatch smiled and pulled out her flip phone. "I'd love that, but it won't do much good with this thing."

"I didn't even think they made those kinds of phones anymore."

For the first time, she saw a spark in the boy's eyes. She rubbed his head, mussing his hair slightly as she took back the piece of paper.

The glimmer of light faded from his face, and he slipped his headphones back in place, replacing the map with the flickering of the game's screen.

Leaving the kids to the care of her mother, Hatch folded the paper and stuffed it into the front pocket of her jeans.

She hopped into the cab of the old F150. The familiarity of the cracked gray leather seat, worn from years of use, brought memories of her father's first few attempts at teaching her the finer points of driving a standard transmission. Learning how to drive at an early age was common around these parts, as many families came to depend on their children's ability to pull their weight around the properties. Hatch's tall frame, even at eleven, made it easy for her to reach the pedals. And so, her father began his lessons.

Her father, a man known for his ever-present calm demeanor, became completely undone with Hatch's incessant grinding of the gears. There was a time not long before his death when she recalled him screaming aloud as Hatch almost launched them off the road and down into the ravine below, a hundred-fifty-foot drop that would have killed or maimed them. Luckily, he'd managed to jerk the wheel, diverting their course. Hatch slammed the brakes, kicking up dust around the truck, and looked over at her father. In that rare moment when life won out over death, the two burst into uncontrolled laughter. Her father's laugh, a rare thing to behold, was infectious to those blessed enough to hear it.

The memories of her father, tucked deep, were flooding back to her with more frequency now that Hatch had returned. With each remembrance came a longing to find closure to his untimely death. Hatch decided right then, as she slid the key into the ignition, to look into the case facts surrounding his death once she'd concluded her sister's investigation.

The truck kicked up a plume of rust-colored dust, clouding the view behind her as she pulled away from the house and headed into town.

"Is Sheriff Savage in?"

"Well, hello again, dear." The woman at the main desk gave a welcoming smile, her bright blue eyes adding to the almost lyrical notes of her voice. Underneath the warm exterior, Hatch felt an unease in the woman's mannerisms. Most wouldn't have noticed the slight change in posture or the flicker of hesitation in her smile. Rachel Hatch wasn't most people. And she noticed. "I'll check."

She rose from her chair and moved out of view. Hatch could hear her muffled voice through the thin walls of the poorly constructed building but was unable to make out any of what was being said. The response came in the deep baritone of a male's voice.

The older receptionist came back into view as the side door opened.

"Aren't you supposed to be at a funeral?"

Hatch turned to see Savage standing in the door, his frame taking up most of the space in the doorway. The brown shirt over khaki pants made most county lawmen look more like a UPS delivery man than a cop, but on Dalton Savage it just seemed to work. The clean lines of his uniform tapered from his broad shoulders down to his trim waistline. His face was serious but softened ever so slightly by his hazel eyes. Hatch didn't often expend mental energy noting such things, and she shook herself from the unwanted distraction.

"It's over. Besides, I said goodbye to my sister yesterday." Hatch didn't mean for the words to be so blunt and cold. But the truth sometimes was. Actually, most truth hit like a jackhammer in the gut. It's the simple reason so many people softened those blows by padding them with little white lies. She found the practice counterproductive.

"Okay. So, what can I do for you today?"

Hatch pulled out the slip of paper from her pocket. "I think you were looking for this."

"And what's that?"

"The username and password information for my sister's phone."

Savage nodded, stretching out his hand. "Thanks. You know—you could've just called. No need for you to come all the way in for this. I'm sure you've got more important things to be doing."

"There's nothing more important than figuring out who's responsible for my sister's death."

"That's not what I meant. I was just saying—"

"Let's pull up the last known location for the phone."

"What's this *let's* stuff? I understand you want to help. I really do. But you've got to trust me on this."

Hatch handed the piece of paper over to the Sheriff. "Fine, but

I think you'll quickly figure out I'm not very good at waiting around."

"Thanks. I'll be sure to keep that in mind."

"And I want to be kept in the loop. Day or night. If something breaks in the case, I'd appreciate it if you let me know."

Hatch turned her back on the Sheriff and walked out the same door she'd just come through minutes before. She had somewhere she needed to be.

As she sat in the cab of the truck, Hatch pulled up her mental image of the map from Jake's iPad. Seeing the green dot in her mind, she pressed the clutch and maneuvered the stick into gear.

"THAT'S JEDEDIAH RUSSELL'S PROPERTY." Littleton was nervous. His voice squeaked when informing Savage.

"Well, it's the last known location for Olivia Hatch's cell phone signal. It's just up that hill and past that cluster of trees." Savage looked at the dot on his phone's screen. The red icon showing his position was rapidly closing on the destination. The map zoomed as the distance between the two points decreased.

"You know he's crazy, right?"

"You sound scared."

"I am. And rightly so. When I was a kid, they used to tell stories about Old Jed taking pot shots with a twelve gauge at anybody who stepped foot on his property."

"Any truth to the stories?"

"Don't know. I was never dumb enough to test it out."

"We're in Sheriff's uniforms. I'm pretty sure nobody's going to be taking any shots at us."

"This ain't the city, boss. People 'round here—especially the recluses like Old Jed—don't take kindly to people traipsing across their land. Especially ones in uniform and driving government vehicles."

They pulled to a stop by the gate defining the man's property. A chain link fence spread out from the gate's end posts. Each one only covered a distance of approximately thirty feet before the thick brush took over, creating a natural boundary line. "No trespassing" signs were posted at spaced intervals along the fence. A hand-painted sign was hammered into the ground a few feet in front of the gate. The words *"Trespassers Will Be Shot on Sight,"* clearly visible in bold black lettering on the yellow backdrop, made clear Old Jed's thoughts on unwelcome visitors.

As if timed to punctuate the young deputy's statement, the distinct rack of a shotgun echoed as Littleton cut the engine. The sound of a round being chambered came from just beyond the rise, in the direction of a ranch house. Littleton gave Savage an *"I told you so"* look.

"I don't know who the hell y'all think you are comin' up here unannounced, but time to leave. Don't set a damned foot on my property."

Savage was about to speak when he heard the old man shout, "Show me your damn hands!"

Savage shook his head. "Sir, my gun's holstered. I need you to lower yours and come to the sound of my voice."

The old man was speaking, but his voice wasn't projecting.

"This is Dalton Savage of the Hawk's Landing Sheriff's Office. Mr. Russell, we need you to lower your weapon and come into view."

"I ain't putting my damn gun down. I need this girl to get to steppin' back to where y'all are at. Trespassing ain't legal. I know my rights."

Girl? Savage thought. He looked over at Littleton, who was shaking but managed to offer an unhelpful shrug.

Rachel Hatch came into view. Her hands were raised slightly above her midline, but not in full submission to the armed man. Savage was impressed by the woman's calm, almost placid, facial expression while a gun was pointed at her back. She rolled her eyes as she walked ahead of the man. Savage read her face as split between anger and embarrassment.

"Hatch? What the hell are you doing here?"

"You're not the only one who can access an app and locate a phone."

"I told you to let us handle this. That was the deal."

"There's no deal. And it appears you two were just going to sit at the bottom of the property line and wait until this case figured itself out. Like I said before, I don't like to wait around."

"Doesn't look like your way turned out much better."

"Now you listen here! Get the hell off my property!" Russell's interruption ended the back and forth.

"Mr. Russell, I'm Sheriff Savage. We'd like to look around your property."

He spat on the ground in the direction of Hatch. "Looks like your friend here already tried that."

"She's not with us."

"Well, maybe she's with those goons from that damned Nighthawk Engineering. Either way and whatever your reasons, you get the hell off my land!"

"Mr. Russell, we're trying to investigate a—"

"I don't give a rat's ass what you want." He spun and turned his back on the trio. The shotgun held low, along his right thigh, as he began walking away from the gate. "Get yourself a warrant or next time I see you sneaking about, I won't be so hospitable."

Jedediah Russell disappeared from view. Savage turned his attention to Hatch. "I don't know who the hell you think you are, but you need to back off and let us work. You're really testing my patience. I've got a right mind to arrest you, but I can't see how that would benefit your family. This is the only pass you'll be getting from me."

"I'm just doing what needs to be done."

"What you're doing is interfering with an investigation. Next time it happens, I will be putting the cuffs on you myself."

"Good luck with that." Hatch turned, walked off the dirt road, and into the thick brush.

"Were you serious?" Littleton asked.

"About what?"

"Arresting her."

"Maybe—I don't know." Savage rubbed his head. "But one thing's for certain, she's got some balls."

8

MILLER'S WALK WAS A DIVE BAR ON THE OUTSKIRTS OF TOWN AND the only watering hole in Hawk's Landing. There were bars in neighboring towns, and those looking for a night-life experience could make the drive into Durango. Most citizens here chose to keep to themselves. And by default, rarely frequented anywhere else.

The bar was named after the first proprietor, Alton Miller. Originally called Miller's, the Walk was added years later when it became commonplace for its inebriated patrons' inability to operate a motor vehicle after spending a few hours in the establishment. Many a person had made the long walk home.

In Hatch's youth, she'd been inducted into the bar's list of Miller's Walkers, as they were known. Every walker ended up getting their name on the wall. On a shelf atop the wall was a pair of sneakers. They belonged to the first patron who'd made the walk. By rite of passage, each walker wrote their name and the distance walked on the wood panel beneath the old shoes. The years had added many to the list, and the space on the wall had become more crowded in the years since Hatch made her mark. It was now a collage of drunken letters, but in it, Hatch knew exactly where she had inscribed her moniker. She eyed the faded-black letters and shook her head at the childish pride she'd taken in writing them.

The other problem with Miller's Walk was everybody would recognize her. The nightly gatherings at the bar were like a perpetual high school reunion dating back to when the school only had twenty students, and that included grades kindergarten through senior year. If this were a movie, the jukebox would've stopped playing as she entered. Instead, people stared as Garth Brooks blared out the lyrics to "The Thunder Rolls."

Hatch stood in the spotlight of the townsfolk's eyes and thought the words couldn't have been more appropriate. *Maybe she never should've come back*, she thought, *because it seemed the storm followed wherever she went.*

Cole Jenson stood when he spotted her. He was at a small table beyond the bar, set away from the others. An island unto itself. Hatch was grateful for his choice of location in the crowded room. At least she could pretend to ignore the other patrons.

Seeing her, he gave a smile and waved her over.

Hatch crossed the peanut-covered wood floor as the others in the room returned to their drinks and conversations. The slurry of spilt beer and peanut shells made the floor slippery. It also gave the bar a unique smell, always reminding Hatch of a circus tent.

"I'm glad you came." He gestured to an empty seat. "To be honest, I didn't think you were going to show."

"Neither did I." Hatch eyed the pitcher of beer and noted it was already half empty. "I see you got a head start."

Cole poured beer into the mug in front of Hatch as she took a seat. "Guess impatience got the best of me. Hope you don't mind Coors Light."

Hatch took a swig as the frothy head quickly dissipated. "I've had beer in places that didn't have running water. No beer snob here." She raised her glass. "Cheers."

Cole smiled. His cheeks dimpled. The same dimples gave him the disarming charm of a sweet boy. In her youth, they'd worked their magic on her. Now, filled with life's unexpected lessons, she knew better. Hatch wondered if he, too, had matured in the years since, but looking at him sitting across from her with the foam of his beer giving him a temporary mustache, she strongly doubted it.

"So, Olivia worked at your company as an administrative assistant?"

"Wow! You don't waste any time. Nothing like catching up over a few beers before we dive into the real stuff."

"Listen, my sister's dead. I'm trying to figure out what happened to her. Sorry if I don't want to spend the night on a long slow walk down memory lane. And if I recall, ours weren't that memorable."

"Ouch. Geesh. It's been over fifteen years. You think you'd cut a guy a break—let bygones be bygones."

"You slept with my sister, Cole."

He broke eye contact and dipped his head, staring into the amber-colored liquid bubbling in his mug. His voice lowered as his smile faded, and with it, the prominent dimples receded. "It was a mistake. I was young and dumb."

"I hope to God you're not going to try and use that bullshit excuse you did when we were kids." Hatch felt her face redden. She took a few gulps, taking the edge out of her voice. "You know the one—where you told me you thought it was me. The whole I-couldn't-tell-you-apart load of crap."

"I was stupid. What can I say?" He looked up. "I'm a different man now. I'm a father. I've got two boys, ages nine and eleven."

This information bothered her. Why had she assumed he wouldn't have a family? Maybe because he approached her at a funeral and asked her out for drinks. "Does your wife know you're out at Miller's with me?"

"No."

Her face warmed. The hurtful memories of the past rolling forward. He wasn't about to end up hurting another woman the way he'd hurt her. Hatch pushed back in her chair, preparing to leave. "Not much has changed."

"You asked me if my wife knew I was out with you. I said no. Because I don't have a wife. I'm divorced." He seemed embarrassed by the release of information. "She left me a few years back. Wanted a different life. Said she needed to get out of this small town. Guess I can't blame her, but I thought I'd be enough—our kids would be enough to keep her here. I was wrong."

"Oh—I'm sorry." Hatch dialed back her annoyance with the man seated across from her and immediately regretted her pettiness of dredging up the past. *Why did he always have this effect on me?*

"It happens, right? This town, this life isn't for everybody. I mean—you left."

She looked hard at him and debated whether to speak her mind. "I've never told anybody this, but you were a big reason I left."

Cole's brow furrowed. "How so?"

"Back then you were my world. I thought we were going to be together forever. I know now that we were just dumb kids. But not then. Back then you were as important as air." She sipped from her mug. "Do you remember we talked about opening a bakery in town?"

Cole chuckled. "Yeah. I still don't know why. Neither one of us knew anything about baking. Or cooking, for that matter."

"I know. That's what I'm trying to say. We were just lost in what we thought life was going to look like. But the point was, I thought whatever we ended up doing, it would be something we did together." She attempted to control the warmth spreading up into her cheeks. "That was until you cheated on me. With my sister."

"I don't know how to make it right. Like I said, I'm truly sorry." His head dropped again. Looking up through the hair that had fallen across his face, he added, "And for what it's worth, I've always considered you the one that got away."

Hatch disregarded the last comment. Dimples and kind words weren't going to change things now. "It was for the best. You—I mean us—was what held me back. The thought of what our future held kept me stuck in this place. What you did actually freed me. I probably never would've left Hawk's Landing if it wasn't for you. So, thank you."

Cole looked genuinely surprised. "Rachel Hatch, thanking me? Well, I think this calls for another round."

Cole flagged the bartender and held up the now empty pitcher. A minute later, the pitcher was replaced with one brimming at the rim. He made a sloppy go of refilling each mug, splashing beer onto the table as he poured.

"To the past. Leaving it where it belongs," Cole said, raising his glass.

Hatch reciprocated, raising hers.

"Now that we've had our stroll down memory lane, tell me about Olivia. Can you think of anybody who'd want to hurt her?"

Cole's light-heartedness faded as he shook his head slowly. "No."

"My mom said she hadn't dated since her husband died. But I've got a feeling that we could fill this bar with the things my mother doesn't know. So, how about it? Any boyfriends lurking about?"

"Not that I know of. She pretty much came to work and went home. Those kids were her life."

"I know. I just can't figure out why somebody would want her dead."

"Why do you say that? I thought she drowned." Cole leaned in and lowered his voice. "You're asking questions like you think she was murdered."

"Things just don't quite add up. Something in my gut tells me there's more to it. I've learned to listen to it, and over the years, that instinct has served me well."

"You're saying things aren't adding up. Like what, for instance?"

Hatch took a sip. "Water in the lungs."

"What do you mean?"

"She didn't have any. There was no water in her lungs."

"I don't follow."

"Drowning victims fight for air. It's a body's natural and instinctive need to survive. A person submerged under water will inhale, and there will be pools of water trapped in the lungs at the time of death. My sister didn't have any."

Cole set his beer aside and seemed wholly mesmerized by the explanation she'd just given. "How do you know this stuff?"

"It's my job to know. At least it used to be."

"In the Army?" Cole crossed his arms.

Hatch nodded, using the mug of beer to deflect any further pursuit into her past. She'd already taken an unintended walk down memory lane and had no interest in talking about the adventures of the last fifteen years with a man who'd never served. "Olivia had no issues with anybody at work? Didn't piss somebody off?"

"No. Everyone loved her. I was the one who'd gotten her the job after her husband died. He'd worked for the company as one of our heavy machine operators. Good guy. Olivia was given a life insurance payout, but it wasn't much. And definitely not enough to keep her family afloat. So, I brought her in as a secretary for Mr. Chisolm. Figured it was the least I could do to help out."

"I'm sure she appreciated that."

Cole shrugged and gave a bashful grin.

"What does your company do exactly? They weren't around while I lived here."

"They're basically a natural resource company. They've been mining the area around Nighthawk Lake. The company has European oversight, but took on the Nighthawk name to make it more endearing to the local community."

"What are they mining around here? Silver?"

"The silver mines that founded this town are long since gone. Nighthawk Engineering found a deep pocket of Uranium here in Hawk's Landing and have been working to excavate it."

"Uranium? Isn't that dangerous?"

"Not the way they do it. Chisolm runs things. It's a green company. The mining is done using state-of-the-art techniques to minimize any risks of contamination. We actually are working to better serve the local tribal lands by redesigning the water lines from the lake's reservoir that feeds those communities. They've basically pumped new blood into the local economy, bringing the town back from the brink of financial collapse. I know you've been gone a while, but after you left and the last silver mining operation closed, we hit hard times."

Hatch remembered tough times. Especially after her father's death. "And what is it you do exactly as Executive of Operations?"

"I'm really more of a face man for the company. Like I said, they're an overseas operation run by Danzig Holdings. The people of Hawk's Landing weren't taking too kindly to a foreign company coming in and trying to dig up the land. Money or not, they were seen as outsiders and met with heavy resistance. So, hiring local boys helped in gathering support from the towns and cities around the world where they operate."

"And I guess you were the man for the job?"

He smiled. The dimples returned in all their glory. "Why not? I was the quarterback who led the team to the state championship our senior year."

She rolled her eyes. "If I recall, we lost that year."

"People still talk about that game around here."

"Continue."

"So, anyway, I help recruit locals to work the mines. Most of the time, I'm stuck in boring meetings with the town council arguing about land restrictions and boundary lines." He drained the remnants in his mug. "My title sounds a lot better than it is. To be honest, it's pretty boring. But it pays the bills. Which is more than I could say before they arrived in town."

"That's important. Especially when you're providing for your kids."

Cole pushed back from the table and stood, looking at his watch. He pulled his phone from his pocket and said, "Reminds me, I've got to check on the sitter. And then hit the restroom. Give me a minute. Don't go anywhere."

"Sure, no problem."

Cole walked around to the other side of the bar and disappeared from view down the hallway leading to the restrooms. Hatch thought hard about using this as an opportunity to make her departure, feeling she'd learned as much as she probably would from Cole regarding her sister and former employer. From his explanation, it seemed as though she'd need to examine other possibilities. To do that, she'd need to retrace the investigation from its beginning. But she'd have to wait until morning for that.

She decided it couldn't hurt to spend a couple more minutes with Cole.

She shifted in her seat and eyed the exit as an outbreak of noise erupted above the sound of the music. A large man in a black and red plaid flannel who could've been a stunt double for Paul Bunyan was in a heated argument with what Hatch deduced was his girl-friend. He towered over the girl. She was standing in defiance, but, even from her distance, Hatch could see her body quaking with fear. It was nearly impossible to hear the exchange of words, but whatever the conversation, it wasn't going in the girl's favor.

Hatch surveyed the other patrons in the bar. None were paying any mind to the developing situation or they were intentionally ignoring it. Knowing the townsfolk the way she did, it was most likely the latter. Intentional blindness had been around since the dawn of time. People turning a blind eye to the injustice of others. Hatch's code forbade her from looking the other way.

Help good people and punish those who hurt others.

The big lumberjack of a man snatched the girl's wrist and raised his hand, slowly closing his fist for added measure. Loud words accompanied the man's gesture, but it was obvious from his posturing, he'd soon be trading them for violence. The two were about ten feet away from Hatch, but she was already on the move, closing the distance.

Hatch caught the tail end of the man's words as she got closer. "—you're never going to open your stupid mouth to me again because it will be wired shut when I'm done with you."

His hand was already in motion, a closed fist hurtling toward the girl's cheek. A massive ball of flesh and bone set on a collision course with the delicate jawline of the girl cowering before him.

The man's expression, one of absolute hatred, changed to one of utter confusion as the direction of his intended blow changed.

Hatch shoved hard on the outside of the man's elbow, using his momentum to guide the descending haymaker out of its intended path and off to the left of the girl's face. Taking advantage of his off-balance state, Hatch dipped low and then sprung upward, slamming her shoulder into his armpit while hooking her ankle around his. The effect was immediate, and the man fell like a tree, crashing noisily into a neighboring table before landing on the hard floor, the impact sending several empty beer bottles into the air.

Dazed, the man rolled to his back in search of his attacker. Hatch now towered over him and the shock on his face at seeing it had been a girl who'd bested him was its own reward. She took a mental snapshot of the expression.

He tried to right himself, slipping on the wet peanut shells coating the floor. "What the f—"

The last word of his sentence was cut short as Hatch's heel stomped down on the bridge of his nose. She felt the crunch of bone under foot.

The man groaned. His hands shot up, covering his face. Blood escaped, oozing through the gaps in his thick fingers.

Not waiting for him to recover, she knelt beside him and snatched his right hand. She maintained control of the wrist with one hand while locking in his pinky finger with the other. "This is the hand you were going to use to damage that girl's face. Yes?"

He squirmed, shifting his weight and spitting the blood draining into his mouth. She tightened the grip, locking his wrist and seizing the opportunity to retaliate. Before he could reply, Hatch torqued the wrist in one direction while she simultaneously pulled at the clasped finger, jerking it in a direction it was never intended to bend. The snap of the break was loud enough to hear over the music playing in the background. But the sound of it was almost drowned out by the man's high-pitched scream.

Hatch stood up, leaving the man to writhe in painful response to his two broken bones.

The girl she'd just saved from certain devastation stared blankly, her jaw slack. "Thanks."

"You can do a lot better than him."

The girl slipped away, moving quickly out of the bar as Cole returned. He was trying to shove his phone into his pocket while staring wide-eyed at the man on the floor.

"My God! I leave you for two minutes and you're in a bar room brawl?"

Hatch moved toward the door, the eyes of the other bar goers following her as she did so. "Probably best we get going."

She stepped out of Miller's Walk. The commotion faded to quiet as the door closed. Cole was one step behind her, rushing to keep up. The girl she'd protected was nowhere in sight. Hatch felt an air of satisfaction from her deed.

Cole grabbed her by the shoulder. She still felt the controlled energy of the short but intense scuffle and spun with her fist clenched. It was a heated response and one that quickly dissipated at the sight of Cole's face. He was worry-stricken, his eyes darting between her and the closed door to Miller's Walk.

"Do you know who that was back there?"

She released her fist and then brushed his hand from her shoulder. She was the same height as Cole and met his worried eyes with a steely reserve. "No. And should it matter? He was about to crush that girl's face."

"That was Bill Chisolm."

"Is that name supposed to mean something to me?"

"Obviously not. But to the people around here, it does. His father, Simon, owns Nighthawk Engineering. He's been here since the company first came to town, and now they pretty much own the place. I told you their money is the lifeblood of the economy around here. And with that comes power.”

“Guess you forgot. I don’t live in Hawk’s Landing anymore. And nobody owns me. His power didn’t seem to help out in there.”

“Everybody isn’t your enemy, Rachel. You’re not on the battle-field. Some of us have to work and raise a family here. We can’t go around biting the hand that feeds us.”

“Even if that hand is hurting people?”

“It’s not that simple.”

“To me it is.”

“He must’ve been drunk. I’ve known Bill for many years, and I’ve never seen him lose his temper like that before.”

“One time is enough.”

Cole sighed. “What do you want me to do? Go back in there and kick him in the head again? Because I’m pretty sure you got your message across loud and clear.”

“I don’t need you to do anything.”

“Yeah, I can see that.”

Hatch walked over to her beat up pickup. Unlocking it, she pulled the driver’s door open with a loud creak.

“Listen—don’t worry about Bill. I’ll try to clear things with him tomorrow when he’s sobered up.”

“I’m not worried about him. Guys like him you can see coming a mile away.”

“Rachel, just let me smooth this over. It’ll be better for everyone if I do.”

Cole walked to his brand-new Jeep Rubicon. It was a dark gray with light specs embedded in the coat, giving it a glittering effect under the parking lot’s yellow light.

“Fancy car. Tell me, Cole, are you doing this for me or for you?”

“In the end, does it matter?”

“Everything matters.”

Cole entered his Jeep and drove away.

Hatch sat for a second, letting the engine settle before putting it in gear. She pulled out and headed in the opposite direction. It wouldn't be long before the news of her barroom altercation circulated its way around town. She knew how things worked and wondered what the fallout would be.

In the morning, she'd be heading to the spot where her sister's body was found. Hopefully, as day broke, so would some clarity into why her sister had ended up floating in the lake. But for now, all Hatch wanted was to get home and wash the stink of Bill Chisolm off.

9

HATCH SHOWERED, LETTING THE HOT WATER ROLL ALONG THE contours of her body. It felt good to wash away the smell of Miller's Walk from her skin, though she wasn't sure about the floral soap her mother stocked. She thought about the big man she'd dropped at the bar. It was a simple response to a simple threat. And at the time, the decision made perfect sense. Her heroics could have backfired, and she had enough experience to know the possible chain reaction of interfering in the personal affairs of others, no matter how outwardly dire. She was happy the girl-friend accepted her protection and didn't rush to her bleeding boyfriend's aid.

It had happened to Hatch more times than she could count in her early years as a military police officer. Working domestic violence cases on military bases was like being on the job anywhere else. The only difference, and one Hatch never took lightly, was each domestic she'd handled was among trained soldiers and their spouses. It's a challenge to walk into a house where you know the perpetrators are combat-trained veterans. Most homes had weapons and the situations were volatile at best.

Many times, she'd be in the middle of arresting an abuser, and the victim would jump in and physically try to intervene, sometimes to the point of violence. On one particular occasion, Hatch had been called to the residence of a twice-passed-over major. His anger and frustration at his latest failure to make the grade to lieutenant colonel sent him over the edge.

He spent most of the day drowning himself in a bottle of Crown Royal. When that failed to placate the rage, he took it out on his wife, who'd just returned from work. After smashing the bottle over her head, he began making preparations to burn his officer's quarters to the ground. A neighbor walking her dog had overheard the commotion and called it in. Hatch was a specialist at the time and was dispatched to the location. Her backup was new to the base, having just transferred in, and couldn't find the house.

Procedure dictated Hatch wait until backup arrived before entering into a domestic disturbance. While standing outside the front door of the residence, she heard glass shatter and a woman scream. Her backup just announced on the radio he'd got his bearings and was two minutes out. Hatch, concerned for the safety of the woman, entered the residence.

As soon as she entered, Hatch smelled an accelerant. The strong odor of gasoline was dizzying. The major was yelling from inside the kitchen. She heard the opening and slamming of drawers. Whatever he was searching for couldn't be good.

Hatch made her way into the hallway leading to the kitchen. He stepped in front of her, holding a lighter. He was so drunk, the shirtless major barely noticed Hatch standing there. She remembered the look of surprise as he registered the MP pointing a gun at his chest.

In the game of rock, paper, scissors, everybody knows gun always trumps lighter. The major must've come to the same conclusion because before any command was given, he broke into tears, dropping the lighter to the ground.

As she placed cuffs on him, Hatch was struck from behind. Her assailant was the abused wife, the same woman who'd taken a bottle to the head earlier. She now clung to Hatch's back, screaming wildly about not arresting him and how this was her fault. Hatch ended up having to shoulder toss the woman off and was in the process of applying cuffs to her when her backup finally strolled in. She learned some important lessons that day. Everybody's a threat until proven otherwise. Be prepared to go it alone should the situation dictate. She was deployed a month later, where those two life lessons proved more valuable than she could've ever imagined.

Hatch turned the shower off and let the water drip from her body, grateful tonight's incident at the bar didn't go that route.

She finished up in the bathroom, grabbed a robe off the back of the door, wrapped herself, and headed down the hallway. As she came to her sister's bedroom, she stopped. The door was closed. She thought about how many times she stood outside this same door as a child after the two had fought. They had a unique way of apologizing, the genesis of which neither could ever pinpoint. The one who'd wronged the other would stand in silence outside the other's door. They'd wait until the door opened. Nothing would be said when the door would open, but once opened, all would be forgiven and the causative event would never be spoken of again. Sometimes the wait for absolution was long, like when Olivia had slept with Cole Jenson.

Hatch exhaled slowly and turned the knob. The door still creaked, as it always had. The hinge hadn't been level when her dad hung it. An item on her father's to-do list, forever to remain incomplete. After his death, the creak of her sister's door reminded Hatch of him, and hearing it now, she was glad it had never been fixed.

She opened the door just enough to snake her wiry frame inside. She hoped the sound hadn't woken the children.

Clicking the switch on the wall threw the room into the soft wash of the light above. The room hadn't changed much over the years. The posters her sister used to decorate her walls were now long gone, replaced by a hodgepodge of family photos and children's artwork. Hatch stepped in deeper and onto the fluff of the shag rug protruding out from the corners of the bed.

There wasn't any one thing Hatch hoped to find. She wasn't exactly sure why she'd even entered. Maybe it was good enough just to be here among her sister's belongings, as if in some small way the connection she'd once had to them would somehow lighten the emotional burden.

Hatch surveyed the story of her sister's life as the images on the surrounding four walls of the room told her tale. Candid smiles captured in the photographs gave Hatch a glimpse of the life lived in her absence. From what she saw, it appeared as though Olivia had a good life in the fifteen years since Hatch set out. The two had sporadically kept in touch over the years, a call here or there. Maybe a letter with a photograph or two. More so in the early years. Not so much over the last few.

Hatch regretted that now.

On the vanity by the window lay a book. Hatch walked over to it. Maybe reading from the last book her sister held would give a sense of peace. To her surprise, it wasn't a novel at all, but a journal. Funny to see it out. Hatch assumed her sister's obsessive need to journal her life's experience would've faded in adulthood. Apparently, this tome proved otherwise.

Hatch picked it up, holding the leather-bound pages closed.

Her sister was dead and gone. Yet the thought of reading from her journal felt like a violation of privacy. It would be the breaking of an unwritten code, but the compulsion outweighed any responsibility to adhere to it.

She opened the journal. The pages separated naturally to a spot in the book held by a marker. The bookmark was a folded piece of paper. Hatch freed the foreign object and unfolded the creased edges, revealing a photocopied portion of a map.

It took only a split second for Hatch to recognize the image. It was an overhead view of the Nighthawk Lake and the surrounding property lines. There was a blue trapezoidal line framing the land surrounding the lake, a boundary line of some sort if she were to guess. Inside the defined area were several red dots. No labels were attached. There was no legend or key on the copied map to denote the meanings of the lines or color-coded dots.

Hatch set the map aside and began scanning the writings in the journal, starting with the last pages first. To her disappointment, there wasn't any reference to the map or anything current. The last entry was made over two years ago and described Daphne's first attempt to ride a bike without training wheels.

Folding the copy of the map and sliding it into the pocket of her robe, she closed the journal and turned to leave.

Standing in the doorway was a sleepy Daphne, rubbing her eyes. "Mom?"

Hatch was standing in her sister's room wearing her sister's bathrobe. Her heart ached for the girl, and she crossed the room quickly. Kneeling to the child's level, she pulled Daphne in tight. "I'm sorry, baby—it's just me."

"I heard a noise."

"It was probably that creaky old hinge. Let me get you back to bed."

"I'm scared."

"There's nothing to be afraid of." Hatch knew this to be a lie. The world she'd come to know was a terrifying place. And for a little girl who by the age of six had lost both parents to tragedy, Daphne was on the cusp of some very hard and scary years of childhood.

"Mom used to let me sleep in here with her when I got scared."

Hatch looked at the bed and then back at the soft face and pleading eyes of her niece. "Okay. Is that what you'd like to do?"

She picked up the girl, cradling her with her left arm while she turned down the covers with the other. Plopping the child into the soft mattress, Hatch took up a position on the other side.

Daphne snuggled in tightly, draping her tiny arm across Hatch's chest and pulling herself close. The girl's breathing quickly settled into a soft snore. In the sweet embrace of her sister's youngest child, Hatch drifted off to sleep.

10

"Good morning." The words were followed by a dainty peck on the cheek and a faint giggle, as sweet as summer rain on a windowsill.

Hatch's eyes fluttered, adjusting to the light seeping in through the blinds. She sat up to see Daphne hovering close, a smile stretching across her face. The child gave new meaning to the saying bright-eyed and bushy-tailed. And if the girl had a tail, it would've surely been wagging.

It was the first time in years since Hatch could remember that she'd not beaten the sun's rise. She was strangely contented by this fact. Whether it was the comfort of being in her sister's bed or lying next to Daphne, or a combination of the two, Hatch felt an uncommon peace.

Returning the smile, Hatch patted the girl's head and slowly sat up. Bringing herself to the edge of the bed, she looked at the digital clock on the nightstand. 7:45 A.M. Her plans of getting an early start were dashed.

Hatch stood, her toes gripping the shag of the carpet encircling the bed as she arched her spine. Reaching skyward, she stretched and then twisted her hips. Her motion sent a ripple of loud pops.

"Does it hurt?"

Hatch looked down at the girl. Daphne was sprawled across the top of the puffy comforter with her hands under her chin. Her eyes held a hint of curiosity. "No. I just popped my back. It gets tight sometimes."

"Not that, silly. Your arm."

The robe's sleeve had slid down when Hatch stretched upward, exposing her damaged arm. "Oh this? It did hurt when it happened, but that was a long time ago. Sometimes it tingles a bit."

Daphne edged closer, reaching her small hand out and touching the raised lines of the web of scar tissue encompassing her right forearm. It felt strange to feel a hand other than hers on the arm. "Are those letters?"

Hatch nodded, smiling that the girl was more interested in the fragments of ink rather than the scars that fractured the words. "A tattoo."

"What's it say?"

"It's no use going back to yesterday because I was a different person then."

"What's that supposed to mean?"

"You tell me."

Daphne thought for a moment, but when the meaning didn't come to her, she traced her finger along the scar. "What happened?"

"Not sure you're ready for that story."

"I'm six." Daphne stood on the bed, striking a superhero stance. "Trust me. I can handle it."

"Maybe another time," she promised, taking the girl by the

hand as she hopped off the bed with a thud. "I'm already behind schedule thanks to you and your snuggly magic."

The little girl's dejected look was interrupted by the loud rumble of her tummy.

Hatch smiled. "Let's get you downstairs for some breakfast."

Daphne scampered out of the room. Hatch quickly made the bed, pulling the sheets into tightly folded hospital corners and stuffing them under the mattress. Not tight enough to bounce a quarter on, but good enough. Old habits die hard.

She slid her hand inside the robe's pocket, feeling the folded piece of paper with the copied image of the map. Leaving the room, she closed the door behind her. The hinge called out its familiar tune.

Hatch went down the hall to her old room, now converted to a study. She quickly threw on a pair of jeans and a long-sleeved shirt, transferring the photocopied map from the robe to her back pocket before departing.

Opening the door, she nearly collided into her mother.

Hatch's mother was standing in the threshold of the doorway with her arms folded. "Sleep well last night?"

"I did."

"Got in late last night, too?"

Hatch didn't bother answering, shrugging off the question. It'd been over fifteen years since she'd had to answer to her mother's inquiry and hearing it now felt contrived. "Gotta get going. Got some things to do this morning."

Her mother's brow furrowed, and she seemed sad at the comment. "You're not going to spend the day with us here? I just thought—"

"You're comfortable leaving Olivia's investigation in the hands of the Hawk's Landing Sheriff's Office?"

"I am."

"Well, I'm not."

"From what I hear, the new sheriff is very experienced."

"Maybe he is. Regardless, he's an island unto himself. The group of misfits he's got working for him are a mess. If they managed a lighthouse, there'd be ships crashing all around. And besides, an extra set of eyes couldn't hurt."

"And why does it have to be you? Why do you have to be the one to stick your nose into things?"

"Because I'm really good at what I do."

"And what is that exactly?"

"I hunt down bad people and make them pay."

Hatch saw her mother's face recoil. Everything about what she'd just said went against the fabric of the woman's essence. The make-love-not-war hippie in her couldn't fathom the thought of people doing violence, even if it was done on the behalf of others. Every soldier and law enforcement officer prayed for the day when their skills would no longer be needed. That time when the world held hands and sang kumbaya. In Hatch's experience, the world had a long way to go before things got better.

Hatch moved past, slightly brushing her mother's arm with her damaged one. She had somewhere to be, already losing a few good early morning hours to unplanned sleep. She wasn't about to lose any more time to a senseless back-and-forth with her mother.

Hatch went down the stairs, grabbed a stainless-steel mug from the cabinet, and filled it to the brim with her mother's special brew. Not wanting to upset the children, Hatch left out the back door.

The engine to the old Ford protested its cold start to the day. Frost melted on the windshield as the defroster began to work its magic. Running the wipers to clear enough to navigate, Hatch headed out in the direction of Nighthawk Lake, the site where her sister's body had been found.

HATCH STOOD on the soft ground and listened in the morning's silence. A breeze forced the lake's water to shore in a rhythmic ebb and flow. She knelt on one knee, and the dampness of the muddy bed penetrated her jeans. Hatch was looking for clues missed by the initial wave of investigators. But more than that, she wanted to absorb every bit of this place, the spot where her sister's body had lain.

A torn bit of yellow police tape tangled in a knot around a nearby tree branch confirmed she was in the right spot. She listened, smelled and opened her eyes to all possibilities. The initial case report the sheriff's office had provided her mother didn't offer much detail other than the time of the call and where the body was located. No formal assessment made. Just a listing of facts. Reading between the lines, Hatch deduced the original train of thought was her sister had managed to drown herself. One thing was certain, she didn't drown. Everything else was open for debate.

The only way to effectively approach any crime scene was to see it with fresh eyes. The problem was, this site had been trampled and disturbed during the processing, making it unlikely that something valuable would still be present. But Hatch planned to trace all potential leads, and this would be one of many stops along the trail.

She remained still in her kneeling position near the water's edge, hoping something would stand out. She had navigated a narrow rocky decline down to the area. Looking back at the trail she'd taken to get here, Hatch thought it an odd place to dump a body. It would've been difficult terrain to carry a body over, even in daylight. But at night, the task would've been damn near impossible. At least not without leaving a treasure trove of potential trace evidence. But according to the police report she'd been given, nothing was located. Plus, the shrubs would've scratched up her sister's arms and legs on the way down. At the autopsy, there were no signs of this. Which led her to one possible conclusion: Her sister's body wasn't dumped here, yet she somehow ended up on the embankment.

Hatch stood and scanned the irregular oval shape of the expansive Nighthawk Lake. The gentle lapping of the water jarred a thought. *Drift.* She'd spent some time in Coronado, and the SEAL she'd lived with during her time there had explained the simple way they'd checked the set and drift each morning. A tennis ball was used to mark out the speed and direction of the ocean's current. It was a daily task for the basic course students, and they were required to deliver the surf report to the instructors before the day's training evolutions began. He told her a funny story about losing the tennis ball on one cold morning and, fearing the reprisal of getting the report wrong, slipped into icy cold water naked while his swim buddy marked the distance and direction as he bobbed along. She laughed, remembering the retelling of the story. Hatch hadn't thought of him in a long time. She pushed the memory back and refocused her thoughts.

Hatch did something essential to all investigations: She put herself in the mind of the criminal. *If somebody was in desperate need to rid themselves of a body, where would she choose? Which spot would provide ease of access and speed of escape?*

Thinking about the ripple of the water and recalling her base knowledge of set and drift, Hatch also took in the terrain and steep angles down to the water. A four-wheel drive vehicle would be a necessity to make the climb. Nobody in their right mind would risk getting stuck with a body in their trunk.

Hatch also took into account the minimal movement of the lake's surface. Some boat traffic would create wakes, disrupting the relatively pristine water with a temporary flux of man-made waves. She also knew most boating took place in the daylight hours and her sister's body had been found during the early morning. The only logical conclusion was the body was dropped close by.

Then she saw it. A small clearing about the length of two football fields away from her. The ground was wide and flat. There was a winding dirt road leading away from it, barely visible through the overgrowth of vegetation. The area was most likely a long-forgotten boat launch. A perfect spot for making a quick drop.

She approached on foot, skirting along the shoreline. The dank smell of mud rose with the rising temperature. Missing her morning run, Hatch was happy to have the opportunity to get in some exercise crossing the rugged landscape. The uneven terrain reminded her of the mountains of Afghanistan. This was much easier, and comparatively so without a sixty-pound rucksack on her back.

It wasn't long before she reached the spot she'd identified. Stopping before setting foot on the sandy packed mud, Hatch retrieved her phone from her pocket and snapped a photo. The image taken by her flip phone would be of the lowest quality, but for her purposes it would suffice.

In the dried mud, leading away from the water, was a set of tire tracks. Cool temperatures helped to lock in the shape, making the deep grooves of the treads clearly visible. Her eyes traced their path, following the wide textured lines as they wove their way upward until they disappeared over a rise of the hill above. The snapped branches and flattened tall grass added to the outline of the departing vehicle. She inspected a snapped branch. The woody innards of the limb were an off-white and still maintained some elasticity, further proving her theory and indicating the trail had been made relatively recently.

Hatch bent low, closely examining the tread marks. The vehicle responsible for them had a distinct pattern in the center, best described as a series of interlocking puzzle pieces. She committed them to memory after taking another photograph, not confident in her flip phone's ability to adequately capture the details should she need it for later comparison.

She followed the trail up, walking the packed earth the vehicle had traveled until she came to a more distinct path that connected with the main road, a narrow two-lane strip of asphalt which wrapped around the lake.

Satisfied she'd gathered her first tangible lead, Hatch walked the shoulder back toward where she'd parked the old Ford.

As she rounded the final bend, the backend of her pickup came into view. Hatch was surprised to see that she wasn't alone. A Hawk's Landing Sheriff's SUV parked alongside her busted old pickup. A female deputy was standing at the overlook, shielding her eyes from the morning's light breaking through the overcast sky.

Hatch approached quietly, using the time to size up the deputy. The woman had her hair pulled into a tight bun and her uniform was neatly pressed. Her boots still held a shine, and it was apparent to Hatch this woman hadn't attempted to follow her down to the muddy bottom.

"Can I help you?"

The deputy jumped at the sound of Hatch's voice. Turning, she quickly worked to settle her unease. "God, you gave me a scare."

"Didn't mean to."

The female deputy eyed Hatch carefully. She seemed nervous, looking beyond Hatch in the direction she'd just come from. Maybe word about last night's bar incident had already snaked its way to the ear of the Sheriff. She watched the deputy's hands. They moved toward her patrol belt and she tucked her thumbs in beneath the front buckle.

Was the deputy here to arrest her? she wondered. Hard to tell from the woman's posture.

"I'm Deputy Sinclair with the Sheriff's office. You must be Rachel Hatch?"

"People just call me Hatch." She stopped a few feet from the woman and looked around. Sinclair was alone. Not a typical tactic if one was planning on making an arrest. But Hawk's Landing was a small department, and it was possible they didn't have the manpower to follow traditional protocols. "What can I do for you, Deputy?"

"Becky is fine."

"Okay, Becky, what can I do for you? I seriously doubt you came out here to admire the view."

She cleared her throat. "The Sheriff would like to see you?"

"Is this some informal Hawk's Landing way of saying I'm under arrest?"

Sinclair looked uncomfortable at the question, and she began to nervously drum her fingers on the plastic of the buckle. "No. At least I don't think so. I mean, Sheriff Savage knows about last night —what happened with Bill Chisolm and all. Hell, everybody knows."

Great, thought Hatch. The small-town speed of gossip had always been fast, but the flow of information was probably made faster by things like Facebook and Twitter. The social media craze hadn't really taken hold when she lived here fifteen years ago.

"Not sure I know exactly what you're talking about," Hatch said, not comfortable with self-incrimination.

"I'm not here to arrest you. This isn't some tricky way of getting you to tell me what went down last night. And for what it's worth

—that asshole had it coming for a long time now. I, for one, am glad it came at the hand of a woman."

It seemed like the deputy was on her side in the matter, but Hatch didn't let her guard down. She'd used this tactic numerous times during her time as an interrogator, working to build trust by showing support. The idea was to lower a person's guard until they let something slip.

"How'd you find me?"

Sinclair was caught off guard by the question, hesitating briefly before answering. "Um—well—I followed you."

Hatch bit the inside of her lip, punishing herself for being careless. She'd been well trained to remain vigilant of her surroundings but allowed tunnel vision to get the best of her. It wouldn't happen again. "Followed me?"

Sinclair sighed, shrinking slightly. "After you went onto old Jed Russell's place, the Sheriff was concerned you weren't going to heed his warning to steer clear of the case. So, he assigned me to keep an eye on you." Her thin lips curled up into a smile, looking at her truck and then back toward the lake. "Looks like he was right."

Hatch shrugged, stuffing her hands into her pocket. It was a test of sorts. If Sinclair was intent on arresting her, she would address the hands in her pocket. If this was a casual conversation, it wouldn't worry her. Sinclair didn't react to the movement. "I was just out for a morning hike."

"Just a coincidence then that this happens to be the same area where your sister was found?"

"Guess so."

"Listen, Hatch, we want to figure this thing out as much as you do."

"Doubt it."

"I knew her, too. Olivia was a good person. We weren't close, but I saw her around town all the time. In fact, I'd bump into her almost every morning at Tomlin's Bakery. Your sister always ordered the same thing, a blueberry scone and vanilla latte. She usually got it to go, but every once in a while, we'd sit and chat."

"You see my sister around town and think you're on equal footing with me about the need to solve this thing?"

Sinclair cowered at Hatch's retort. "All I'm saying is we're on the same team here."

"We'll see about that after I speak with Savage."

Curiosity got the best of Sinclair. "Did you find anything down there?"

"No. Looks like you all got everything during the initial investigation."

Hatch wasn't sure about Sinclair, or the sheriff's office for that matter, and decided now wasn't the time to talk about the dump site she'd located and the tire tracks leading away from it.

"So, I'll let him know you'll be on your way?"

"Aren't you going to follow me?"

"Not sure I'll be able to. You drive like a crazy person. I actually lost you for a bit this morning. Took me a while to find your truck after you turned onto the lake road."

"Never been much for speed limits. See them more as a caution sign for inept drivers."

"I can see that."

Hatch got into her F150 and pulled out onto the roadway, quickly losing sight of the deputy and her SUV behind a curve in the road. She had other places to visit this morning and hoped the unexpected detour to meet with Savage wouldn't interfere.

11

"I'VE SEEN MORE OF YOU THIS WEEK THAN MY OWN GRANDDAUGHTER, who I might add is just about your age." The woman seated behind the glass smiled. "I failed to introduce myself the other day. Things were a bit crazy around here. I'm Barbara Wright."

Hatch inhaled Barbara's perfume, which lingered just beyond the counter. "Nice to meet you, Mrs. Wright—officially, I mean."

"Please, just call me Barbara. The missus stuff makes me sound old." She gave a friendly wink.

Hatch gave a rare smile. "I think Sheriff Savage is expecting me."

"I am."

Dalton Savage stood in the doorway. He wore a pair of well-worn jeans and a brown button-up long-sleeved shirt, the silver star pinned above the pocket. He had a ruggedness to his features, well-suited for this town's landscape. If he'd been wearing a Stetson, the ensemble would've been complete. The Marlboro Man would be jealous.

"Sheriff, you wanted to see me?"

He stepped aside, opening the door wide and ushering her in.

Hatch felt as though she was back in grade school and had been sent to the principal's office. A feeling she had multiple experiences from which to draw comparison. She moved past Savage, and he fell in behind her.

The hallway was narrow but quickly opened up into an office space with a cluster of desks in the center. Deputy Littleton was typing at a computer, using the painfully slow hunt and peck method. *Didn't every Millennial grow up with a computer in hand these days?* He'd probably quadruple his output had he been able to use his phone and text the report.

Littleton, seeing her enter, perked up and waved. The young deputy reminded her of a puppy dog, eager but relatively clueless. Hatch nodded, acknowledging him.

She turned and faced Savage. "Where are we doing this?"

"In my office."

He took the lead, stepping around her as he moved to the open office door on the far side of the room. As he passed, Hatch smelled black licorice again. With no formaldehyde to overtake the scent this time, it was more pronounced.

Hatch stood as Savage took his seat behind the cluttered desk. There were partially filled boxes scattered about the floor. She couldn't tell if it was old stuff to be discarded or his things left in mid-stages of unpacking.

"Don't mind the mess. I'm not normally this disorganized."

"I don't judge. I've basically lived out of an Army duffle most of my adult life. If I couldn't fit it in, then it never made my next move. Traveling light has always worked for me."

"Maybe that's a better way to live."

"The jury's still out on that."

Savage pushed aside a stack of papers. "Have a seat. Grab you a cup of coffee? Some water?"

"No offense, but I don't plan on spending much time here."

"In town or in my office."

"Neither if I can help it."

"Let's slow things down a bit." Savage eyed the chair near where Hatch was standing. "Please, have a seat. There are some things I'd like to discuss with you."

Hatch heard the change in the man's tone; a slight firmness filtered into his otherwise laid-back demeanor. It was clear enough for her to notice, so she decided to pick her battles.

"Okay."

Pulling the chair toward the desk, Hatch sat with eyes firmly fixed on the Sheriff's. She wouldn't play coy. And she definitely wasn't the least bit intimidated by her current surroundings. She'd sat across from terrorist leaders who had wanted her dead. This was pleasant in comparison.

"I did a little digging into your background."

"Find anything interesting?"

"Not really. Not to say you're not interesting. I'm just saying there isn't much out there about you. Your military record is pretty light for somebody who served the better part of fifteen years."

"Not for nothing, but how'd you get access to my military record?"

"Like I said before, I wasn't always local. I networked and built up some solid connections in a wide variety of arenas during my time in Denver. Been assigned to a few federal task forces, including the FBI's Counter Terrorism Unit. There were military attaches in supporting roles."

"And so you reached out to an old Army buddy and had him poke around?"

"I did."

"You know that's illegal. There are reasons why obtaining military records outside of proper channels isn't allowed. Some things aren't privy to the general population."

Savage glanced down at a pile of papers to his right. "In the end, it didn't really matter anyway because there's not much to it. Most of your service history was redacted."

"Or beyond the means and abilities of your contact."

Savage raised an eyebrow. "Kind of hard to believe if you knew who my point of contact is. He's a pretty powerful player within the Department of Defense."

Hatch said nothing. She knew why they couldn't access her records, but there was no need explaining it to the Sheriff of Hawk's Landing. Whoever his contact was, high ranking official or not, there were only a few who had access to her and the members of her old unit.

"You did rack up an impressive list of awards. Whatever you did, classified or otherwise, it appears you served admirably. That being said, I've got to ask—why did you get out after fifteen years of service? Five years, and you'd be on a full retirement."

"Medical." Usually this was enough to shut down most follow-up questions, but she could see from Savage's face, he was already prepared with another.

"Is that what the Purple Heart was for?"

Hatch nodded but didn't want to go into the details. It was a story she shared with few and one she wasn't ready to discuss with a man she hardly knew. "I hope you didn't call me in for this. Going over my military history seems like a gigantic waste of time. Why worry about me and my past when you've got a real case to work going on in the here and now."

"Because you've made it a point of looking into your sister's case. And I'm thorough in what I do. I can't have you poking around this case on your own."

"And why not?"

"Because you're getting in the way of my investigation."

"How so?"

"I've got one of my three deputies assigned to keep an eye on you."

"Doesn't seem like the most effective use of your limited manpower."

"It isn't, but I heard about the assault last night."

"What assault?"

"C'mon, Hatch, do we really need to do this? Are you going to fight me every step of the way? I'd like to think we're on the same team here." Frustration was layered thick in his plea as Savage methodically rubbed at his temples.

"So, that's the real reason you brought me here—to talk about last night?" Hatch shifted back in her chair, expanding her peripheral vision to include the door to Savage's office. She didn't want one of his deputies to pop in to make the arrest. Her mind was still not fully convinced this wasn't a slow country way of doing business.

An uneasiness shrouded her. She couldn't let them arrest her. Hatch was already operating at a disadvantage in working the case, arriving several days after Olivia's body had been discovered. Leads in homicide investigations dried up quickly with the passage of time. Every hour mattered in a death investigation.

Hatch committed her mind; nobody was going to be putting handcuffs on her today. The odds against her were daunting with two deputies and the Sheriff inside the station, but she'd faced worse and come out on top. And those were trained men. This ragtag group would be at a disadvantage should she try to escape. The downside, if it came to that, would be she would be on the run while trying to solve a murder.

Decisions like this were simple at their core—act before reacting, commit fully and adapt to the variables. These were lessons taught by her father at an early age and honed under the crucible of her Army training.

Savage watched her and must've sensed her unease. "I'm not going to arrest you. I heard about Chisolm getting his ass handed to him. I also heard he was seconds away from caving in a girl's face. Plus, a big guy like him would never make a formal statement of being beaten up by a woman. They'd pull his man card."

"Then what? Why am I here?"

The Sheriff leaned forward and his voice hushed to a whisper. "I'd like to ask for your assistance."

"My assistance? How so?"

Savage reached into his drawer and pulled out a silver starred badge, resting it on the desk. "I know you've got the investigative experience. One of the members of my Homicide Unit in Denver was former Army CID. He had a depth of knowledge that proved very useful on the cases we worked together. He'd told me about some of his cases."

"Let me get this straight, I beat a guy up in a bar while sticking my nose in your investigation and you think offering me a job is the best course of action?"

"I trust my gut and I need another real investigator on this. You're already doing the work anyway, might as well put it to good use."

"I don't plan on sticking around here when this is over. Don't really need a job."

"It's temporary. When this is done, you can cut and run."

Hatch sat quietly, processing the sheriff's train of thought.

"Ever heard of posse comitatus?" Savage didn't wait for Hatch to answer. "It's an old law that never came off the books here in Colorado. Basically, it allows a sheriff to deputize a citizen for a specific task. It was used back in the day with more regularity but has been utilized in recent years in places like Hinsdale County when the local sheriff was murdered. It was used in Larimer County in response to a devastating flood. And I'm invoking it now with you, here in Hawk's Landing."

"And you want me to work for you?"

"It's better than working against me. What's that saying? The enemy of my enemy is my friend. Plus, I could use your eye on this case." Savage shot a glance toward the outer office. Littleton was trying to work the copier with great difficulty. "My department is limited in experience. And this case is proving to be well above their skill level. I really could use an extra hand around here. Somebody who knows their way around a crime scene and can see things others can't."

"How do you know I'm capable?"

"You quickly picked up some oddities during the autopsy. And you were digging around the initial crime scene this morning. For starters, it tells me you've got good instincts. It's what I would've done if the roles were reversed."

"I can probably get more accomplished without being tied down by the procedural rules and regulations."

Savage pushed the badge closer. "It will give you an all access pass into the investigation, so you don't have to be such a continual pain in my ass."

"Who says wearing that thing will change that?" Hatch picked up the tin badge and rolled it between her fingers.

"Well, for starters you'd know a small needle mark was found in her right foot near her big toe."

"Not sure what you're implying, but my sister wasn't an addict."

"I didn't say she was. But it's something we're looking into. I'm still waiting to hear back on the bloodwork. Things move a little slower on that end around here. I miss the ability I had to expedite things back in the big city. Working on getting the lab to move this to the front burner is like pushing a boulder uphill."

"I'm telling you I know my sister. You're looking in the wrong direction. Drugs were never her thing. Even out here in rural Colorado, she never once smoked marijuana when all her friends were doing it back in high school."

"You've been gone a long time. Things can change. People change." Savage softened. "I've seen it before—people using in secret. They shoot up in their foot because the marks are less noticeable. Hell, we almost missed it during the autopsy. The doc didn't catch it until after we left, and he was about to put her back into the locker."

Hatch wanted to scream and grab the man by the collar. Her sister didn't do drugs. But something stopped her from saying anything. The anger she felt was directed more at herself and not the man seated before her. She'd been out of her sister's life for years. Maybe things had gotten so bad Olivia had sought escape in a needle. Hard to swallow. But Hatch had seen some tough operators follow a similar path when trying to run from the invisible scars of war.

"I will add that I don't think this was the case with your sister. There were no other signs of abuse and no other track marks to indicate any prior use. But if I'm going to do justice by your sister, then I need to explore all the angles. And if you're going to help out, you should, too."

Savage slid over a worn leather badge carrier. "So, how about it?"

She inserted the silver star into place and then clipped it to her waist. "Is this a clerical position, or do I get a gun?"

"What would a cop be without their duty weapon?"

From a locked drawer on the other end of the desk, Savage retrieved a small black case. Unlatching it, he revealed a Glock 22

.40 caliber semiautomatic handgun with two spare magazines. Savage tossed her a box of hollow point ammunition. Hatch caught it.

Loading up the mags, she gave Savage a playful smile. "Sure you want to do this?"

"No. But things being what they are, it seemed like the best of all options—unless you'd prefer I lock you up for interfering?" This time it was Savage who was smiling.

Hatch stood, guided the magazine into place and tapped the butt, seating it with a click. She racked the slide back, chambering a round. No point in having a gun if it wasn't in battery. Hatch looked at the holster and then held up her left hand. "Got another holster?"

"A lefty?"

"Wasn't always." Hatch cast a glance at the exposed scar tissue creeping up her hand and disappearing into the sleeve of her shirt. Savage didn't follow with a comment or question and she appreciated his discretion.

Savage went into a storage closet and fumbled through some boxes. He returned with a holster, still in its original packaging, and handed it to her. Hatch clipped it into a spot along her belt line behind the silver star and slid the weapon in place with a click.

"Well, Deputy, what do you have planned next?"

"Thinking of paying a visit to my sister's employer."

"Really? You think somebody at Nighthawk Engineering had something to do with this?"

She shrugged. "Not sure, but like you said, at this point, I'm not ready to rule anything out. I've already seen what the owner's son is capable of. The apple may not fall far from the tree."

"I just thought you'd be interested in helping me serve a search warrant at old mister Russell's place."

"Why didn't you say so in the first place? My plans can hold."

"Figured you'd say something like that. You didn't like him getting the drop on you."

"Can honestly say it hasn't happened much in my life. And I'd like to even the score. When are we going to execute it?"

"Now." Savage stood, looking past Hatch at the other deputies milling about the office. "I need some qualified backup before I approach that crazy shotgun-wielding coot again."

"He's a sneaky bastard and won't be too excited to see us again so soon."

Hatch exited the office and stopped. The jaw-dropped expression on Littleton's face was equaled only by the scowl on Cramer's. It became readily apparent Savage hadn't informed his deputies of his decision to bring her onboard the department's roster.

Savage stood alongside her. "I'd like you all to welcome Deputy Hatch. She's been brought in to assist with this investigation. She's got experience in this type of work and will be granted access to any and all resources at our disposal."

Cramer's arms folded tightly across his chest. "This is bullshit. You can't just give somebody a badge and gun! That's not how this works!"

Savage's face reddened. "Title 30, Article 10, Section 506 of the Colorado Revised Statutes says different. If you've got a problem, I'd be happy to have you step down so I could offer her a full-time position."

Cramer got up, storming out of the rear door and slamming it behind him.

"He's probably running off to tell his uncle." Littleton walked over to the two.

"Let him. He'd slow us down anyways."

"Welcome aboard." Littleton extended his hand.

Hatch shook it. The thin deputy's grip was limp and damp. "Thanks."

"It's about time we had another woman around this place." Barbara Wright rolled her chair into view.

"I agree." Becky Sinclair entered from the hallway. "Plus, that means I don't have to follow you around anymore."

"Littleton, you and Sinclair ride together. Hatch will come with me."

"Where're we going?" Sinclair asked.

"To serve a search warrant at Jed's place." Savage slapped the paperwork in his hand as he threw on a ballistic raid vest and moved toward the rear exit of the building. Hatch followed close behind. He called back over his shoulder, "Make sure you guys vest up. Jed doesn't seem to take kindly to strangers."

12

"Let me out here." Hatch was already gripping the door handle of the Suburban.

"What? Why?"

"I'm not going to repeat the same mistake as last time. Plus, I'm pretty sure your police vehicle isn't going to calm the old man's nerves. So we need to be ready with a plan B."

The vehicle slowed. They were still at least a half mile outside of Russell's property line. "Let's hear it. What do you have in mind?"

The car was almost at a stop when Hatch pulled the door open. Savage slammed the brakes. Dust kicked up and coated the insides of her nose and mouth as she leapt from the SUV. Littleton and Sinclair, following behind in their vehicle, stopped short with a shocked look of surprise at her hasty departure.

"I'll let you know when I know."

"I don't thi—"

Hatch didn't wait for Savage to finish his statement, shutting the door and picking up a quick jog into the wood line to the left.

She had a plan, just didn't want to waste time explaining it. Better to ask for forgiveness than permission. She found the trail she'd used the first time she snuck onto the man's property.

Within a minute she was out of sight. She heard the roar of the engine as it accelerated up the road.

Knowing it was imperative she arrive in time to assist in wrangling the old man into submission, Hatch picked up the pace of her trek. Her arrival time needed to be as close to Savage's and the others as possible so she could be in a position to provide assistance if Russell's temper flared. A likely probability based on the last exchange with the man.

The ground was an uneven smattering of rock and brush surrounded by tall pines. There was a low area, a naturally eroded water runoff from the hill. Hatch found it easier to navigate in the dry gully, and to keep her footing as she moved up to the property line. Being lower than the surrounding forest also gave her additional concealment from view, enabling her to run upright instead of moving along in a low crouch.

A steady cool breeze billowed past, drying the sweat on her forehead as it formed. She caught a hint of a dying campfire.

Savage had briefed her on his plan during their ride from the station. To avoid an unwanted confrontation, he decided the best course of action would be to stop at Russell's entrance gate and communicate using the Chevy's PA system. In his opinion, safety outweighed the element of surprise. Hatch agreed with his approach but felt it essential to have a backup contingency plan. Time and experience had proven Murphy's Law to be a fickle beast and thinking outside the box was critical to winning on the tactical field of play.

"Mr. Russell, this is Dalton Savage, Hawk's Landing Sheriff. We met the other day. I need you to exit the premises empty handed."

Hearing Savage's voice reverberate through the thin mountain air, Hatch quickened her pace.

A blast from a shotgun scattered birds in the nearby trees, causing them to take flight in a noisy panic. Hatch paused only momentarily. Not out of fear but out of a need to pinpoint the direction of the blast. It was off to her left, toward Russell's house. She also paused to listen for any sounds of anguish following the discharge. Unlikely at the distance he would've fired from, unless he was using slugs. A more likely scenario was the weapon had been a warning shot, but she wanted to make sure the others weren't injured. Silence followed the birds' ascension.

There was no return fire from the law enforcement side of the house. This was obviously because of Savage's control. It spoke volumes of his experience and his ability to think under pressure. And there is no greater pressure than that involving gun fire.

Hatch was on the move again. This time as she hurried along the makeshift path, it was Russell's voice she heard.

"I told you not to set foot on my damned property again. Not without a damned warrant!" The loud metallic *thunk* rang out as the shotgun's pump racked another round, punctuating his rant with the unspoken threat of violence.

Hatch was now on his flank. His voice gave away his exact location. She needed to time her next move carefully.

The PA's feedback echoed as Savage tried to continue the long-range communication. "Mr. Russell, we have a warrant in hand. I need you to lay down your shotgun, and I'll be happy to show it to you."

"How do I know this ain't one of your damned tricks?"

"I'm not here to trick you or harass you. You're going to have to trust me on this. Only way I can prove it is if I can show you this piece of paper. And the only way I can do that is if you put the gun down."

Jedediah Russell stood in line of sight with Savage and the other two deputies. He was atop the crest of his grassy hill and was standing next to a rusted-out shell of a pickup truck, a twelve-gauge Mossberg held at his hip line with the barrel pointed downrange. The man's long gray hair and beard flared out with a gust of wind, giving a wildness to him.

Nothing more was said by either side. A silent debate was being waged and both sides had decisions to make. The wrong one would no doubt be deadly.

"Do what the Sheriff said and put the weapon on the ground." Hatch whispered the words so as not to further startle the frazzled older man.

"What the he—"

Hatch stood three feet back from the man. She wanted to give herself distance should he spin on her. Pressing the gun up to his head, as seen in movies, only gave the other person a frame of reference, making it possible to counter and disarm an opponent. Being close yet far enough away added an element of the unknown. Unknowns cause hesitation, and that is how control is won.

"Don't turn. Just listen." Her voice was calm but assertive. "I've got a gun to the back of your head. I don't want to shoot you, old timer, but all that depends on you. And for what it's worth, I never miss."

Russell spat, just as he did the other day. His final protest made before yielding. Without an utterance, he slowly bent and placed the shotgun on the ground.

"Now, take two steps forward away from the sound of my voice."

The man complied.

Seeing that his resistance had ended, Hatch proceeded to walk the man down to Savage and the awaiting deputies. She maintained her distance and kept her gun trained on the back of his head until they reached them.

Savage took Russell by his wrist and turned him so he now faced Hatch. Keeping the man's hands behind his back, Savage searched the man for any additional weapons. None found, he released him.

Russell squinted his eyes at Hatch as she lowered her gun and holstered it.

His eyes then widened in recognition. "You're that girl I caught snooping the other day."

"I am."

"But I thought you weren't with the Sheriff's office?"

"I wasn't. Not until an hour ago."

Russell was obviously baffled. The bewildered look on his face spoke volumes.

"Mr. Russell, here's the warrant to search your property." Savage handed the man the copy of the warrant, identifying the legal right to conduct a search of the premises.

"I still don't understand. I did nothing wrong."

"I'd be happy to explain it to you. Let's head inside."

Littleton cleared his throat, making a squeaking sound. He then whispered, "Sheriff, mind if I sit this one out."

"I thought you were eager to learn."

"I am it's just—" The young deputy shot a glance down, drawing attention to the damp stain on the front of his khaki pants.

"Okay, just wait in the cruiser."

Littleton's face blotched red in embarrassment as he turned.

Hatch, Savage, and Sinclair escorted Russell back toward his house.

The old man muttered, "Well, that saying finally makes sense."

"What's that?"

"I guess I literally scared the piss outta that boy."

Hatch fought the urge to laugh.

Savage picked up Russell's shotgun as they passed it, cradling it across his forearm. He then caught up to Hatch and walked in step with her. The two took up the rear, walking behind the old man. Sinclair walked beside Jed, keeping a loose hand on the man's elbow.

Savage leaned in. "Would've been nice to know your plan before you bailed out of my car and went Lone Ranger on me."

"Sometimes I go on autopilot. I'm more accustomed to working alone."

"I can see that."

"At least it ended peacefully."

Savage nodded and tapped the butt of the twelve-gauge. "Thanks for taking the fight out of him before things went sideways. I'm glad we had you with us today."

"For what it's worth, you did a good job maintaining control while I got into position. Not an easy thing to do when guns are involved."

Neither comfortable with receiving compliments, the two finished the walk to Russell's ranch-style home in relative silence.

Hatch stepped up on the front step, hoping answers to her sister's death lay within.

13

THE INTERIOR OF THE HOUSE WAS SIMPLE IN FUNCTIONALITY. THE one-level ranch had decor one would expect from a man who lived alone in the mountains of Colorado. Most of the furniture looked hand-made, presumably by Russell or maybe purchased in town. Lemon and orange lingered heavy in the air. What surprised Hatch most was the cleanliness. The place wasn't just tidy, it was damn near spotless. A total contradiction to the man's unkempt personal state.

"I'm going to place your gun over here." Savage pressed the slide release and then pulled the pump grip, sliding it back and forth, releasing the unspent slug from the magazine tube. He racked it two more times for good measure and then visually inspected the ejection port, ensuring the weapon was empty before resting it against the wall nearest the door. "Why don't you have a seat over there?"

The old man let out a huff as he plopped into the living room recliner. "You showed me the warrant paper, but I still don't understand what this is all about."

Savage took up a seat on the couch across from Russell. "I tried to talk to you about it during our last visit, but you weren't in much of a mood to listen."

"I guess that's changed."

"Did you hear about the woman found dead at Nighthawk Lake?"

"I don't have a television. And the local paper is written by a bunch of idiots. The only news I get comes from when I head into town. I usually go in for food and supplies once a month. Sometimes I talk to Ruby Musgrave at the diner. But I ain't been in to town in about three weeks. Guess I'm due. Y'all gonna haul me off to jail anyway."

"Why would we do that?"

"Because I popped off my gun in the air."

"The way I see it, you were just trying to protect your property. Can't do that if you let anybody come up here whenever they please. And it isn't like anybody was hurt."

"Except, maybe that young deputy's pride." Russell gave a weak smile.

Hatch watched the change in Jedediah Russell's face. Savage's diplomacy melted away the old man's resistance in a matter of seconds.

"What about this dead woman has to do with me?"

"We're not sure. But her cell phone's last GPS location showed it was on your property."

"You tellin' me somebody was on my property and I didn't know?"

"I'm saying her phone's data showed it was here on Friday night."

"This past Friday?"

"Yes, why?"

"You're not going to believe me, but I was out."

"I thought you said you haven't been to town in a few weeks." Savage spoke and Sinclair wrote notes into her pad. Hatch stood by, taking it all in.

"I did."

"Then where were you on Friday night?"

"Fishing. I got this sweet little honey hole. I don't much like people, as you can plainly see, so I go at night. They bite better at night, too."

"How long would you say you were out at the lake?"

"I don't fish the lake. I fish the river. The Animas is much better."

"Okay. If you had to guess, how long would you say you were at the river?"

"I left just before dark and probably got back sometime after three in the morning. I don't have the same stamina I once had."

"Did you notice anything when you got back? A car or truck? Anything that might help us?"

"I'm sorry. Nothing was out of the ordinary until y'all showed up."

"The GPS gave a five-hundred-meter radius of your property. Any other structures out here on your land?"

"I've got a detached garage. And a shed where I do woodworking. Other than that, you're standing in it."

"Sinclair, you stay here with Mr. Russell."

Sinclair nodded her agreement to the task, but her eyes widened, and the fear on her face was palpable.

"I'll stand by in here," Hatch said. "You guys can run the search."

"You sure?" Sinclair offered, but was visibly relieved.

"I think we'll be just fine." Hatch replaced Savage on the couch as he stood.

"I'll let you know if we find anything."

Savage and Sinclair left out the door they had come in, leaving Hatch with the wild mountain man.

———

"How long have you been living up here, Mr. Russell?"

"Been about fifteen years, give or take. And please call me Jed."

"It looks like you and I swapped out."

"How's that?"

"I was born and raised here but left around the time you apparently arrived in town." She glanced around at the sparse interior. "If you don't mind me asking, what brought you out here to Hawk's Landing?"

Jed Russell's head dipped lower. The shag of his hair flopped over his blue-gray eyes. "Long story. And one I don't much tell strangers."

"I think we're more alike than you realize. Not too many people get to point a gun at me and live to talk about it."

"Me neither." At this, both of them broke into a soft chuckle. "You move quiet as a cat on wet moss in the springtime. I can't remember a time somebody got the drop on me."

"Don't feel bad. I had good trainers, some of the Army's best. And old habits die hard."

Russell rolled back his sleeve and exposed a faded tattoo across his right forearm, a black shield with a face of an eagle and above it the airborne tab. The ink was more blue than black now, the lettering, and details of the eagle were blurred, but Rachel Hatch would recognize the patch of the 101st Airborne Division anywhere. "Me, too."

"Fort Campbell, Kentucky. That was my first duty station."

"I'm pretty sure I was there a long time before your day. Vietnam was a wild time to be a paratrooper." Russell traced his finger over the tattoo one time before rolling his sleeve back down. "How about you? Ever deploy?"

"Four times. Once to Iraq and twice to Afghanistan."

"I thought you said four times?"

"Nothing gets by you, Jed. There's another, but that one's off the books."

"Did you see combat?"

Hatch knew why the veteran soldier asked. There was an invisible barrier between those who served in a combat environment and those who served in actual combat, fighting for your life and the soldier standing next to you. Both deserved respect, but among soldiers, the latter was less common and therefore held in higher regard.

This time it was Hatch who rolled up her sleeve. Her right arm was a tangled web of raised scar tissue. She kept the underside out of view. "I got a different kind of tattoo. A gift from a not-too-friendly group of people in the mountains of Afghanistan."

Russell gave a solemn nod, one conveying both understanding and respect. "Were you with the 101st when you got that?"

She shook her head as she covered her damaged arm. "No. I was with a different unit at the time."

"Which one?"

"Some things can't be shared. I think you'll understand my discretion."

The old man pressed no further.

Hatch surveyed the room again. A series of pictures in a neat line on the fireplace mantle caught her eye.

Jed followed her gaze. "Those were taken a long time ago."

"Where are they now? Your family, I mean."

He sighed, and with it his demeanor changed. The crazy look dissipated, giving way to a thoughtful gaze. "Gone. Lost my daughter years back to a rock-climbing accident. Came here with my wife to escape. My daughter Camille would've been about your age. She was tough like you, too. In a different world, you might have even ended up serving together." He stared up at the pictures, focusing his gaze on one of a younger Jed with his arm tightly wrapped around a teenage girl. The two were on top of a snow-capped mountain and looked truly happy. He sighed. "Every nook of our old house carried with it some memory of Camille. So, we left it all behind to start anew."

"Did it work?"

Russell gave a weak shrug. "Not really. We quickly found that no amount of running would give us peace. When somebody is a part of you, as our daughter was for us, then no matter where you go, their memory will follow. My wife was taken from me a year after we moved here. Lost her to cancer. By the time we learned of her condition, it was too late for treatment. All the doctors could do was help with pain and keep her comfortable until the end."

"I'm sorry to hear that."

"At least she's with my daughter. Not sure my take on the great beyond, but the only peace I've found is in the hope there's something out there where our spirits can rest. I've been waiting for my time to join them." He eyed the empty shotgun resting against the wall where Savage had placed it. "Never got the nerve to pull the trigger. Thought about it plenty of times. Not in my nature to quit. But one thing's for certain, I'll welcome death when it comes."

Hatch battled with her own demons when it came to the dead. Her father's tragic demise coming at an early age caused her to question the purpose of life and the meaning of its end. None of which she'd ever fully resolved. She held off on debating the topic any further with the man.

"You said something to the Sheriff the other day when we were on your property. I've been meaning to ask you about it. You thought we might be with Nighthawk Engineering. Why would you think that?"

"Those bastards have been harassing me for years. Ever since they came to town. I own a large bit of land. When they took up business here, everybody was excited to have jobs. A boost to the economy, ya know? Old silver mine towns have a tendency to turn to dust when the well runs dry. But I wasn't fooled by their knight-in-shining-armor routine. I saw what they were up to."

"And what's that?"

"Well, I understand how a company like theirs works. I wasn't always the man you see before you. After the Army, I went to work in corporate America. Believe it or not, I rose through the ranks, becoming a CEO of a biotech firm before tragedy brought us to Hawk's Landing."

Hatch's eyes widened. She never would have guessed this man to have been capable of trading his jump boots for a corporate suit. She was impressed by the transformation.

Russell pushed his long hair out of his face and gave a tug of his beard for good measure. "I know, right? I look like I was raised by wolves. I even started talking like an uneducated mountain man to add to the subterfuge."

"Well your disguise worked. I never took you for management. Tell me more about the harassment."

"A few years back, the company started buying up all of the land around Nighthawk Lake. They made me an offer. An offer twice what this land was worth. That type of buyout strategy is common, especially if a natural resource is at stake."

"And how did you respond to their offer?"

Russell smiled and thrust his chin in the direction of the Mossberg. "I politely refused. Told them to stick it where the sun don't shine. I wasn't going to leave. I ran after my daughter's death and learned that didn't work. I definitely wasn't going to leave the last place to hold a memory of my wife. I'm terrified if I left, over time, I would lose any and all connection to my life."

"I understand that better than you know."

"It didn't stop there. These guys were pushy. The last time they came to me with an offer, it was four times the value. Big money. But I didn't budge."

"And when you turned down all of their financial offers?"

"Then came the threats. Nighthawk sent some big guys to rough me up and get me to sign the papers."

"How'd that turn out?"

"I showed those young muscle heads what an old paratrooper was capable of. I took some licks, but I gave as good as I got. And those bastards ran off with their tails tucked between their legs."

"Did it end there?"

"That was three weeks ago. Was the last I heard from them. That's why when you showed up, I figured I was in for another round."

Hatch believed him. She noticed the yellowed mark of the nearly healed bruise under Russell's left eye. "Makes sense. Why didn't you call the sheriff's office and tell them about the threats?"

"The former Sheriff, Larry Jeffries, was as corrupt as they come. I'm sure, without a doubt, he had his pockets full of Nighthawk money."

"But Savage's in charge now. Why didn't you go to him?"

"He'd just been appointed. Didn't have an opinion, but figured if he was elected over Jeffries, then Nighthawk already had him under control. It seems they've got a hold on everybody else around here."

"My positive opinion of people is hard earned. For what it's worth, I think it's safe to say you can trust Savage. He's one of the good guys."

"If you say so." Russell sat back and looked around his small living room. "For the life of me, I can't figure why that girl's cell phone was on my property. Any thoughts?"

"I don't know. I've been trying to figure that out since you and I began talking. Doesn't make sense."

His eyes widened. "They're trying to set me up. Frame me."

"Frame you? Why?"

"If they can put me in jail, I'd default on my mortgage. The bank is tied in with Nighthawk. They'd oust me while I rot in prison. I know it sounds like a conspiracy theory, but—"

Hatch thought about the photocopied map in her back pocket with Jed Russell's property circled in red. "No, it doesn't."

"They deputized you just for this case?"

"Yup. I guess the Sheriff wanted a little extra manpower. Plus, he was tired of me poking around on my own and figured it better to join forces."

"And why are you so interested in this investigation?"

"Because that dead girl was my twin sister."

Jed's gaze lowered to the floor as he nodded. "I'm sorry to hear that. Guess we are more alike than I realized."

"Guess so."

"And whoever's responsible is going to rue the day they pissed you off."

"That's my plan."

The door opened, allowing a chill to sweep across the room. Savage and Sinclair entered, both their cheeks pinched with red from the cool air. Sinclair walked over and stood behind the chair where Jed Russell was seated.

"Hatch, you got a minute?" Savage dipped his head in a silent beckoning.

Savage stepped into the kitchen and just out of earshot of Russell.

Hatch followed. "What's up? Find something?"

"I need you to stay cool. I don't want you to react to what I'm going to tell you."

"I'm calm. Just spit it out." Hatch's voice was raised just above a whisper. She could feel Russell's eyes upon her.

"We found rope. It was hanging loose around the arms of a metal chair. If I had to guess—it was used to tie up Olivia."

Hatch listened to the words and then looked over at Russell. She replayed the conversation they'd had just moments before. Either the old man had lied and was a killer, or he was telling the truth and they had a much bigger problem on their hands. Her gut told her which direction to lean. It had served her well in the past and she trusted it now.

"There's another thing. Looks like we found the murder weapon."

"What?"

"There's a syringe on the floor. I'm going to go out on a limb and say whatever's in your sister's system is going to match any residue found in the needle."

Savage looked past Hatch, eyeing Russell. Sinclair stood nervously behind him, aware of the findings and whatever follow-up course of action they'd planned.

Hatch gently grabbed Savage by the elbow. "It's not him."

"What are you talking about?" His voice teetered just beneath the threshold of a whisper.

"I talked to him. He's not the killer."

"Then who is?"

"I don't know."

"I'm going to ask Mr. Russell to come to the station with us. We're going to need to do a full interview. I put a call in to the State Police to provide mutual aid and assist in processing the crime scene. They've got their crime scene techs on the way. Should be here within the hour."

"I think it's a waste of time to bring Jed in. We should be looking at another angle."

"Like what?"

"Nighthawk Engineering."

"You think it's more plausible that there's some conspiracy afoot than a trespasser who came across paths with a deranged old man?"

"He's not deranged. You brought me on this case for my insight, and I'm telling you to trust me."

"We can explore your theory after we've had time to talk with Mr. Russell at the station."

Hatch didn't argue further and turned away. She walked over to the seated man and stood before him. "Jed, the Sheriff's going to need you to come down to the station and give a statement."

"What did you find?"

"Enough that they're going to need to hear your side of things." Hatch bent low and gently gripped the man's forearm at the spot of his tattoo. "It's not a trick. From one Screaming Eagle to another, you have my word. Just tell them what you told me, and you'll be back home before you know it."

Russell stood without any protest. Hatch followed Sinclair and Russell. Turning to Savage she said, "I'm going to ride in with them and help out."

Sinclair looked relieved at Hatch's offer.

Savage pulled Hatch aside with a gentle tug on her arm. "Listen, Hatch, we've got to run this one by the numbers. I'm more than happy to entertain all possibilities, but let's gather as much as we can before we shift gears in another direction."

"Fair enough." Hatch offered no further resistance.

Her next move was already in motion. And she preferred to make it alone.

14

THE LAYOUT WAS UNASSUMING. A FEW DOUBLE-WIDE TRAILERS IN line with a high chain link fence enclosed a fleet of construction equipment. All were embossed with the company's logo, a black hawk swooping downward set against a full moon.

Hatch parked her truck. Not comfortable with the idea of driving a sheriff's vehicle, she drove her own. The badge and gun were concealed under a lightweight gray parka. Her hands rested on them, separated only by the pocket lining. A gust of cold wind blew through, kicking up dust. She blinked it out of her eyes as she headed toward the trailer marked main office. As she stepped toward the door, a man exited a port-a-john off to the right, near the fence line. She recognized the large man immediately by his bandaged nose and hand.

Bill Chisolm scowled. The dark circles under his eyes gave him a menacing look. Hatch smiled back. Chisolm began approaching as she stepped inside the office space.

"Can I help you?" a man asked, looking up from a file. He was slender, in his mid-fifties, with a pointy nose and glasses.

"I'm looking to speak with Simon Chisolm."

"And who, may I ask, are you?"

"Rachel Hatch."

The man took off his glasses and gave a warm smile. He stood from his chair and made his way around his large desk over to where Hatch stood. "Miss Hatch, I'm terribly sorry for your loss. The resemblance—I can't believe I didn't notice it when you first entered. These eyes aren't what they used to be. Your sister was a valued employee and dear to our hearts."

"Thank you for that. I really need to speak with Mr. Chisolm."

The man outstretched his hand. "You are."

Hatch shook it and was taken aback by the man's outward kindness. He was not as she had pictured. Especially after hearing Jedediah Russell's claims. Maybe Savage was right to probe deeper with the mountain man.

"Please have a seat, Miss Hatch."

"Hatch is fine." She took an empty chair on the opposite side of the desk.

"So, what is it I can do for you?"

"I'm not sure. I'd like to find out what my sister was working on at the time of her death."

"Not sure I get what you mean. Your sister, God rest her soul, was an administrative assistant with us. She didn't have any particular assignment besides keeping me organized." He fanned his hands out at the stacks of paperwork and rolls of blueprints. "Heaven knows I need it. To be quite blunt, she was a secretary, albeit a good one."

"What about co-workers? Anybody she had problems with or a recent disagreement?"

"Absolutely not. She was loved by all."

The door to the office swung open. Standing in the doorway,

his massive hulk blocking out the daylight, was Bill Chisolm. "That's the stupid bitch who did this!"

Hatch stood and faced the massive man, preparing herself to provide him a follow-up lesson to the one she'd given him the night before.

"Bill, shut the door and your damned mouth too!" The kind demeanor of the elder Chisolm was now replaced with anger.

The door shut. The big man continued to seethe, his thick shoulders rising and falling in an exaggerated fashion.

"You're telling me this nice young lady did that to you?"

"She sucker-punched me."

"Not exactly, but I definitely caught you off guard." Hatch winked.

"You told me it was a bar fight."

"Well—" The big man appeared at a loss for words.

"He probably also failed to mention that he was seconds away from punching his date in the face when I interrupted."

"I'm going to file a complaint with the sheriff's office," Bill Chisolm said, folding his arms across his massive chest.

"Would you like to do that at the station?" Hatch opened her jacket, exposing her gun and badge. "Or would you prefer we do it right now?"

He went wide-eyed at the sight of the silver sheriff's star.

"We'll be doing nothing of the sort. Bill, step outside and let me finish my conversation with Miss—correction—Deputy Hatch. I'll deal with you later."

With that, the large man disappeared through the door he'd just entered, slamming it loudly.

"I'm sorry about him. He's really not a bad kid. Just has a bit of a temper on him."

"I guess you can see why I came to talk with you."

"Don't get me wrong, Bill's no angel, but he's my son and I can vouch for him. He got along well with your sister. And if it's not too inappropriate to say, I think she fancied him."

"I'm not seeing it. But I've been gone a while."

"And you've been hired by the sheriff's department?"

"It's a temporary thing. Just until I figure out what happened to my sister."

"That's good. Hopefully, you'll be able to figure this out. It was a tragedy. And you think her drowning had something to do with her working here?"

"I'm not sure about anything. Just covering all the bases."

"One of the deputies already stopped by a few days ago. A nice kid, a bit young, but he seemed well-intentioned."

"I know. But I like to double check things."

"As a businessman, I can appreciate your thoroughness."

"Speaking of which—what is it your company does?"

"We mine uranium."

"Isn't that dangerous for the environment? I remember reading that most of the mining operations were closed down because of contamination issues."

"That was the case in years past, but at Nighthawk, we've refined the process. Zero contamination. I'm proud to say we're an environmentally-conscious company."

"Do you think I could have a look at your records?"

Simon Chisolm blinked twice in rapid succession. A minor facial tic, but Hatch had learned not to dismiss such observations. "I don't think that would be a problem. I would, however, need to see a warrant. I wouldn't want my shareholders thinking I disseminated company information without going through the proper channels. I'm sure you understand?"

Hatch felt he was stalling, but also knew without his consent she'd have no legal access until a search warrant was in hand.

She'd played her hand and was angry at herself for even asking. By the time a judge granted a warrant, anything of value would be destroyed or electronically buried. "I do. I wouldn't want them to think you were violating their trust."

"Thank you for understanding. Without trust, what do we have?"

Hatch turned to leave. "I'll be in touch."

"And good luck in your investigation. I hope you find what you're looking for."

"Me too."

Hatch left the trailer. She looked out on the site and saw Bill Chisolm standing with a group of men in hard hats. They were smaller than him, but not by much. One looked like a Fabio stunt double with his long, light brown hair tied back in a ponytail. She wondered if he was gathering reinforcements to take on the girl who kicked his ass.

She stepped down to the dirt lot. None from the group approached. They never broke eye contact as she entered her pickup, staring at her until she drove away.

Hatch's phone vibrated and she flipped it open, answering her mother's call.

"What's up?"

"I thought you would've been home by now."

"I'm working on something."

"I need you to pick up Jake. I dropped him at karate, but Daphne's not feeling well, and I've got her soaking in an Epsom bath. Could you get him?"

"Where's the karate school?"

"It's at the old gymnastics studio where you went as a kid."

"I thought it would've been torn down after it went out of business."

"Guess not. Anyway, he finishes up in about half an hour. If you could make it before he's done, I know he'd love it if you were able to watch him. He's quite good."

"Okay. I'm on my way."

15

It was strange seeing the sign for Flying Dragons where Sally's Gymnastics used to be. She'd only attended until the beginning of middle school, but standing in front of the glass panes brought back a memory of her father. He would wait for her to finish the class, watching through the glass.

Hatch watched, just as her father had done with her, while Jake moved around the mat. He wore bright red sparring gear as he bounced lightly on his feet. His opponent was a heavier boy. Jake threw a jab-cross combination followed by a roundhouse kick. Her mother was right, he was good. He delivered the trio of blows quickly. The bigger boy parried the punches, but the kick found its mark, striking him in the side of the head with enough force to spin the boy's headgear.

The instructor separated the two and brought them back to a neutral ready position. They faced each other and bowed. With the match over, all of the students formed a line facing the instructor and gave a synchronized bow.

Jake turned as Hatch entered. She watched his face shift from elation to disappointment in the blink of an eye. Seeing her had to be a painful reminder of his mother and a twisted play on his fragile mind.

He stepped off the mat and sat on a bench to begin loading his duffle with his training gear. Jake slid on his shoes and put on his jacket.

"I didn't know you were into martial arts."

Jake had a vacantness to his eyes. "Yeah. Been doing it for a little over a year."

"I would've guessed you've been training for a lot longer."

Jake smiled. It was the first time she'd seen him do this since arriving home. And with it, his protective shell seemed to melt away.

"If you want, I'd be happy to teach you a couple moves."

"You know karate?"

"I do."

The two walked out as the sun was beginning its descent. The air had chilled ten degrees in the time she had been inside. She took Jake's bag as he climbed into the truck and put it in the storage space behind her seat. As she was closing the outer cabin door to the cab's stow area, Hatch felt as though somebody was watching her. She looked up to see Fabio, the ponytailed construction worker who'd been standing with Bill Chisolm when she'd left. The man was across the street, near Gabe's Hardware. He wasn't wearing the hard hat anymore. He'd exchanged it for a ball cap and his hair was no longer tied back, now hanging loose. But Hatch never forgot a face, and she was certain it was him.

The two made eye contact. Fabio immediately broke away. Odd seeing him here. Odder still was his reaction to her seeing him.

The man got into a newer model red Dodge Ram and drove

off. She made a mental note to take a look into him. Something was definitely off. In her world, coincidence didn't exist. Had she not been with her nephew, Hatch would have followed to see what he was up to and where he was headed. She looked over at Jake as she entered the truck.

"Everything okay, Auntie Rachel?"

"Yeah, I just thought I saw somebody I knew."

She popped the emergency brake and shifted the truck into gear, pulling out from her parking space and heading out in the opposite direction of the man she wanted to follow.

"What moves are you going to teach me?"

There was an eagerness to the boy's voice. She was glad to hear it. The sound gave her confidence he'd find the strength to get through the loss of not one but both parents. "It's called a feign. And it works great against bigger opponents."

"A feign?"

Hatch was happy for the distraction. After seeing the place where her sister had been killed, she welcomed the conversation. "It's like a fake punch or kick."

"Oh, okay. Feign means fake. How does that help with the big fighters?"

"You don't want to try to stand toe to toe with them and bang it out. They can usually absorb more punishment, and you'll just tire yourself out." She looked over at the boy. His eyes were ablaze, soaking up the information like a dry sponge. "You're quick enough to use this effectively. I watched you with the boy you were sparring."

"That was Derek Milton. He's a jerk. Bullies a lot of kids around school."

"Well, you did a nice job smacking him in the face with your right foot."

Jake's grin widened into a full smile. "Yeah, I sure did."

"Next time, instead of wasting time trying to land those initial punches, throw a low kick but don't connect."

"I don't understand."

"Shoot your knee out like you're going to throw a front kick. When he lowers his guard to block, shoot that jab cross combo and double tap his face."

"I can't wait to try it."

Hatch gave him a wink as she approached a yellow traffic light on the downhill side of Main Street. "After dinner, maybe you and I can give it a try?"

"Sounds good to me."

Hatch applied the brakes. The pedal sunk to the floorboard. The truck continued to roll full speed toward the intersection. The light changed from yellow to red. She pumped hard on the pedal. Nothing. She pressed down on the e-brake. The cable locked and the worn tires screeched as the truck slid into the intersection.

The pickup jerked to a full stop. Hatch turned to Jake, whose face was white with fear. She spun just in time to see a Suburban closing the distance, the driver's eyes wide.

Time seemed to slow in those final seconds before impact. Hatch threw herself over to Jake's side in an effort to shield him from the impending collision.

The back-left quarter panel took the brunt of the impact and sent the truck into a wicked spin. Metal on metal boomed as glass shattered, sending bits and pieces throughout the interior like mini spears hurled by angry Lilliputians.

Hatch did her best to shelter Jake, but with the truck's emergency brake locked in place and the torque from the impact, the old Ford rolled hard onto the passenger side. The momentum slammed Hatch into something hard, either the window or dash. Her mind immediately became hazy.

Jake? Hatch searched for him as she fought against the closing blackness. Regardless of her will, she was swallowed into nothingness.

16

THE DARKNESS GAVE WAY TO LIGHT IN THE WAY MORNING FOG LIFTS from the foothills. A pulsing throb spread from the back of Hatch's head, across her forehead and nose. With every heartbeat the pain intensified. Even in her haze, the softness of the bed coupled with the steady beep and whir of a nearby machine clued Hatch to her whereabouts. The former Army investigator had spent numerous days and weeks in one. She was in a hospital.

Her mind couldn't sort how or why. Details of events leading up swirled in disjointed fashion. One by one they began to find order, an assembly line of images being fastened together until clarity was reached.

Jake! She thought of her nephew and the terrified look on his face. The last image of the boy's horror was etched in her mind.

Hatch jolted upright. The room spun and a searing pain resonated from her right arm. She looked down at the bandage. It was neatly dressed, and the sterile cotton wrap covered the majority of her forearm, masking the old scar tissue. She labored to pull air into her lungs. The beeping in the background sped up as her heart pounded in her chest.

She was in the emergency care section of a hospital. Only a wrap-around curtain separated her from other patients. Hatch saw no sign of Jake and worried. She didn't let her mind dwell on the worst of possibilities but prepared herself for it regardless. *Prepare for the worst and hope for the best.* Dad's mantra offered little comfort to her fear.

Hatch swung her feet off the edge of the bed. Prepared to move, she heard the voice of a woman beyond the partition on the left.

"Is he going to be okay?"

Hatch listened. The voice was soft, almost delicate. But it wasn't her mother.

"We've run him on an IV. The increase in fluid should flush out his kidneys. The pain should subside in a day or so. I want you to pick up a couple bottles of Pedialyte and continue the hydration process. Give him six ounces every hour he's awake."

"Doctor, do you know what caused this?"

"I'm not quite sure yet. His blood work is showing elevated levels of Alkaline Phosphatase. You mentioned your family drinks from well water?"

"Yes. Do you think there is a problem with the water?"

The doctor tapped his pen against his clipboard. "I don't know. To be on the safe side, use bottled water until I know more."

"Okay." Her voice quivered. "Should everyone in my family get tested?"

"Let's focus on your son first. There are a lot of possibilities to consider, and as of right now, he's the only one showing any symptoms."

"What does that mean?"

"It means I'd like you to bring your son back in a couple of days so I can further evaluate him. In the meantime, please ensure he's hydrating."

Hatch slid off the bed, the cold of the floor on her bare feet sent a chill up her spine. She took the IV stand in hand and dragged it with her as she shuffled over to the curtain.

"Knock, knock." The doctor pulled back the curtain and almost dropped his clipboard as he came face to face with Hatch.

She staggered back a step. "Sorry to startle you. I was looking for my nephew."

"You shouldn't be out of bed yet." He aimed a finger at the cot.

"Well, I am. And I need to see my nephew."

"He's okay. He's with your mother in the waiting room."

Relief washed over Hatch like cool rain. "Oh, thank God. He wasn't hurt then?"

"Broken arm. But it was a clean break. It's been set and cast." His face drew tight. "My concern is for you. Head trauma is nothing to take lightly. And you've been out for a little over three hours."

"I'm up now and feeling fine."

"You've got a concussion and two lacerations. Seven stitches above your left eyebrow and nineteen to the arm."

"Then it sounds like I'm all patched up."

"I really would like you to stick around for another couple hours—maybe even stay overnight."

"Out of the question. I'll sign the release."

The doctor threw his hands up in defeat. "Have it your way. I'll send the nurse in with the paperwork. Your clothes are over there on the chair."

"My gun and badge?"

"It's in the bag underneath." He parted the curtain and then looked back at her. "I didn't know we had a new deputy in Hawk's Landing."

"It's just temporary." Realizing she'd come off a little strong, Hatch added, "Thanks for patching me up, Doc."

"I can see you've been through some rough stuff before. Fire?"

"War."

"Oh." The doctor was at a loss for words and used the moment to break away. He retreated from the room, closing the curtain behind him.

Hatch, alone again, removed the tape securing the IV and pulled out the needle. She taped the bit of gauze back over the small hole to sop up the blood. Walking over to the chair containing her folded clothes, Hatch disrobed. She pulled up her jeans and threw on her shirt. As she buttoned the last button, the curtain opened again. Expecting to see the nurse, Hatch turned and instead found herself staring at Dalton Savage.

"Nothing like knocking first, huh?"

"Sorry, I wasn't thinking. The doctor said you were alert and I just—"

"Worried about me?"

"Well, you are my newest deputy. It'd look pretty bad on me if you died on the first day."

Hatch's grin shifted to a grimace as she adjusted the sleeve of her damaged arm, rolling it up to the elbow.

Savage looked at the scar damage covered by the pristine white of the bandage. "Must hurt."

"Everything is relative. A splinter doesn't hurt somebody who's pulled shrapnel out of their body."

"Guess so. What's that tattoo say?"

Hatch held up her bandaged arm. "What tattoo?"

"I saw it before, but didn't want to pry."

"And now you do?"

"I think we're close enough now." He smiled.

"Just a quote from *Alice in Wonderland*."

He nodded, withholding comment.

"Surprised?" she asked.

Savage shrugged. His face turned serious. "What were you doing at Nighthawk Engineering questioning Simon Chisolm?"

"I was checking a lead."

"You were supposed to be assisting Sinclair with the interview of Jed Russell. Instead, you disappeared to go off and run your own investigation. And then you wind up in a car accident."

"It was no accident."

"What do you mean, no accident?"

"Just that. My brake lines had to have been cut. They were working fine before I spoke with Chisolm. And then presto—they're not."

"Your truck is about as old as Jed and you're starting to sound about as crazy as him, too."

"So, you don't believe me?"

"I don't know what to believe. But if we're going to go after the wealthiest and most influential individual in town, then we'd better have some hard evidence."

"I saw a guy from Nighthawk just before the accident."

"Most of this town works for that company."

"I mean he was at the construction site with Chisolm Junior, and then he was across the street from me when I went to pick up my nephew from karate."

"There aren't a lot of places in town. Isn't that karate school on Main Street?"

Hatch saw his logic, and Savage's play at devil's advocate was starting to rub her the wrong way. The pain in her head was also intensifying. She decided to drop it until she had something more concrete than intuition and hunches. Her answer came in the form of a shrug.

"Your truck is at Bo's Automotive. Total loss, by the way. I'll call over and have them check out your brakes. In the meantime, you can ride with me."

Hatch pulled the gun and badge from the bag. She looked at Savage before donning the items. "You still want me to have these?"

"As long as you still want them."

Hatch answered by clipping them onto her belt.

She walked out into the main hall of the small ER. A nurse flagged her down and hustled over. Winded from the short burst of energy, she held out a clipboard with the release attached. Hatch signed it and walked out to the lobby.

Jake was sitting in the chair tucked under Hatch's mother's arm as she gently stroked the top of his head. The two looked up as Hatch entered the waiting area.

"You doing okay?" Hatch squatted down in front of the boy.

He nodded, holding up his cast. "Are you?"

"Just a couple of scratches. Nothing to worry about."

Jake held up his cast. "I guess it'll be a while before you can teach me those moves."

"Nonsense." She lifted her scarred arm into view. "When this happened, my arm was useless for a very long time. I adapted and overcame it, learning to shoot with my left."

A glimmer of hope spread across his face. "You can still show me how to feign an attack?"

"Of course. Sometimes an injury can be one of the best ways to lull an opponent into a false sense of security, making the attack an even bigger surprise."

"Enough of all this talk of surprise attacks and violence. I think Jake's been through enough today." Hatch's mother stood. "We're going to head home. Are you coming with us?"

"I've got some work to do with the Sheriff."

Her mother looked down at the gun and badge. She whispered, "Whatever you do, please be safe."

The sentiment shocked Hatch, and she had no witty reply. The automatic sliding doors opened and a cold wind enveloped Hatch as her mother and nephew slipped into the night.

Hatch turned to Savage. "How about we get a bite to eat? Nearly dying's got me famished."

"Sounds good to me. I know just the spot."

17

CLAY'S DINER SMELLED THE SAME AS SHE'D REMEMBERED FROM HER high school days. A mix of maple syrup and coffee. The moment the aroma hit, her mouth watered and her stomach knotted. Hatch surveyed the scattered pockets of patrons sipping coffee or having a late meal. For being in a town with a population of less than three thousand, the restaurant always seemed to have customers. More so now. And Hatch assumed it had to do with the shift work at the mine.

Danielle Franklin walked over as Hatch and Savage took a seat in a booth. "Well, my goodness. Look what the cat dragged in. If it isn't Rachel Hatch?"

Danielle had been two grades below Hatch in school, but in Hawk's Landing the two knew each other well enough. The years had not been good to Danielle. She was frumpy, not fat, but she had a look of perpetual exhaustion. Sadly, Hatch remembered the girl bragging about getting her first job, starting out as busser here at Clay's. The first job apparently became the only job Danielle would know.

"Hi, Danielle. It's been a long time."

"My gosh, girl, what happened to you? Looks like you've been to hell and back."

"Aw this? Been through worse. Got in a car *accident*." She shot a glance at Savage.

"That one over on Main Street?"

"That's the one." Hatch didn't need to ask how the waitress would know about it. In this town, everybody had heard the news before her truck finished spinning.

"I'm sorry to hear about Olivia. She was a real sweetheart. She'd come in here from time to time with her kids. They love Clay's milkshakes." Danielle paused and looked over at Savage, as if she'd just realized he was there. "Oh goodness, I'm just over here running my trap. I didn't even see you there, Sheriff. Would you like the usual?"

"That'd be great."

"How about you, Rachel?"

"I'll do the meatloaf with a side of mashed potatoes."

"Sure thing." Danielle gave a slight bat of her eyes toward Savage.

As Danielle started walking away, Hatch called out to her, "Can you add a short stack to my order as well?"

Danielle gave a thumbs up without breaking stride.

"Did you just add a side of pancakes to your meatloaf dinner?"

"Yup. I told you I was starving." Hatch smiled.

"What?"

"Looks like you've got yourself a little bit of a fan club."

Savage shrugged her off and changed the subject. "Why don't you lay out your theory on why you're hell bent on going after Chisolm's company?"

Hatch reached into her back pocket and pulled out the piece of paper, unfolding it on the table between them.

"What's this?"

"Take a look and you tell me."

Savage leaned forward, looming over the table as he examined the image. Hatch again got the scent of licorice. "Looks like the lake. Not sure what the boundary lines are. Where'd you get this?"

"Olivia's room. I found it in her journal."

Savage sat back. "Any idea why she had it? Anything noted in her journal?"

"No. It was just stuffed inside."

"And you think this has something to do with her death?"

"I do." Hatch tapped her finger on the red circle. "That's Jed Russell's property. Speaking of, what did you end up doing with him?"

"Sinclair got a sworn statement from him. He denies having any contact with your sister and continued his claim that he was fishing on the night she disappeared. He added his conspiracy theory about members of Nighthawk Engineering coming by and harassing him after he refused a buyout option. And then he was returned home."

"So, you believe him?"

"Not necessarily, but we have his statement. Once I compile the evidence, I'll determine if we've got enough for an arrest warrant."

"You've got to be kidding me?" Hatch pushed back in her seat. The old vinyl squeaked. She sipped her bitter coffee. "I just showed you the map. Russell's property is being sought after by Chisolm."

"Land deals happen all the time. Hell, from what I understand, that company has bought up a bunch of places around the lake over the last few years." He tapped on the map. "I've got a different theory. This map with Russell's home circled was in your sister's possession. Maybe she went to his place to try and sway his decision. Maybe Chisolm decided using a softer approach might yield a more positive result. Your sister goes to the house and Jed decides to take out his anger on her."

"Please tell me you're not seriously entertaining this idea."

"I don't know. All I'm saying is sometimes the simplest solution is the right one. Your sister was murdered on his property. He's obviously got some anger issues."

"Does he seem like the type of guy to tie up a girl in his shed? I'd be more apt to follow your train of thought if she'd been found with a gunshot wound. And you still haven't accounted for the fact that I saw one of Chisolm's guys moments before my crash."

"Bo's shop is closed. I put a call in. Hopefully, I can ease your suspicion."

"Or confirm it."

Savage slid the paper back across to Hatch's side of the table, and she returned it to her pocket. The waitress returned and halted the conversation. She placed Savage's plate first. "Here you go, Sheriff."

Hatch received her food but with less care. "Anything else I can get you two?"

Savage shook his head. "I think we're good for now. I wouldn't mind a top off on my coffee when you get a chance."

Danielle smiled and then went to check on her other tables.

"Something I've been meaning to ask," Hatch said.

Savage stopped before taking a bite into his tuna on rye and waited. The sandwich hung in front of his mouth and he sighed.

"Licorice."

"What?"

"I've noticed it several times. Do you have some secret obsession with the candy?"

Savage laughed. "I used to smoke. Tried quitting a million times. Nothing worked. Then one day a guy I arrested had a bag of it on him while he was being booked. I asked him about it. And he told me it was how he quit. Of course, I was leery to take the advice of a murderer, but low and behold—it worked." He pulled a bag containing bite-sized squares of black licorice from the inner pocket of his jacket. "Never leave home without it."

She laughed. "Tell me—how did a licorice-eating homicide detective from Denver end up in little old Hawk's Landing?"

Savage took a bite of his sandwich, chewing slowly as if buying time. Hatch waited and dug into her meatloaf. It tasted as she'd remembered. The hot sauce Clay blended into his ketchup topping lingered on her tongue with just the right amount of heat.

Savage swallowed his sandwich, then cleared his throat. "I shot a kid."

Hatch stopped chewing. She nodded and held no judgment in her eyes, though inside she played out a short film of what might've happened. In her core, she felt every emotion Savage might have in the moments and days following the incident. But nothing in her world was ever black and white. In the blurred gray was a truth few could understand, unless they'd walked the same path.

"Well, he wasn't a kid," Savage said. "He was nineteen, but a kid to me."

"Did the department hammer you for it?"

"No. That's the thing. I was heralded as a hero. But it just made it worse."

Danielle came back over with her pot of fresh coffee. Steam rose as she refilled both cups. She must've noticed the intensity of the conversation because she made no attempt at flirtations or small talk before departing.

"I was assisting the robbery squad. They were tracking a crew hitting a bunch of Burger Kings at closing. A real professional group. They timed their hits when the stores were empty, just before locking up. Three of them. They used guns to threaten the workers and control them, pushing them into the manager's office where they would go for the safe's cash." He paused to add a spoonful of sugar to his coffee. He stirred, staring at the swirling black liquid mix with a fading foam head. "They were good. Fast and effective takeover. And long gone before any units arrived. We had no leads."

"Then how'd you catch up to them?"

"They'd hit most of the Burger Kings in that section of town. We later learned the ringleader was a former employee who got fired for stealing. That's why they were so familiar with the store's layout and routine. There were only three more restaurants in the area, so we staked them out. Every night for a week. On the seventh day, we saw the crew pull up. The orders were to take them upon exit, once they were clear of any potential hostages. Their M.O. had been to lock the employees in the manager's office after each hit."

A plate crashed in the kitchen, causing Savage to snap his head. Retelling the story had put him on edge.

"I didn't mean to dredge up the bad stuff," Hatch said. "Feel free to tell me it's none of my business."

"No. It feels good to talk about it. Not something I've done enough of."

"I understand that completely."

"Everything was going according to plan. While the crew was inside, my partner and I staged behind their getaway car. A few minutes later, they exited. When the three men were within a few feet of their vehicle, we revealed ourselves and began giving commands. It went sideways quickly. One of them ran and my partner broke into a foot chase, leaving me alone with the other two. I told them to drop their guns and get on the ground. One kid complied, the other didn't. He raised his gun. I got off three shots before he could fire on me."

"Sounds like a clean shoot to me. Kill or be killed. He made the choice and you answered."

"I guess." He slid his mug from his left hand to the right, and back again. "Except it wasn't a gun."

"What do you mean?"

"It was a pellet gun. Realistic as hell, but it wasn't real."

"Under those circumstances nobody would be able to tell. I mean, some of those things are perfect replicas. How manufacturers get away with it is beyond me."

"It doesn't take away from the fact that I killed a nineteen-year-old boy holding a plastic pellet gun."

Hatch could see the pain in his face. She could feel it tightening her lungs and diaphragm, knotting her stomach. Her words didn't console, and they were ones he'd probably heard a thousand times over from friends and coworkers and therapists.

She bit her lip. "Maybe it's time you heard my story."

Savage looked relieved, as if shifting the topic lifted his burden.

Hatch said, "I was assigned to a unit tasked with locating and interrogating high value targets. I won't talk much about that for reasons you already assumed when trying to backdoor my military records. To say the job was dangerous would be an understatement. I was in charge of interrogations but was brought on the capture missions so I could begin the rapport building immediately when the target's mind would be the most unprepared and disorganized."

"I can only imagine the training you had to go through."

"Good reason you should probably listen to my gut on Jed Russell. I rarely misread a person or situation."

"Point taken. Please continue."

"We were deep in an area of the country not too fond of American soldiers. Not many places are, but this was worse than most. We were pinned down by a sniper. Our team leader was working on calling in air support when I saw this girl. Hard to tell her age because of the abaya she wore. It's like an outer garment cloak. Her face was covered. But I remember her eyes, a golden brown. If I had to guess, she was in her teens. Something was off. She kept approaching our Humvee, taking small steps. In the dress, it almost looked as though she were floating across the terrain. I raised my gun and gave her commands in Arabic to stay, but she kept coming, step by delicate step. By the time I saw the cellphone in her hand, it was too late. I'd allowed her to get too close. I pulled the trigger, but the bomb strapped to the girl's torso exploded."

Pain seared through her arm. She unclenched her fist and traced her hand along the web of scar tissue.

"That's how you got that?"

"The tattoo? No, that was at a parlor in Florida." She gave him a weak smile.

Savage returned it with about as much emotion as he could in the moment. "What's it say?"

She held her arm out. "You can't figure it out?"

He took her hand in his. His touch was gentle. His fingers rough. "It's no use...uh, going back...to yesterday? Is that right?"

Hatch nodded. "Because I was a different person then."

"And that's from Alice in Wonderland?"

"That's right."

"Why?"

"It's the last thing my mother and I enjoyed together."

He glanced at the table as though he had another story to tell. "Back to the scar."

"Got it that day," she said. "A constant reminder to never let my guard down. And to always trust my instincts. But this arm is nothing. I lost a good friend to that blast. A blast I could've prevented. Now, do you see why you made the right call in that Burger King parking lot? You saw a threat and addressed it. Hesitation costs lives."

"Is that why you left the Army?"

"Yes and no. Rehabilitation of this arm took a while. It functions at about sixty percent of what it used to. So, I learned how to use my left. Retraining my firearms and hand-to-hand skills to my weak side took time. I had to prove myself to my old team. Go back through the Q Course a second time."

"The Q Course? Isn't that the Green Berets?"

"Yes. But any member of our task force, regardless of position, was required to successfully pass the twenty-four-day selection course. It was one of many obstacles to become part of my unit. I was the only female to have ever attended and completed the course on two separate occasions."

"I'm impressed. But I'm not shocked. I'm looking at a person who's eating meatloaf and pancakes after being crushed in a brutal car crash."

All the memories of the day and the past escaped with Hatch's burst of laughter. Savage joined in. The lightness was welcome, if brief.

"Well, the Army didn't see it that way," Hatch said. "Even after passing the requirements and with the endorsement from my former unit's team leader, the Army said no. I was allowed to remain on active duty, but I was assigned a desk job. You probably wouldn't guess this, but I'm not exactly the office type."

"Could've fooled me."

"Yeah, right. So, I packed up and left. The Army was gracious enough to give me a medical retirement. It's not much, but it supports my drifting habit." She sliced up a pancake with her fork. "I've been trying to find my way since."

"You're here now. Maybe the silver lining in this whole thing is you belong in Hawk's Landing. Maybe this is your second chance at things."

"Let's figure out who killed my sister before I start worrying about second chances."

"Fair enough. What are you thinking?"

"Trust me enough to make decisions now?"

Savage shrugged.

"Got access to the town hall after hours?"

Savage took the last bite, finishing off his sandwich. He extended a large key ring from a lanyard clipped to his belt. "I've literally got the keys to the city."

18

"WHAT ARE WE LOOKING FOR EXACTLY?"

Hatch popped her head up from a file cabinet. The musty smell of dirty carpet and old manila folders filled her nose. "Not sure. I'll know it when I see it."

"Makes it kind of hard for me to help with the search."

"You did help. You unlocked the door."

Savage rolled his eyes.

"Basically, I'm looking for all the land deeds and records of sale since Nighthawk Engineering came to town."

Savage walked over to a closed office. The stenciled letters read, Town Manager. He jingled the keychain. He tried several before caving to the fact the key was missing. "Any of your special training ever include picking a lock?"

Hatch returned a file to its rightful place and stood, closing the cabinet. It squeaked on uneven tracks and banged shut. She walked toward Savage with a broad grin. "Of course."

Within a matter of seconds, Hatch had the door open.

"MacGyver, eat your heart out," Savage said.

"Just wait until you see what I can do with a bobby pin and a couple of rubber bands."

Savage chuckled as he entered the office space of Town Manager Thad Cramer. He walked over to the four-drawer file cabinet near a bookcase by the window. He toggled the latch and pulled the handle and the top drawer rolled open. "Shall we?"

They rifled through the files, going drawer by drawer without luck. Until they reached the bottom drawer. In the very back was a thick file, banded closed. Savage retrieved it and set it down on Cramer's desk.

Releasing the band, the file spread open and several documents slid out. Hatch picked up one of the packets and quickly thumbed through it, scanning for some connection. It was a land deed, but the buyer information didn't say Nighthawk Engineering. The purchase was made by Danzig Holdings.

"Damn it!"

"What is it?" She looked up from the paper to see the Sheriff staring out the window.

"We've got company. Cramer."

"The town manager is here? At this hour?"

"No. It's Donny. Probably just doing a security check."

"I thought he didn't *do* anything."

Savage sighed. "He doesn't when it comes to work, but Sinclair told me he likes to pretend he's doing work by putting himself out here. But he really just goes into their break room, watches television, and eats."

"Regardless, he's here now. Going to be hard to explain why the two of us are in his uncle's office after hours."

"At least we parked on the opposite side of the building."

Hatch grabbed another stack of paper and began flipping through the pages.

"What are you doing?" Savage reached for the folder. "We've got to put this back in the cabinet and slip out."

"Hold on a sec. Just keep an eye on Don." Hatch found what she was looking for. She looked up at Savage. "The same company is buying up all these properties."

"He's out of his car." Savage bounced on his heels.

Hatch began putting the files back in the folder when one caught her eye. "Here's the unsigned offer Jed Russell was talking about. Looks like he wasn't lying about them offering about four times what the property is worth."

"Sounds like we're going to be digging a little deeper on this."

Hatch finished closing up the file and was working on stowing it back in its original position when Savage whispered, "We're out of time. He'll be coming through that door any second."

She finished clicking the cabinet closed. Savage ducked down behind the desk and Hatch maintained her already crouched position. In the quiet, they heard the old hinges of the front door of the building creak open followed by the heavy footsteps of Donald Cramer. It wasn't lost on Hatch the strangeness of seeing the Sheriff hide from one of his deputies.

If Savage was correct about Cramer's night-shift routine, then he'd be entering the main office space at any moment. His boots clapped loudly against the tile floor of the hallway.

The break room was on the opposite side of the office they were in. Hatch was hopeful the careless deputy wouldn't all of a sudden develop any police sense and notice the office was open.

Savage pulled out his cellphone.

Cramer walked into the break room and clicked on the light. The television came on soon after as the overweight lawman undid his duty belt and set it on the table. "Son of a bitch." The set went off.

Hatch didn't have a visual of the man but heard him donning

his gear again. She duck-walked around the desk, keeping her profile beneath the glass partition wall that faced the main space of the office. She tucked low near the entrance, ready to spring into action should the deputy enter.

The deputy didn't enter. He shut off the light to the break room, and Hatch could hear him lumber down the hall and out the door he'd entered only a minute before.

The two waited in silence for several minutes. Savage stood and looked out the window. The deputy's car was gone from the lot. He gave a relieved sigh. "That was close."

"That was weird. He came and then left. I didn't hear a radio call."

Savage held his cellphone in the air. "He got a message from me to get back to the station ASAP."

Hatch laughed.

"What was your plan?" Savage said.

"I was going to neutralize him."

Savage's face went rigid. "You were going to kill him?"

"I was going to knock him out. And hopefully before he saw either one of us."

His shock lessened. "Thank goodness for technology then."

"For once, I agree with that sentiment."

The two tidied up Cramer's office, putting things back exactly as they'd found them. They shut the door, made sure it was locked, and then walked out to Savage's Suburban parked by the back dumpster.

"Mind dropping me at home on the way?" Hatch asked. "We can pick this up tomorrow."

"Sure thing. What time do you want me to pick you up?"

"Let's make it seven. I'll let you sleep in."

"If seven's late, I'd hate to see what early is for you."

"There's a lot that can be accomplished in those early hours before the rest of the world is up and moving."

Hatch sat in the passenger seat as a wave of heat and exhaustion crashed over her. It might have been her body finally giving in to the physical stress of the car accident. And everything else. But deep down, she knew it was the emotional release of sharing her story with Savage. He was now in a very small group of people who'd ever been granted access to that memory. And with it an unspoken trust was given to him.

19

Sore would be the understatement of the century for the way Hatch felt. The rigid tension of her muscles when trying to shield Jake at the point of impact was the source for the achiness. It took a great amount of effort to sit up on the leather couch. Move an inch, wait for the knifing pain to subside as the muscles relaxed, and repeat. It was dark. A sliver of the moon doused the end of the couch with pale white light. It wasn't quite four-thirty in the morning. With no Daphne to aid her sleep, Hatch's insomnia had returned. Twisting and stretching slowly as she sat with her bare feet on the cold floor, a ripple of cracks and pops sounded as her joints released their pressure.

During her second round through the Army's Special Forces Qualification Course, Hatch rolled her ankle on a night land navigation training. Alone and in pain, she laced her boot tighter and pushed forward to the finish. Knowing she was under extra scrutiny for being both female and war wounded, Hatch kept the information from the medics. She wanted to give them no excuse to roll her back into another session or dismiss her completely from the program. The injury occurred on day eighteen of the twenty-four-day course. Each day she bound her damaged ankle as best she could and kept her boot tight against it for additional support.

Hatch continued to pass each evolution thrown her way over the six remaining days. Only when she was advised of passing the course did she notify the medical team of her injury. The ankle wasn't broken, but the surrounding ligaments were torn. She remembered the look on the doc's face when he saw her foot, discolored an odd mix of purple and yellow, and how his eyes widened when she told him the injury occurred six days prior.

She'd learned some valuable lessons that second time around. The biggest being that pain is a limitation capable of being overcome. The truest test of mind over matter is doing it when things matter the most.

Hatch stood. Throwing on a long-sleeved shirt, shorts, and sneakers, she left the room and headed out the back door. Her muscles seized again at the onslaught of thirty-degree air. The first mile of the jog was stilted. Her body remained tight and her breathing was out of rhythm. With every passing minute, the movement loosened things, and ten minutes in, her body fell into step with her mind's determined guidance.

She remained at her father's rock longer than usual, enjoying the meditative state the stillness put her in. She returned to the house to see the sun cresting over the roof. Savage's Chevy Suburban sat in the driveway. The hood was hot. The engine ticked. She hustled through the door.

Dalton Savage was seated at the table, bookended by her niece and nephew. Her mother came around from the kitchen and into view holding the coffee pot. "Rachel, the Sheriff was just telling us that he'd recruited you."

Savage silently mouthed, "Sorry."

"It's just temporary." Hatch turned her attention to him. "I lost track of time on my run."

"You went for a run after what you went through yesterday?" He shook his head. "Kids, if you got me a dictionary and opened it to the word crazy, there'd probably be a picture of your aunt there."

She waved him off, catching Jake's eye. "If you only train when it suits you, then you'll never be ready to function when it matters."

Hatch walked over and patted Daphne on the head. Then she went over to Jake, who was struggling to butter his toast with his left hand. She leaned in close and whispered in his ear, "It'll get easier. And don't forget we've got some training to do."

His face shifted from obvious frustration to one of stalwart determination as he moved the butter in a small arc across the crusted bread.

"Your mother makes a heck of a cup of coffee. Better not tell the customers at Clay's or there will be a mutiny."

Jasmine giggled. Something Hatch hadn't heard in ages. And the sound of her laughter brought with it a memory of her father and mother, holding each other right where her mother stood now, her father whispering in her ear sweet words Hatch never heard. It was the last good memory she had of them together. Hatch was twelve then. It was the morning her father died. That memory had been buried in the awfulness of the later events of the day. Hatch was grateful for its return.

"I'm going to shower up and then we'll get going."

"Don't hurry. I'm going to try and fill up on as much of this coffee as I can before we go." Savage winked at Jasmine.

Hatch heard her mother's laugh again as she bounded upstairs.

HATCH RETURNED A FEW MINUTES LATER. Her wet hair dampened the area of her shirt near the neckline. "Ready?"

Savage emptied his mug and carried it to the sink.

"I filled a thermos for you." Her mother handed it to Hatch as she passed by.

Hatch stopped and looked her mother in the eye while touching her elbow. "Thanks."

Savage thanked her mother, too, and gave each child a sticker badge before leaving. Then the two departed into the crisp morning air and entered the still warm suburban. Hatch shielded her eyes from the intense sun. She carefully sipped the coffee as Savage drove the vehicle down the windy dirt-covered driveway.

She broke the silence. "So, how'd it go with Cramer last night?"

"I read him the riot act about a bunch of incomplete paperwork. The guy really is one of the laziest people I've ever come across. He's got seventeen open cases. Seventeen." He paused for emphasis. "Most of which could be completed with a sentence or two."

"He was that way in high school, too. I guess when you come from money, you don't have the same drive mechanism."

"Where'd their wealth come from? It's not like the town had much to offer before Nighthawk Engineering rolled in."

"From what I remember, the Cramers were silver miners back in the day. Hit a big payload that's still paying out today."

"I'm sure the previous generation of hardworking prospectors would turn over in their graves if they saw the byproduct of their success."

"That's it!" Hatch almost dropped her thermos.

Savage looked over as he rolled the SUV to a stop in front of the main road. "What is it?"

"Let's head to the Emergency Room."

"Are you okay?"

"It's not me. It's something I overheard while there. It didn't click until now."

"Okay. Was it something I said?"

"*Byproduct.*"

Savage turned onto the road and headed in the direction of the hospital. "I may be wrong, but if I'm not, this investigation just got a whole lot messier."

"Messier? How?"

"My guess is Chisolm's company isn't as environmentally conscious as they'd like you to believe. I'll explain on the way."

20

THE HOSPITAL WAS SMALL, BUT APPROPRIATELY SO FOR THE population it served. There was an older man half asleep in one of the waiting room chairs. He looked half dead. Smelled that way, too. Hatch wasn't sure if he was waiting to be seen or waiting for a patient. She let Savage take the lead when dealing with the main desk's receptionist, figuring his position as Sheriff would hold more clout.

"Good morning. We're trying to find some information on a patient who was seen by the ER yesterday."

"Sheriff, you know we can't divulge patient information to you. Unless you have a warrant. Do you have one of those?"

"No. I understand the privacy laws, but this may be critically important to an ongoing investigation."

"I'd really like to help. But I could get in serious trouble. Lose my job. I can't risk it."

"How about we speak to the doctor then?" Hatch asked.

"I guess you could. Do you know which doctor you'd like to speak with?"

Hatch searched her mind to her very brief conversation she'd had with the doctor, trying to recall the stitched name on his lab coat. "I think it started with a T."

"Well, that would be Doctor Talbot." The secretary leaned and lowered her voice. "Short and a bit on the plump side with a pinched nose."

"That's the one."

"He's off for the next three days. He just finished up his rotation."

"Can we have his address? We really need to speak with him."

"Afraid that won't do you any good either. He just got a new boat and is on a fishing trip with his son."

Hatch bit her bottom lip in frustration.

A nurse walked into the reception area. "Mr. Caldwell, your wife's ready to see you now."

The half dead man snorted loudly as he righted himself. He shuffled slowly across the linoleum of the waiting room.

Hatch turned her attention back to the receptionist. "Listen, this information could save lives. That boy who was in the room next to me, he was sick. And I think I know why. If we don't have the information, then a lot more people are going to be filling these beds."

"I'm truly sorry. If it's as you say, I'm sure you could get a warrant for the records."

"That's time we may not have," Savage said.

The nurse cleared her throat loudly, and Hatch cast a glance in her direction. As the nurse began gently guiding old Mr. Caldwell into the doors of the ER she mouthed, "Out back."

Hatch acknowledged her receipt of the message with a barely perceptible nod of her head. She then faced Savage. "We're obviously not going to get anywhere here. Best we head out and look at getting that warrant."

Savage raised an eyebrow, baffled at Hatch's sudden change in tactic and temperament. "Okay."

"I'm sorry about not being of more help."

"No harm done. You're just doing your job." Hatch turned and Savage followed.

Outside of the hospital, Savage looked over at her. "You're up to something. I'm just not sure what exactly."

Hatch didn't say anything. She began walking away from where they were parked and around to the back side of the building.

Standing by the back door, Hatch waited as a harsh wind lashed at her face, causing the fresh laceration above her eye to tingle.

Savage took a fistful of licorice from his pocket and popped them into his mouth. "Waiting is always when the craving strikes hardest." His words were muffled by the chewy mass lining his cheeks.

A few minutes later, the door opened and the nurse from the lobby appeared. Her gaze swept the parking lot multiple times before she stepped out to meet them.

She approached with a file tucked under her arm. The nurse paused before handing it over to Hatch. "I could get in a lot of trouble for this."

"Thank you."

"I overheard you and felt something needed to be done. Doctor Talbot didn't seem to care much when I tried to explain to him it was the fifth case like that this month. Isolated events happen all the time, but patterned ones need to be analyzed. He told me he's aware and that it's being looked into. But I know he's lying. This medical chart was in his desk drawer. Along with the other four cases. Not normal protocol."

"You're doing the right thing in getting us this," Savage said.

"It's a copy. All five cases are in there." Rubbing her arms against the cold, the nurse began a hasty retreat back inside. "I hope you can put a stop to whatever's going on."

The nurse disappeared inside, leaving Hatch and Savage to themselves.

Hatch tucked the file inside her jacket and started walking back to their SUV.

"I don't know what we've gotten ourselves into, but one thing's for certain, Hatch. You've got us crossing over into some dangerous territory."

"Story of my life. Hopefully, it won't be my last chapter." Hatch opened the file folder and began thumbing through the medical charts.

"Anything to go on?"

She flipped back and forth between pages. "Looks like each patient was noted as having higher than normal levels of Alkaline Phosphatase. Not sure what that is, but I'm guessing it's not good. Each patient came in experiencing stomach pain. The youngest, age four, was experiencing some sort of issue with his kidney. That's the one I overheard yesterday."

"I guess we start there then."

Hatch gave Savage the address listed on the medical form. She knew the area. A small trailer community at the city limits.

21

SAVAGE SLOWED THE VEHICLE AS HE PULLED INTO HIDDEN GEM Trailer Park. Hatch took in the sight of the poorly kept double wide trailers interspersed among high pines. Hidden, yes. Gem, no.

A woman gave a wary eye as she swatted a rug hung on a clothesline extending from the corner of her home. Dust exploded into the air around her with each strike, mixing with the smoke seeping out of the corner of her mouth. A cigarette dangled from her lower lip and miraculously, the long ash didn't fall, in spite of the violent swings of the fan-shaped carpet beater. Its odor greeted them through the Suburban's cracked windows. Judging by the sharpness of the woman's glare, the sight of law enforcement was not a welcome one within this community.

"Looks like you've got a real fan club in these parts," she said.

Savage gave a bleak smile and focused on the road ahead. "Haven't had much dealings with this area since taking over. From what I hear, the last sheriff did his very best to make them feel unwelcome."

"Why's that?"

"Don't know. Might've grown up around here and developed a disdain for the residents. Or maybe he didn't like poor people? Whatever the reason, there was no love lost between the trailer park and sheriff's office."

"Could've been his intentions were influenced by somebody else." She stared at a porch missing its top step. "Somebody who needed them oppressed."

Most of the numbers on the homes were either faded or had fallen off. The last number they'd been able to make out was fifty-seven. The medical form said the boy lived at sixty-eight. As they came around a bend in the dirt path, they saw a trailer up ahead with a big wheel in the front yard.

Savage slowed as he came up to the overgrown driveway leading to a dilapidated home. "No numbers on this one, but if I had to guess, we're here."

They pulled to a stop. Savage cut the engine. Hatch saw a woman in her early twenties wearing a thick bathrobe and slippers sitting in a rocker on the trailer's small porch. The condition of the robe matched those of her surroundings. Tattered and torn bits of the once white cloth hung from the sleeves. A maroon thermal shirt, worn as an undergarment, came into view as the sleeve of her robe slid down to her elbow when the young woman raised her hands to sip from her coffee mug. Steam rose. The woman's eyes widened at the sight of the police vehicle.

Hatch exited the Suburban, stepping down onto pine needle-covered ground. The chill in the air was cooler than before. The shade cast by the pines dropped the temperature ten degrees. The faded remnants of dinner seared on a charcoal grill lingered. Could've been steak. Might've been possum.

The woman looked nervously back toward the front door as they approached. Hatch couldn't tell if she wanted to run away or call for help. Savage was definitely right about the community's perception of the police.

"Hi there, I'm Sheriff Savage and this is Deputy Hatch. We'd like to talk to you for a minute if that wouldn't be too much to ask."

"Am I in some kind of trouble?" She hugged her robe tight.

"Not at all. We'd just like to talk with you about your son Gabe."

Her eyes scrunched, pulling the chub of her cheeks into tight, rose-colored balls. "I don't understand."

"I was in the hospital yesterday," Hatch said. "Overheard the doctor speaking with you about your son."

"What's the police care about a sick boy? Got nothin' to do with the law. Hell, y'all never gave a damn about us out here before. And whenever you venture out this way, it's to harass or haul our asses off to jail."

"I've heard." Savage adjusted his posture to appear less intimidating. "However you've been treated before isn't going to pass muster on my watch. Without sounding like an old western, there truly is a new sheriff in town." Savage gave a tip of an invisible hat.

Hatch watched the former city homicide detective as he embodied the role of small-town sheriff. She was impressed at his ability to shift gears. A true chameleon. He must've been pretty good in an interrogation room.

"Well, 'round here talk is cheap." The young mother stood up and made for the door. "I don't think there's anything I've got to say to you two."

Hatch threw a Hail Mary. "There are others. More people who got sick just like your son. Probably more still to come." She softened her tone. "We really could use your help."

The woman paused with her hand on the door handle. "I don't think so."

Hatch stepped closer as the door opened and the woman

slipped inside. She closed it and the deadbolt locked into place. With her hands on her hips, Hatch threw her head back, then turned toward Savage. "Guess we move on to the next one."

"Not sure anybody in that file's going to be willing to speak with us."

Hatch met Savage's gaze. "And what makes you so sure of that?"

He pointed to the other side of the trailer. The front end of a Range Rover peeked out. Its highly-polished red exterior shimmered. The vehicle was worth more than the double wide when it was brand new. Hatch was surprised she hadn't noticed it before, but her focus had been on the woman.

"Something seem a bit out of place?" Savage walked around to take a closer look at the vehicle and Hatch followed.

"That thing's fresh off the lot. It's still got the purchase sticker on the driver side window." She cupped her hands against the glass and looked inside. "Are you thinking what I'm thinking?"

"They've been bought. No way living here under these conditions that young mother would be able to afford anything like that. Hell, I couldn't afford it."

"First, we learn of a doctor buying a brand-new boat. And now this. I wouldn't be surprised if we went to the others on this list, we'd find a similar set of circumstances."

"This isn't a wealthy town. Whoever's responsible probably figures it's easier to pay them off early, rather than in a class action lawsuit."

"If that's the case, then I'm going to assume they've signed a non-disclosure agreement of some sort to indemnify the company from any civil or criminal liability."

"Let's head back to the station and regroup."

THEY ENTERED through the front of the small headquarters. A heavy floral fragrance greeted them. Hatch glanced down and saw a plug-in air freshener hanging out of the first receptacle. Barbara perked up as Savage entered followed by Hatch. The thick plexi-glass partition separating the small lobby from the inner workings of the office gave a clear view into the cluster of cubicles set back from the receptionist's desk.

Hatch could see Cramer's boots propped up on his desk and crossed at the ankles. The lowest performing member of the department was either hard at work on a word jumble or fast asleep. Figuring him for the type of man who wouldn't be using his intellect during his spare time, Hatch assumed the latter.

"Looks like your little talk last night didn't take."

Savage closed his eyes and shook his head. "Can't polish a turd."

"One of my instructors used to say that on a regular basis. You never mentioned being prior military."

"Honorary. My father was Army. Master Sergeant. Always said I got it worse than any of his guys. We ended up at Fort Carson for his last duty station and I liked it so much I decided to make Colorado my home."

"It suits you."

Savage shrugged as he used his fob, swiping it over the dark gray pad to release the door's lock. He opened it and Hatch followed him in. "I'll get you a key card to the office later. Once things settle down."

"Don't worry about it." Her injured arm caught on the bulky lock hardware. She stifled a grunt. "I'm not planning on sticking around."

"This place hasn't won you over yet?" He smiled.

"It's not that," she said, rubbing her wrist. "I've just never been one for staying in one place for long. Especially since I left the service."

Cramer was snoring softly. His tranquil mid-morning siesta didn't last long. Savage walked by the man's small office space and swiped his boots off the desktop. Cramer's feet fell noisily to the floor. The portly deputy's legs a cantilever and his round buttocks the fulcrum, Don Cramer launched forward, throwing the newspaper in the air as he caught himself before face planting into his desk.

"What the hell?" Cramer yelled. His face turned red and his eyes darted back and forth as his brain sought to reconcile the sudden shift.

"My apologies for interrupting your beauty sleep." Savage leveled a heavy dose of sarcasm in his words.

"I was reading."

"Try again."

Cramer huffed. "You know I was working late last night. You're lucky I even came in this morning."

"Work is an understatement for what it is you think you do here. And lucky is not the word I'd use for describing my feelings toward you being here."

Barbara laughed. Her seat rolling into view, she gave two thumbs up followed by a golf clap. Savage didn't see because he was intently focused on his slack-jawed employee, but Hatch did and smiled her silent agreement.

"So, what's next?" Savage ignored Cramer's disgust, turning his attention back to Hatch.

"I'd like to look at your case files."

"What cases did you have in mind?"

"I want to take a look at those addresses." Hatch was vague. Cramer might be a slug when it came to work ethic, but she didn't want to risk exposing the focus of their investigation. Or more importantly, last night's break in at the Town Manager's office.

"We've got a digital report system, but all of them are printed and then filed."

"Where do you keep them?"

"Basement. Been meaning to go through them myself and do a little spring cleaning."

"Lead the way."

Savage headed toward the back. Hatch followed. There, just past his office, was a closed door. He used his fob to unlock it. Savage flicked on the light illuminating a metallic staircase leading down to a gray concrete floor.

A musty dampness assaulted Hatch's nostrils and the noisy hum of a dehumidifier filled the silence as she shut the door behind her. Lining the wall was a long line of six-foot-high cabinets. Even the newest additions to the metallic column looked to be at least ten years old.

"As antiquated as it is, these cabinets are filed in order by date. The farthest goes back nearly eighty years. A lot longer than we'd keep records in Denver. We had an archive, but mostly it's all digital now. But there's something about keeping a physical record of events that just feels right."

"Like turning the pages of a book or newspaper, rather than reading them on a phone or tablet." Hatch lightly rubbed her thumb and forefinger, imagining a piece of paper in between.

"Exactly."

It was dim, but she noted the smile forming in the corner of Savage's lips. Hatch pulled a small Maglite from her back pocket and illuminated the first cabinet she came to. There was a small handwritten label at the top, noting the files were from this year. She looked at the date of sale on the property list and moved to a drawer containing files from five years ago.

"What are we looking for exactly?" Savage asked.

"Not sure. Maybe wishful thinking, but it was something that mother said back at the trailer park that got me thinking."

"What's that?"

"She said whenever deputies came by it was either to harass or make an arrest."

"Nothing too unusual there. Sometimes that's the way people see us. You know as well as I do, public perception is often misguided." Savage gave a slight shrug. "Like I said, the prior Sheriff didn't have much fondness toward that community."

"But it made me think about old Jed and the pressure to sell."

"You think the former sheriff had something to do with these land deals?"

"Would it shock you if he did? I mean, didn't you tell me the only reason you were able to oust him from office and take the seat was because he'd been implicated in some misappropriation of the town's budget money?"

"There wasn't enough to formally press charges, but he was definitely dirty. People here knew it."

"That's my point. I'm guessing if you have an elected official who's filling his pockets, it's not a stretch to assume he may have diversified his sources."

Savage took a break from looking through files and glanced at Hatch. "It makes sense. Chisolm works hand in hand with Thad Cramer. Small town politics."

Flashing her light on the outside of a drawer, Hatch found the date range she'd been looking for. She pulled on the handle. The rolling mechanism squeaked loudly as it slid open. She put the end of the flashlight in her mouth. The grooved grip had a sour taste. The cone of light shone on the labels, each marked with a last name, address line, crime, and date of report. Hatch rifled through, her fingers rapidly pawing at the tabs as she scanned for what she hoped would be there. Savage leaned in over her shoulder.

Wedged in between a burglary file and a missing child case was the file containing the name and address she'd been looking for. Hatch slid the file out and Savage stepped back, giving her space as she stood. Pulling the flashlight out of her mouth, she wiped off the excess saliva on her shirt and handed it to Savage. He moved alongside her and shined the light down as Hatch opened the thin file.

The report, a town ordinance violation, was one page long and dated from last fall. The name of the person cited for illegal dumping was Jedediah Russell. Deputy Don Cramer had filed the report.

"Son of a bitch," Savage said.

"Looks like the former Sheriff had his hand in Chisolm's pocket and was doing his dirty work."

"He had a little help from our lazy friend upstairs. Makes more sense why he's hated me since day one. When I took over as sheriff, it must've cost him financially."

"If we can get some hard evidence to connect these, it may do more than hurt his bottom line." Hatch handed Savage the file and took back her flashlight. She then followed the row of cabinets going further down the line and deeper into the historical archives.

"I don't think we're going to find anything related past the five-year mark."

Hatch barely heard him. Her mind was focused on the dates. She muttered, "I know."

"Then what are you looking for now?"

"An answer."

"To what?"

"My past."

And with that, Hatch saw the block lettering, 1998. Her heart beat faster. A tingling sensation vibrated throughout her body comparable to the jittery feeling the first time she'd fired her weapon in combat. Her eyes lowered until she found the cabinet where the file would be. A momentary wave of doubt flooded her, and she questioned the rationality of what she thought might be inside.

Her gut instinct told her the answer, or potential answer, was somewhere in the rusted drawer before her. Hatch's gut was seldom, if ever, wrong. She pushed through her doubt and yanked open the cabinet. The filing system had been a little less organized twenty years ago, but there were a lot less reports, making the search easier. The file was thick and the corner of an eight-by-ten glossy photo was sticking out. She tapped it in place, not ready to see the images it contained. She closed the drawer and tucked the file under her arm.

Walking back to Savage, he gave her a weighted glance. "Did you find what you were looking for?"

"We'll see."

"Is this something I should be concerned about?"

"No." Hatch was evasive. She wasn't ready to bring Savage into this part of her past.

"I won't press. You'll let me know if and when you need me?"

"Yes." She appreciated him for giving her space. Hatch didn't need a knight in shining armor and he recognized this. "For now, let's stay focused on the case we're working."

"Fair enough. Looks like we've got plenty to follow up on."

The two spent the better part of the next hour seeking out other homeowners on the buyout list who'd had a police report filed about some minor infraction. Each report they found had been written by the same deputy.

They climbed the stairs and exited the basement. Hatch half

expected to see Cramer asleep in his chair again. But he was nowhere in sight.

"Where's Cramer?" Savage asked more to himself than anybody in particular.

Barbara rolled into view as Savage closed the door. "He left as soon as you two went downstairs."

"Did he say where he was going?"

"No, but he sure did look to be in a hurry. He's a man not known for speed." She chuckled at her own observation.

Hatch took into account the woman's words. Savage's eyes seemed to deepen, and she knew without asking he'd deduced the same thing. Cramer had scurried off like the rat he was to relay his observation.

"Do you have GPS in your vehicles?"

It was commonplace among most police departments to have a way of tracking the whereabouts of a shift. There were agencies that used the locators as a means of enhanced safety protocols. If a transmission for help went out, it was good to know where to send additional units. Dispatchers also used this for priority calls so that units in closest proximity to an incident could be sent first. But this was Hawk's Landing, and basing her question on the antiquated filing system she'd just witnessed in the basement, she wasn't sure the small sheriff's office was current when it came to technology.

He was already moving toward a computer terminal. A few rapid keystrokes and the monitor came to life, showing a two-dimensional map. "He's in the one marked four-oh-six. It's his badge number."

Hatch watched the rectangular icon with the 406-tag jitter forward on the map. "I wonder where he's going?"

"I don't." Savage trailed his finger up a path on the screen and stopped on a house set in a clearing, far away from anything else. "That's Larry Jefferies' place."

"The *former* sheriff?"

"He's running off to warn him."

"I guess old habits die hard." Hatch placed her hand on Savage's shoulder.

Savage looked back at her, his face hard to read. "This thing keeps growing. Pretty soon everybody in the town will be suspect."

"Maybe they all are."

Hatch's phone rang. Looking down at the caller ID, she recognized the number. Cole Jensen. She stepped back and looked at Savage. It was his turn to try to decipher her reaction. To do so was impossible because Hatch didn't have one. Hatch didn't know how she felt about Cole. Looking at the rugged features of the man standing before her as the phone continued to chime and vibrate, she felt conflicted.

"Are you going to answer it?"

Hatch snapped out of her trance-like state. "Yeah. Sorry. Give me a sec." She walked away from Savage toward the back door. "Hello?"

"Rachel? My God—I just heard. Sorry—if I had known, I would—"

What was he talking about? Her mind shifted gears. And then it hit her—the accident. "The crash?"

"Yeah. What else would I be worried about? Should I be worried about something else? For a girl who just came back to town after being gone for so long, you sure as hell know how to make an entrance. Bull in a China shop comes to mind."

She found herself smiling at the man's mile-a-minute speech and genuine concern. It'd been a while since somebody was truly worried about her. And if she were to be completely honest with herself, it felt good. "Slow down. I'm fine. How'd you hear about it?"

"I called your cell a few times and you never answered. You know you don't have voicemail set up?" Cole didn't wait for an answer. "Anyways—I couldn't get a hold of you and got nervous."

"Nervous about what?"

"That you'd left town again."

Hatch let the words filter past her barrier. He was worried she'd left. "I didn't go anywhere. At least not yet."

"I called your mom. She said you were in an accident."

"I was. And I'm fine."

"She also said you're working with the sheriff's office now."

"I am."

"Does this mean I need to call you Deputy?"

Hatch let a giggle slip out. She caught Savage out of the corner of her eye. She turned away, shielding her face from view. "Okay, funny guy, I'm in the middle of something right now. Anything else?"

"I'd like to see you again."

Hatch began to raise her emotional shield. Don't attach to anything, anyplace or anyone. And yet here she was, making a conscious effort to fight back the longing for normalcy. "Look, Cole—I just think it's better we don't. I told you I'm not planning on sticking around. Us going on a date isn't going to change that and will most likely complicate things."

"Whoa! Who said anything about a date?"

Hatch immediately felt the heat rush over her cheeks and was glad she'd turned away from Savage prior to her color change. "I guess I—"

"Just kidding. I was going to make it a date, but since you're opposed to it, we could just go as friends. There's this great little restaurant, opened a few years ago."

"I don't know. I've got a lot going on with this case."

"Everybody needs to eat. Hell, I'll even let you pay if it makes you feel better." He laughed, the same laugh she remembered from their teenage years. It was an infectious cackle that went from a deep baritone to a high-pitched squeak.

The laugh sealed the deal. "Fine. I'll meet you there. What's the name of it?"

"Lumpy's"

"You're taking me to a place called Lumpy's?"

"The food's better than the name implies."

Hatch felt the color in her face had faded enough. "See you at eight." She didn't wait for a response, clicking her phone closed. She slipped it in her pocket and walked back over to Savage.

"Everything good?"

She felt odd answering. "Old friend."

"I think we've got an idea where this thing is headed. We've got to go through those files and do some comparisons with the paperwork we found in the town manager's office."

"It'd be great to see the bank records too."

"That's not going to happen without a court order. After we get enough evidence, we may be able to gain access to that. But let's focus on making a solid connection first. We can use my office."

She followed him in. Savage set the stack of files on a small circular conference table set off in the corner. Hatch kept her personal file separate, placing it aside.

They set about organizing the files so comparisons could be made more easily. Her mind drifted and she looked at her watch. Three more hours until she'd be seated across from Cole. Whether or not she wanted to admit it, things just got a lot more complicated.

22

Hatch's mother placed a dish in the sink. The children scampered up the stairs to get ready for bed. The porcelain disappeared, sinking into the foamy water as Hatch entered the kitchen. The mix of soap and leftovers permeated the air and reminded her of the makeshift dining halls during deployment.

Her mother turned to face her, drying her hands on a dishrag adorned with butterflies. "You didn't eat tonight. My meatloaf recipe used to be your favorite."

"I remember. Maybe I'll have some of the leftovers when I get back."

"Leaving again and so soon? You just barely got here, missed dinner, and now you're off before the dishes are wiped clean. Not sure what you're doing or what it is you've gotten yourself into, but if you want to talk, I'd be willing to listen."

"I've got something I need to do."

"Dressed like that, I'm assuming it's not work related."

Hatch looked down, giving her appearance a once over. She had on a pair of jeans and a long-sleeved cashmere sweater. The outfit accented the slight curves of her body. To a normal person, whatever that was, Hatch's attire wouldn't have drawn attention. But to her mother, who was accustomed to seeing her in a t-shirt or sweatshirt, it must've been a shock to see her in something different. That or the fact that the sweater she was wearing belonged to her sister, whose sense of fashion had far exceeded hers.

"Cole asked me to meet him for dinner."

"Cole Jensen? Now that's a name I haven't heard mentioned around this house in ages." Her mother folded the rag and hung it over the edge of the sink, giving Hatch her full, undivided attention. "The fire still burns."

Hatch couldn't decode her mother's tone in the last comment. It fell somewhere between playful and sarcastic. "Never a fire. Only a flicker. And trust me when I say this—that burned out long ago."

Hatch grabbed her coat off of a nearby hook in the hallway. The air outside was colder now that the sun had gone down, but the outer garment also served another purpose beyond being an additional layer of warmth. The coat hung just below her belt line by a couple of inches, further concealing the pistol tucked neatly against the small of her back. It did no good if people knew you were armed. She'd never seen the purpose for openly carrying a firearm, even though the practice was legal in Colorado and several other states. Hatch felt it weakened the element of surprise, a cornerstone in her ability to survive many encounters in her past.

She had just opened the door to leave when she heard the patter of footsteps on the stairwell closing in behind her. Hatch knew without looking who they belonged to.

"Auntie Rachel, you're not going to stay tonight?"

Hatch had hoped to slip out before the kids noticed. She

turned and saw the sullen eyes of her niece staring unblinkingly at her. "I'm sorry, Daphne. I've got something important I need to do right now."

The girl's shoulders slumped, and she huffed softly. "You look pretty. Are you going on a date?"

"No, silly. I just have to meet up with an old friend who invited me to dinner."

Daphne reached out and rubbed a piece of the soft sweater protruding out from under the jacket. "Is that mommy's sweater?"

"Yes, it is." Hatch paused, evaluating the little girl's face. "If it bothers you that I'm wearing it, I'll run upstairs and change out of it right now."

She shook her head. The child's curls swayed freely. "It looks good on you."

Hatch was grateful for the approval. "Tell you what. When I get home, I'll sneak into your bed and we can snuggle. Just like we did the other night. How does that sound?"

Her head perked up and her posture straightened. "Sounds great to me!"

"Then we have a deal."

"Seal it with a kiss." Daphne looked up expectantly. "Something mommy used to say."

Hatch bent, kissing the soft cheek of the sweet girl. She inhaled the scent of innocence. Daphne, in turn, kissed her upon the tip of her nose, sealing the deal.

Without further protest, Daphne returned upstairs. Hatch left. She got into the older model Bronco that Savage had loaned her until her truck was repaired, if it could be. He'd told her it was one of several vehicles in the motor pool and had come by way of asset forfeiture during a meth raid in the previous sheriff's administration. Since learning of Jeffries' propensity for criminal activity, she wondered about the legitimacy of the seizure and its legality. But she needed a vehicle and, for the time being, this would do.

The door wailed its high-pitched metallic creak, as if the truck had somehow overheard the exchange with Daphne and was now begging for her to stay. In the stillness of the night, the sound echoed out into the surrounding darkness.

Hatch snaked down the dirt driveway and out onto the main road. Heading to see Cole, her head was filled with uncertainty and she worried her buried emotional connection to their past was leading her astray.

COLE WAS RIGHT. The restaurant's moniker didn't do it justice. Lumpy's wasn't the hole-in-the-wall diner she'd expected. The establishment had a wraparound porch for outdoor dining. Gas lamp heaters were spaced evenly among the tables to provide relief from the cold, but few patrons seemed willing to face the rapidly dropping temperatures and the seats outside the restaurant remained empty. The exterior design made it look like an oversized log cabin with hand-sanded timber shellacked into a high gloss. Through the large window panes, she could see the shimmer of candles. The dancing light gave the place an air of sophistication with a quaintness few restaurants in the area could match. Hatch could understand its popularity, especially among the town's younger adults.

Cole's fancy Jeep was parked in the lot a few spaces away, and she assumed he was inside the restaurant.

She stood in the entrance and was greeted by the warmth of a fire from the stone set fireplace on the far side of the restaurant opposite the bar. The smell of pine filled the air. A hostess standing behind a nearby podium smiled at Hatch. "How many in your party?"

"I believe the other half is already here." Hatch craned her neck and then saw the back of Cole's head. His back was to the door, facing the fire. Her first thought, strangely, was of his lack of situational awareness. Hatch never sat with her back to a door or window if possible. Survival 101, you can only react to a threat if you see it coming. "He's over there."

Hatch walked into the dining area and pulled out a chair across from Cole. The hostess followed and placed a menu in front of her as Hatch sat down.

"You're punctual. Something I never expected from you. Not the guy I remember."

"Rachel, who I was back then and who I am now are worlds apart." He spread his hands until his arms were extended all the way out.

"You and me both."

She noticed he'd taken the liberty of ordering some red wine. A full glass was waiting for her. Cole had already drained half of his and she wondered how much earlier he'd arrived. She looked at her watch and it was just turning eight.

"That's one nasty gash you've got on your forehead."

Hatch playfully batted her eyes and fanned her face in an over dramatic flair. "Oh, Cole Jensen, you say the sweetest things. I bet you tell all the girls that."

His eyes rolled. "I can't believe you're so relaxed about this. You seriously could've been killed."

She dropped the act. "Killing me is harder than people realize."

"I can see that. And I, for one, am glad." He picked up his glass by the stem and gave it a gentle swirl before sipping. "I still don't understand what happened. Did the other car blow the light?"

"No. I did."

"Why? Were you running late or just not see it?"

She gave him a measured look. He leaned in and his concern was genuine, but the why of it bothered her. The man did work for the same company as the man who severed her brake line. And that alone gave Hatch a deep level of skepticism. "I pressed on the brakes and they failed. Looks like some kind of mechanical issue. I probably should've taken the old Ford to the shop and had it inspected before I started driving it. I don't think my mom uses it much and it was obviously in desperate need of a tune up."

"Well, that truck was old as dirt. I think we had a couple of good nights in it if I recall."

"You don't say? My memory's a bit foggy since the crash. Maybe the impact erased all the bad ones."

He winced. "Ouch."

Hatch sipped from the wine, inhaling the oaky notes while the tannins bit at the back of her mouth. "Let's stick to the present. Shall we?"

"Sure thing."

"I'm not sure you're working with the most upstanding group of citizens."

"Billy's an ass." Cole leaned back in his chair and crossed his arms over his chest. "He's got an overinflated ego. You already proved you're more than capable of putting the big man in his place."

"He's not who I'm talking about."

"Who are you referring to?"

"Fabio."

"Who's Fabio?"

"The big blonde with the long ponytail. You know, the one who looks like he could be the spitting image for the model who adorns all of those trashy romance novels."

"Silas Calhoun? How do you even know him?"

"He was outside the main office when I went to speak with your boss." She was still on the fence with regard to Cole's loyalties and where he fell in the company's pecking order. But sometimes in an interrogation you had to give a little to get something back in return. "I can't put my finger on it. Something about him rubbed me the wrong way. Maybe it was the way he eyeballed me when I left. He strikes me as a guy who looks for trouble."

Cole gave a shrug. "I guess I really don't know much about him. He's always been cordial in the few times we've spoken. We're not drinking buddies or anything like that. He mostly keeps to himself. I do know that he used to work with the main branch in Europe and came here when Chisolm first arrived."

"Did he have any issue with my sister?"

"Silas and Olivia? Nah, no way. She's probably had less contact with him than I have. The guy isn't even around the site that much. He handles our demolitions logistics. If you want, I can do some digging. Pull his personnel file for you? Maybe there's something in it that will help you find what you're looking for."

Cole's eagerness was etched across his face.

Hatch gave a dismissive wave of her hand. "I don't want you getting mixed up in anything and getting yourself hurt."

"I can handle myself. Maybe not as good as you, but I can hold my own. I kicked Bobby Lancaster's ass back in the day."

"Not that story again? It wasn't even a fight. You pushed him and he tripped over a tree root."

"Well, I still won."

Hatch laughed. She'd heard him tell that story for years. The fight, or pushing incident, actually occurred at the end of their eighth-grade year. He'd stuck up for her when Bobby Lancaster made a snide comment about her father's death. Cole stepped in, putting an end to any further comments from the larger boy. She fell in love with him that day, but the two never took their relationship beyond the friend zone until the summer before junior year.

Cole finished the glass and flagged the waitress, tapping the rim of his glass. She came over with the bottle in hand. "They make an amazing smoked trout here."

"Sounds good to me."

The waitress filled Cole's empty glass and topped off Hatch's before going to place their order.

"I should've asked if you're a wine drinker." He gave a bashful smile.

"I'm not picky." She raised her glass. He did likewise. Reaching across the table, he gently tapped his rim to hers. "Remember, this isn't a date."

"Understood. Friends only."

Friends? Strange to hear the words come out of his mouth. Something she'd never thought possible when she left Hawk's Landing behind fifteen years ago.

"You can't stand alone in a town like this," he said. "You're going to need someone beside you if you plan to take on Chisolm."

"Who said I'm taking on Chisolm?"

A ripple went along his rigid jawline. "Small town. People talk."

"That's not what I asked."

He hid behind his glass of wine.

She was about to press him further but decided to drop it for now, making a mental note to return to it again.

"How's things been going at your house with your mom and the kids?"

"It's not my house."

"It used to be."

Hatch took a sip of wine. This time she was the one hiding behind the glass. Setting it down, she looked over at the man whom she'd once thought would be her future husband. He looked the same. Better if that was possible. But this Cole Jensen was not the same man she'd known. He was different. An intangible change. Like her, the years had added their burden. She suddenly felt silly for agreeing to meet him. For thinking there could be a lingering hope at finding any semblance of the feelings she once had. Normalcy? It didn't exist for Rachel Hatch.

"Listen, Cole, this isn't going to work."

"What isn't?"

"Anything between us."

"I know. You've made that abundantly clear on multiple occasions since you've been back." He spread his arms again. "And I told you, I just want to be your friend. Bury the hatchet between us and see where things go."

"I don't think you get it. There's no place where things can go. I'm leaving Hawk's Landing as soon as I figure out who's responsible for Olivia's death."

"You loved it here once. Maybe you could find something or someone to make you feel that way again. I mean—is this place that bad?"

"It's not that."

"Then what?" He leaned over the table, his face a mere foot from hers.

"I keep moving. It's who I am. I don't expect you to understand. But I need to rely on me and me alone. I don't want to be tied to anything or anyone."

"Is that really how you plan to live the rest of your life?"

Hatch shrugged. The debate had raged on in her mind for years. How long could she continue drifting? It was a question she continually posed to herself. The answer always eluded her.

"Look, let's have a nice dinner and catch up. I'd love to hear about your time in the military." He cocked his head and did his best puppy-dog impression. "You may be surprised to find I'm a pretty good listener."

She returned his efforts with a weak smile. "Next time."

Hatch stood and dropped a twenty-dollar bill on the table. Cole looked hurt.

"I've got to go."

"Why?"

The real reason was she already got what she'd come for. She was leaving with Fabio's name and, now that she had it, she wanted nothing more than to run him through the police database and do a little fact-finding. In the tennis match against her teenage feelings, the adult in her had won. Wasting two hours on dinner with a man who'd cheated on her when they were younger didn't seem like the best use of her time. But she held back from unloading and let him off easy.

"Work stuff," she said. "Something I've got to check out. I forgot about it until now."

"You're not even a real cop."

She felt her cheeks burn. "Maybe, but I'm the best chance this town has of finding the killer."

"I'm sorry. That came out wrong. You running around town with the sheriff just seems kind of dangerous to me, that's all."

Hatch brushed it off and was already moving toward the door. "We're all victims in waiting. But don't worry about me. Danger only exists when you're not prepared."

Outside, an icy wind kicked up as she moved across the parking lot. Getting into the Bronco and closing the door, she sat in silence. The wind battered and rocked the vehicle. The old springs croaked. She looked back at the restaurant and could faintly make out Cole, his back still to hers, now sitting alone, draining another glass of wine. Part of her felt foolish for leaving

in such a hurry. Then again, Hatch knew where it could poten-
tially lead and the complications it would create if it did.

Things were better this way, she thought as she turned the
ignition, bringing the engine to life in a loud roar.

She drove away from Lumpy's restaurant and began heading
back toward the center of town.

About a mile away, she noticed a pair of headlights appear in
her rearview mirror. The approaching vehicle was closing the
distance fast until it was only a few car lengths away. Hatch could
tell from the height of the headlamps it was a large vehicle, maybe
a truck or SUV. The road she was on had no streetlights, cloaking
the shape in darkness and leaving her to guess.

Cole? She wondered. Had he decided to chase her down and
beg her to come back to dinner?

She slowed down in an effort to bring the car behind her into
view. The vehicle following slowed as well, but not before her
brake lights cast the front end in a red glow, enabling her to make
out the truck, and more importantly, the driver in it. Fabio's long
flaxen hair was a dead giveaway for the man. The passenger also
had a unique identifier. Bill Chisolm's bandaged nose was clearly
visible through the windshield.

Hatch immediately accelerated. The old Bronco was no match
for the newer model Dodge following. Whatever Fabio's intention,
it couldn't be good.

If it was a fight they wanted, she'd give it to them. But Hatch
liked the odds to be in her favor, and she knew just where to go to
even the score. She just hoped she'd get there before they overtook
her.

23

THE BOXED END OF THE BRONCO CRASHED THROUGH THE GATE. A piece was trapped in the undercarriage of the beastly SUV, pulling down a portion of the attached chain link fence, which now whipped wildly behind like a superhero's cape. Fabio's truck had nearly spun out on a dark corner a quarter mile back, giving Hatch about a thirty-second lead. And she'd need every second to prepare for whatever was coming her way.

Hatch pitched and swayed as she crested the incline of the hill. The cool air made the patchy spot of grass slick. Throwing the Bronco into park, she jumped out and rounded the smoking engine. While on the move, she withdrew the Glock from the small of her back and took up a stable shooting platform. Her left arm rested on the warm hood. Steam from the radiator spit out from the dented grill.

"What in the hell—"

"Jed. It's me. Hatch!"

The man, already toting his home defense Mossberg, ran from his front porch down to where Hatch was positioned.

"They're coming. Chisolm and his boys. I understand this isn't your fight but—"

Jedediah Russell's eyes narrowed with an intensity that would've made Clint Eastwood blush. "The hell it isn't!"

She kept her focus on the opening where the gate stood only seconds before. "They'll be coming any second now."

He didn't rack a round. The shotgun was already in battery. "How many?"

"At least two, but probably more like four. These pricks don't like to fight fair."

"Ten of those soft ass bastards ain't gonna be enough for us!"

"Well, we're about to find out."

The Dodge's hemi engine bellowed as the headlights came into view. The truck slowed and didn't recklessly barrel through and onto the property, as she'd thought they might. It stopped at the property line. Flood lights activated from the beefy truck's roof, casting anything behind the cone of light into darkness. Good tactic. Maybe these guys weren't as dumb as she'd thought.

Hatch dipped her head, shielding her eyes from the light in an effort to keep some semblance of night vision. The brim of Jed's hat was tilted, dipping his face into a shadow and giving the old timer a menacing appearance.

"They'll be fanning out." His raspy voice crackled.

Then Hatch saw something of concern, a tactical maneuver which made her realize these men were well-trained. She momentarily regretted bringing the older man into the fight. The Dodge was now creeping along slowly. The only sound was the tires' slow roll over the uneven incline. The flood lights kept them blind to whatever was coming.

"They're stacked," Hatch said. "Using the truck as a mobile shield. Bad news, we're blind to their movements. Good news, somebody's in the driver's seat."

"Let's deal with the knowns. I'll flush them into the open. And then see if we can even the damned playing field." Without another word, Jed dropped into a prone position. Low crawling over to the tire on the opposite side, he took aim.

The bang ripped through the silence, giving the first jolt of the fight to come. Every battle, big or small, requires a first punch. In this case, it came in the well-placed shot delivered by Russell. Buckshot struck the KC lights atop the cab, taking out ninety-percent of them, disabling the blinding beams.

Hatch's eyes adjusted in a manner of seconds. The truck stopped in its tracks and the driver, Fabio, exited quickly just as Jed peppered the windshield with his second shot. The door hung open, and in the seconds that followed the shotgun blast, the annoying chime was all that could be heard.

Two deep breath cycles in and out. Hatch controlled her heart rate as she homed in with focused concentration. Hatch wasn't going to change positions. She planned on letting them come to her. The engine block and wheel she was tucked neatly behind would provide adequate cover for whatever assault was coming their way.

Movement came from the rear of the Dodge, on Hatch's side. A silhouette of a man was all she could make out. The dark form crouched low, moving out to her left. Taking aim, she centered her front sight post, the glowing green dot of the Trijicon night sight resting on center mass.

Hoping it was Fabio, Hatch pulled the trigger. The explosive muzzle flash caused by the release of superheated gas as the bullet left the barrel threw her into a temporary state of night blindness. She closed her eyes momentarily, while ducking low, knowing that her shot just gave away her position.

An eruption of gunfire broke out from the Dodge. A rhythmic staccato of semi-automatic rounds tore into the metal frame of the

Bronco she was tucked behind. Glass shattered, falling like sharp bits of hail around her. The familiar zip and snap filled her ears as one almost found its mark. The proximity of the round was unnerving. A couple inches closer and she'd have been dead.

As quick as the barrage started, it ended, plunging the night back into silence. They were now listening, as she was. Both sides waiting for the cries of the dying, an indication the volley of shots had found their target.

Hatch took a split second to look over at Jed. He was still in the same position. *Good*, she thought. He'd been able to make it through the first wave. She hoped to bring this skirmish to an end before the next one began. Then, to her horror, she saw it. In the limited light provided by the moon's momentary break from cloud cover, she observed a small dark pool slowly expanding outward from the old man's right side.

A moaning sound broke the silence. She was surprised the noise didn't come from Jed. It originated from where she fired her one and only shot. Squinting, she peered into the darkness at what first looked like the twisted branches of a bare, leafless bush, but she knew better. The contorted figure was the man she'd shot. A low gurgling escaped, followed by a high-pitched wheezing sound. One thing was certain, her bullet had found center mass. The unmistakable sound of the man's collapsed lung left no doubt. He didn't call out for the others, and nobody broke cover to render aid, further demonstrating the trained discipline of the group.

The dying man released an agonized breath, a blood-choked release like that of a person waking from apnea. The death rattle confirmed what Hatch already knew. The man in the grass was no longer a threat. He was dead. And with that, the odds were evened.

Hatch turned her attention back to Jed, who remained motionless on the ground. She crawled to his position, grabbing his ankle and squeezing tight to check for responsiveness and alert him of her presence before getting closer. His wiry calf tightened, and his foot moved. She let out an audible sigh of relief. He was alive. At least for the moment.

"Jed? How bad?"

He spat into the dirt. As she got closer, Hatch realized the battle-hardened veteran remained steadfast with his eyes sighting down the shotgun's long barrel. "Hard to tell. Son of a bitch hit me in the shoulder. Right side. Stung like hell. Forgot how much I hate getting shot."

Hatch edged up closer and began running her right hand along his back, gently searching for the exit wound. Hard to do in the dark. She found it between the scapula and armpit. "Found it. Through and through. I'm going to pack it."

"I got a rag in my back pocket."

Hatch fished it out and began stuffing the bandana into the hole. Jed whimpered softly with each push, but he was tough. Stayed steady on his sights while she worked. Meeting max resistance, she stopped. Her hands were slick with the warm blood. She grabbed a handful of dirt to absorb the moisture before wiping it on her pants. "Good to go?"

"There's plenty of fight left in me. Now, how about we show these boys how we handle business in the 101st?"

"Don't worry, the cavalry is on the way." She paused, taking a second to assess the effectiveness of the bandage she'd applied to the wound. The pool around him appeared to have stopped spreading, or at least slowed to an imperceptible level.

"Jed, I need you to put a couple rounds on the driver side of that truck. Send them my way."

Hatch pushed up into a crouch, duck walking back to the side she'd originally fired from. The first blast from Jed's gun was like a starter pistol. She was already in full stride at the second shot. The buckshot plinked off the metal frame of the Dodge and popped the front tires.

Hatch moved wide. Ten feet away was the man she'd killed. Close enough, even in the darkness, to see it wasn't Fabio or Bill Chisolm. The deceased was a person she'd never seen before.

An assault rifle began firing in three-round bursts. It took only a split second to realize the shots weren't aimed at Hatch. Jed had drawn their fire as she'd intended. The shots gave away their positions and, in the night, the sporadic flashes from their weapons clearly lit their faces up and gave Hatch the point of reference to focus her aim.

Hatch closed the distance, maintaining a stable shooting platform and firing two controlled shots. Fabio never saw the rounds coming. He was knocked sideways by the impact with a second round striking him square in the right side of his head, near the temple. His body collapsed, and with it his flowing locks dropped out of her sight.

Bill Chisolm spun. Shock stretched across his face. Hatch's front sight post fell in line with the bandage taped over his broken nose. Her trigger pulled to the break point. And then in the split second needed for her to complete the action, the big man did something she hadn't expected. He dropped his gun and raised his hands.

"Please don't kill me. It wasn't my idea. I swear. Arrest me—do whatever—I'll cooperate. Just don't kill me!" His voice was pitchy, almost to the point of squealing.

Hatch didn't speak. She didn't move. The picture was clearer with each passing second. Her heart rate dropped. She was in total control. And she wanted nothing more than to bring resolution in the form of a single gunshot. Yet she didn't pull the trigger. The man before her might hold the key to finding out exactly what had happened to her sister.

"You're in a world of shit. Do you understand that?"

Chisolm nodded his head. His eyes glistened as tears formed.

"If you change your mind about cooperating or hold back in any way—the bullet in this gun will find you. Is that clear?"

"Yes." The man's hands were still held high, but she saw the slack in his shoulders.

Sirens echoed nearby, calling out their impending arrival. Hatch had called Savage while being chased and had given him a brief synopsis of her plan.

"Step away from the gun and get down on your knees."

Blue and red danced in strobe pulses through the high pines of the wooded pass leading to Jed Russell's property. Hatch brought her weapon down into a low ready, indexing her trigger finger while waiting for Savage and his team to roll in.

The sheriff led the caravan of cars, stopping his big Suburban just short of Hatch's position. His headlights illuminated her and the downed men lying nearby. Jumping out, he ran to her, assessing the carnage as he approached.

Hatch watched him scan her up and down, evaluating her. She couldn't read the expression on his face. Part of her hoped he was worried for her safety, not because she was now one of his deputies, but because of some other more personal reasons.

Savage's head swiveled between the dead man on the ground and Hatch. "Are you okay?"

"I'm good. Jed's been shot. He's up by the Bronco's driver side front tire. He was hit in the shoulder, but there was a lot more gunfire, and I haven't been able to check on him. I've been busy babysitting this cornfed crybaby."

Chisolm sniffled loudly, adding merit to her statement.

Savage turned and barked orders at Sinclair and Littleton.

Sinclair handcuffed Chisolm, needing two sets of cuffs to lock the big man's hands behind his back. She returned after stuffing him in the back of the cruiser.

"Is he crying?" Sinclair asked Hatch in amusement.

"I guess he didn't like being bested by the same girl twice." Jed staggered down the hill, using Littleton as a human crutch. "Looks like they underestimated you."

"No. They underestimated us." Hatch walked over to the old man and kissed his damp forehead.

"She told you that you were wrong about me." Jed directed his ire at Savage. "But you didn't listen. Maybe you will from this point forward. She's as smart as she is tough."

Savage bowed his head. "No truer statement's been said. And I owe you a great debt."

"You want to do right by me? Then arrest that son of a bitch Chisolm and every other crooked asshole in his employ. Anything less, you'll still owe me."

"We're working on it. You need to get to the hospital. Best if Littleton takes you. You'll probably bleed out if we wait for the medics to get out here."

Russell pointed to the blood-soaked bandana sticking out of his shoulder blade and gave a weak smile. "She did a pretty good job keeping that from happening." Then, turning to Hatch, he said, "You ever need me again, don't hesitate to call."

"Careful what you wish for, old timer. I may just collect on that someday."

"I'm counting on it." He leaned in close enough so that only Hatch could hear. "You take care of yourself, and remember, sometimes we can't outrun our ghosts."

"You want this?" Savage extended Jed's hat toward the older man.

Russell reached for it. The front and back were adorned with seared holes. Through and through, like his own injury. Lowering his chin to his chest, he dropped it to the ground. "Goodbye, sweet hat."

Littleton escorted the injured man down to his cruiser. Russell gave Hatch one last smile before taking his seat in the passenger side. They sped out of view, leaving those behind to sort out the scene before them.

"To say this is a mess doesn't do the word justice." Savage rubbed at the gray of his temples and then shoved a fist full of licorice into his mouth.

Hatch looked around, noticing they were shy a member. "Where's Cramer?"

"I figured we were better off without him." Savage looked over at Sinclair, who nodded her agreement. "Good thing, too. We didn't need him running off to tattle before we got a handle on this thing. All we need is his uncle and members of the town council to get wind of this during its infancy."

"Well, there's not much to it besides the fact that these two guys are dead and I shot them." Hatch pointed toward Fabio. "You might want to take a close look at him."

Savage walked over and squatted down. He shot a glance back at Hatch. "Is this the brake job guy from your accident?"

"I told you he looks like Fabio." She glanced at the head wound. The once-chiseled features of the man's face were now distorted. The .40 caliber rounds that passed through his skull left a wake of destruction in their aftermath. "Well, at least he used to."

Savage turned his attention toward the twisted man who she'd first shot when the battle began. "And who's the other guy?"

"Your guess is as good as mine. I've never seen him before."

Hatch took a moment to survey the damage. Both vehicles

were bullet-ridden and looked as though they'd been in a war zone. Sights like this were commonplace overseas, but it was strange seeing it in Hawk's Landing.

"Kind of ironic," she said. "I was just heading to the station to do some fact checking on our supermodel mercenary here. I just learned his name from an old friend who works at the company."

Hatch decided to leave out the fact she'd learned the information while on a non-date with none other than Cole Jensen. For some reason she was worried what Savage would think. *Why would he care?* It's not like there was anything between them. And why on God's green earth would she even be worrying about this while standing between two dead bodies? This town was kryptonite to her otherwise impervious emotional balance.

"I'm going to call this in to the state police to assist working the crime scene. I hate to do it because it may open a lot more questions than we're ready to deal with right now, but there's no way with our limited manpower that we'd be able to handle this while trying to figure out who the hell's behind this."

Hatch turned the Glock butt forward and held it out toward Savage. "With that being said, I figure you're going to need to take this."

He took the duty weapon and then handed it over to Sinclair. "Becky, we're going to need to tag that and keep it as evidence."

Deputy Sinclair nodded and walked back toward the trunk of her car. She secured the weapon, opening the trunk and stowing it inside.

An awkward silence followed as Hatch and Savage stood facing each other. The cruiser lights continued to pulse red and blue, washing them in the flickering light. There was no worse feeling than turning over a weapon after its righteous use. It added a feeling of wrongdoing no matter how justified the actions. Hatch fought against it now.

Savage bent over, kneeling as he lifted up his right pant leg. Withdrawing a snub-nosed .38 from his neoprene ankle holster, he stood. He held out the nickel-plated wheel gun. "No cop should be without."

"I'm not a cop."

"You are until you give me that badge back." He handed Hatch the gun. "I know it's not much, but it will get the job done if needed. Seeing your handiwork, I'm confident you're more dangerous with it than I'd ever be. But let's hope you don't have a reason to prove that."

Hatch slipped it into the small of her back, in the same place she'd fit the Glock earlier. The gun's metal frame was cold against her skin. "Bill Chisolm is primed and ready to talk. And if my instincts are right, he's going to have a lot to say about Nighthawk Engineering. He made me a promise to fill us in. One that I'm confident he'll keep."

"Do I want to know how he became so cooperative?"

"If you have to ask, then you probably don't. But seeing your friends die in front of you is a very persuasive argument for telling the truth. More effective than Wonder Woman's magic lasso. Some would even call the experience life-changing."

"I'll leave Sinclair here to maintain scene security until the state arrives. You and I will take our cooperative friend to the station and get the ball rolling."

Sinclair transferred the big man from her cruiser into the back of Savage's Suburban. The backseat of the oversized SUV was fitted with a half cage, which put Chisolm behind Hatch for the ride back to the station.

Hatch sat in the passenger seat, feeling the hot breath of their prisoner on the back of her neck. They pulled away from Russell's property, leaving Sinclair to watch over the deadly fallout from the standoff.

Chisolm said nothing on the ride, but Hatch knew he'd be singing a different tune once he was locked in an interrogation room.

24

A LARGE METAL-COATED GARAGE DOOR ROSE UPWARD. THE GRINDING screech of the door's wheels rolling along the track could be heard over the engine's rumble as Savage pulled the Chevy into the sally port. He waited until the door shut behind him before exiting and walking around to Hatch. She stood by the rear door containing their prisoner.

The sheriff's office had a small prisoner holding area containing two jail cells. Typically, these were used for temporary detention prior to prisoners being sent to the correctional facility located in Durango. More times than not, these cells remained empty. On the rare occasion when they were used, it was typically to allow a drunk the opportunity to sleep off a bad decision or two before being released.

Bill Chisolm's massive frame shuffled alongside Savage as he was escorted inside, his head hung down low in defeat.

Hatch watched the broken man. She thought about the small window of opportunity she'd had to end his life before Savage and the others arrived. Nobody would've been wiser had she pulled that trigger. But at her core, she knew she'd never be able to execute a person in cold blood. Chisolm didn't know that, and her bluff now gave them leverage in the interrogation to come. She hoped her decision to let him live would prove to be a wise one.

Using his fob, Savage unlocked the door leading from the sally port garage into the main building. The entrance led them into the small hall containing the two cells. The floor was a poured concrete coated in rubber, making it easier to clean up blood and other bodily fluids. Their boots squeaked as they proceeded. Hatch smelled the familiar odor. Every jail she'd ever set foot in during the many bases and countries she'd travelled to all had a similar stench. There was a failed sterility to the air quality, as if whatever cleaning solvent used was incapable of fully removing the actual source. And the small holding area of the Hawk's Landing Sheriff's Office, set in the rural mountains of Colorado, was no different.

Savage stood outside the first cell they came to. A large secure door, approximately eight feet high and four wide, separated them from the confined space inside. The heavy metal was painted an awful shade of beige. Much of the paint was peeled and cracked, revealing the rusted underbelly. The facility was in desperate need of a facelift.

Keeping one hand on the meat of Chisolm's thick elbow, Savage pulled his radio from the holder on his waist. "Barbara, do me a favor and open the door to cell number two, please."

Acknowledgment came in the sound of a buzzer, which was then followed by a loud mechanical click. The hydraulics hissed and the door released, opening an inch gap that separated it from the frame.

The pungent smell of urine spewed out from within and filled her nostrils as Hatch pulled the handle, sliding the door the rest of the way open. Savage gave a controlled shove, moving the big man into the cell.

"Listen, Bill, these cuffs are coming off now. You're going to have a few minutes in here while we take care of a couple things. Use that time wisely to think about what it is you need to tell us. I'm going to send in somebody to fingerprint and book you. Any trouble and the cuffs go back on. Understood?"

Chisolm bobbed his head in an almost imperceptible nod but said nothing.

The two sets of handcuffs were linked in the middle to provide the broad-shouldered man a modicum of relief during the transport. Savage unlatched one wrist, maintaining control of the other while he did so. As he took off the cuff, he blindly reached back, handing it to Hatch. Savage repeated the process on the other side. With the stainless-steel restraints removed, Savage took a step back. Chisolm remained facing away as they backed out of the cell, leaving him to silently occupy the small space. He looked like a circus elephant after being loaded into a trailer. The man's impressive girth swallowed up the area around him.

Savage slid the door closed. The latch banged noisily against the hook. He gave the handle a firm tug to verify the lock had seated and the door was secure before turning to face Hatch. "We'll give him a little time to reflect. I'm sure he's got a lot to think about. I'll send Cramer in a few minutes to pull Chisolm. He can handle the booking and processing. I've always found it beneficial to have a gap between an arrest and any subsequent interview."

"Sounds like a plan. Plus, it will give us time to do a little digging into Fabio. Guys like him have got to have a past."

Savage started down the hallway, moving away from the cell. Hatch took a moment to peer into the cell containing the man who earlier in the night had been hell bent on killing her. He sat on the aluminum bed which was bolted into the concrete wall.

Chisolm never brought his eyes up to meet Hatch's gaze, but by the way he shifted uncomfortably, she could tell he was aware of her, the girl who'd broken his nose, his fingers, and now his spirit.

She walked away from the cell, quickening her step to catch up to Savage as he opened another secure door. Inside was a room only slightly bigger than the cell. In it was an AFIS machine, the Automated Fingerprint Identification System. The boxy unit, which looked more like an oversized photocopier than a high-tech digital instrument, was set against the right side of the wall. On the nearby floor next to the machine was a box marked with red electrical tape for the intake photographs. Across from it was a wall-mounted camera. It was a small but efficient processing station.

They passed through the booking room and out into a narrow hall connecting them to the backside of the office space, near the basement access door. Before reaching the basement door, there were two doors simply marked Interview 1 and Interview 2.

When they rounded the corner into the main cubicle area, Cramer was seated at his desk, inattentively scrolling the newspaper's sports section. Savage walked directly over to the portly deputy. Towering over the man, he leaned in closer. "I don't have much confidence in what you can do, but booking a prisoner is something a boot rookie can handle. Do you think it would be too much to ask for you to process Bill Chisolm for us?"

Cramer set the paper down and looked up. "What are the charges?"

"Let's start with attempted murder. I'm sure there will be more to come, but I can add them on later. I need him processed so we can conduct an interview."

Cramer's eyes widened. Hatch could see from the lazy deputy's reaction that he hadn't been brought up to speed on the incident at Jed Russell's place. She wondered who he'd run to tell when he was done booking the big, broken man. And in that thought, Hatch realized the genius of Savage's ulterior motive having Cramer assist in the processing. It controlled him, even if only for a short amount of time.

Cramer got up without his normal protest to all things work-related and disappeared in the direction they'd just come from. Hatch followed Savage into his office. Without any needed explanation, he began quickly typing into his computer. Within seconds, the screen was filled with a law enforcement-only digital inquiry form. Every agency used different programs, but they all accessed the same state and federal informational databases. Some search requests did local checks, while others ran information provided against national and international records systems.

Savage's fingers hovered above the keyboard. "What's the name you've got for your recently deceased friend, Fabio?"

"Silas Calhoun. Probably in his mid-thirties. I don't have a date of birth and neither man had an ID on their person. Which I guess makes sense. If you're planning on killing somebody, you don't usually carry your license."

"And you know this how? Or is this another question I don't want the answer to?"

Hatch let silence be her answer.

A couple keystrokes later and they were staring at a message. *No info found.* Savage tried to narrow the scope of the search by providing a possible age range. A few possible hits came up, but looking into the physical descriptors provided in the return, nothing came close to matching up with the dead man. No state driver's license.

"This doesn't make sense." Savage rubbed at his salt and pepper temples. "Maybe no criminal record is possible, but if he was working in this area and doing any type of machine work, there would be a commercial license. Or, at the bare minimum, a driver's license. But we're batting zeros on this name. You're sure your friend gave you the right name?"

"I'm positive." She thought for a moment. "I've got an idea on how to clear this up. How long until the state police are on scene at Jed's?"

Savage looked down at his watch. "If I had to guess—half hour. Maybe a touch more. Why?"

"Then we best get a move on." Hatch was already throwing her jacket back on and moving out of the office toward the back door. "I'd rather not be there when they arrive. Not a huge fan of being questioned. Especially, if those questions are about a couple of people I've recently killed."

"Justified."

"Justified doesn't always play out the way it should in the real world."

Savage gave a nod. She knew he understood her reality was different from most others.

The sheriff grabbed a spare set of keys out of his drawer. "We'll take Cramer's vehicle. My Suburban is still parked in the sally port."

They entered the cold night air of the parking lot and set off in the direction of Jed Russell's, leaving Cramer to handle Chisolm.

SINCLAIR WAS CROUCHED LOW, snapping a photograph when they pulled up to the property line. Savage stopped where the gate used to be. Leaving the engine running, he and Hatch stepped out. The air no longer held any scent of the gunfight. It was crisp, cool, fresh.

"How's it going, Becky?"

"Just finishing up with photos. I know the troopers are coming, but I figured we'd need something for our files, too."

"Good thinking."

Sinclair paused, glancing over at Hatch. "I thought you guys were going to be handling Chisolm's interview?"

"We are. Cramer's doing the booking right now, but we needed something—"

Hatch didn't wait for Savage to finish. She'd explained her idea to Savage while on the ride over. The men who'd tried to kill her were well-trained, well-disciplined, and most likely ex-military with a covert ops background. They needed to positively identify them before the state police took over the scene. After that, everything would be on the state's timeline and it was critically important to know who they were dealing with now.

She'd already donned sterile nitrile gloves and held a small pack of fingerprint lifters in her hand. Hatch walked directly over to Fabio. His once flawless Rapunzelesque hair was no longer a bright gold. Blood coupled with bits of skull fragments and gray matter muddled the color, turning the mass of tangled wisps into Medusa-like tendrils.

"Um—are you supposed to be doing this?" Sinclair looked as surprised at asking the question as Hatch did in hearing it.

"It's important," Hatch said dismissively. "I need to get their IDs. We're dealing with some bad people here, and unless we can figure out exactly who they are, then we're going to be one step behind."

"I just mean—I thought we weren't supposed to touch bodies on a crime scene."

Savage approached, interrupting the stalwart resistance being offered by his deputy. "It's okay, Becky. We need to identify these men and the name we had for one of them isn't coming back. Good chance they're not who they said they were."

"Aren't the crime scene guys from the state going to do all this?"

Hatch stopped what she was doing to end this line of inquisition once and for all. "Yes, they will. They'll also take their sweet time in processing things, and since they'll have assumed the overall investigative responsibilities for a case of a shooting involving a sheriff's deputy, they will be slow to release the information to said agency. Basically, they'll halt any chance we have of getting a foothold on this thing. And I am done with surprises."

Sinclair cowered at the berating. Hatch took a breath. She actually agreed with Sinclair's logic and had worked numerous crime scenes in which she'd had to block higher ranking officers from entering. But she'd also learned during her time in service that, on rare occasions, the rules needed to be bent or broken if timely results were the end gain. This situation fell into that category. Sinclair didn't have the experience to understand the distinction.

"I understand what you're trying to do, but this is one of the times where protocols get trumped by the overall need of the situation."

Sinclair stepped back. "Fair enough."

Hatch set about pressing the cards to the man's cold fingers. The chilled air added to the stiffness setting into the body, increasing the rigidity of his appendages. For their purposes, she only needed a few good prints for comparison and decided to lift them from his left hand, the one not gripping the assault rifle.

"And I know this goes without saying, but when state arrives, this never happened. We aren't here right now."

Sinclair nodded. "I think that's going to be harder to explain."

"What do you mean by that?"

Hatch looked up from the dead man to see Sinclair staring past Savage and off into the distance. She followed her gaze and immediately understood the meaning of her words. The state police were winding their way along the road leading up to Jed's property. There were no sirens, but the LED strobes of the emergency lights flashed in the trees above. Headlights came into view in a long procession of vehicles. In a matter of minutes, the troopers would flood the area and take over the scene.

Savage looked down at Hatch. "Shit."

"Understatement of the year. If I'm on scene, they're going to hold onto me for interrogation. No way are they going to let me move about freely with two bodies to account for. Justified or not." Hatch stood, handing the fingerprint cards to Savage. "And that just can't happen."

"Then what? One road in and out of this place. We can't just drive off."

"I can't, but you're the sheriff. You can leave. Turn the scene over. Leave Sinclair here as a liaison and tell them you need to check on the status of the prisoner."

"And what are you going to do?"

"Run."

"What?"

"Remember where you dumped me off when we executed the search warrant?"

"Sure. But if I recall, I didn't drop you off—you jumped out of a moving vehicle."

"Semantics."

Hatch took off into the darkness, her long legs striding effortlessly on the downhill stretch of property leading to the cover of the thick brush as the troopers arrived on scene.

Hatch navigated the creek bed lining Jed's property, moving quickly under the cover of night.

SHE'D FINISHED her trek through the creek bed, a harder task to accomplish in the pitch dark. What little light was provided by the intermittent moonlight was completely obscured by the high pine and thick brush.

Hatch waited in the dark. From her position, she could see the lights, but the sound didn't carry far enough to reach her. The state police's crime scene technicians had erected several flood lights, bathing the hilly rise in a pale white. She could barely make out the spots where the dead men lay, frozen in time by the bullets Hatch had fired.

Even in the cool temperatures, Hatch managed to work up a bit of a sweaty lather while on her run. As she remained crouched and waiting, the dampness of her blouse amplified the effect of the rapidly dropping temperature. A taste of winter was in the air, and she knew it wouldn't be long until the landscape harshened to its hold. Hatch hoped to be long gone before that came to pass.

The sound of an engine pushed through the quiet stillness surrounding her and moments later headlights swept over Hatch's hiding place. The tires slowed, crackling along the unpaved surface of the road. The vehicle was close. She waited, not wanting to reveal her position prematurely in the event it wasn't who she expected.

"Hatch?" Savage's voice was just above a whisper.

She stood up. The suburban was stopped ahead of her position by a few feet. Hatch moved around the back of the vehicle, avoiding the bright white of the headlights and only temporarily silhouetted by the red of the brake lights. She saw Savage's face in the rearview mirror, his attention focused on the area illuminated by the cone of light.

She approached the passenger side and rapped on the window. Savage jumped, nearly coming out of his seat. His nerves were on edge.

"You scared the life out of me."

Hatch climbed inside. "I bet you say that to all the girls you pick up from a roadside ditch."

"Just the cute ones." He smiled, tossed the cards with the prints at her, and drove off.

She hoped their gamble would provide some insight into the man she'd killed.

25

SAVAGE ENTERED THE MAIN SPACE OF THE SHERIFF'S OFFICE WITH Hatch by his side. It was empty, except for Barbara, who was manning the main desk. Did she ever go home? "Where's Cramer?" he called out.

Barbara rolled into view from behind a four-drawer filing cabinet and thumbed in the direction of the bathroom. "He's in his personal office. You know—the one he spends most of his patrol shift in. From the sounds of it, he's been hard at work in there."

Savage rolled his eyes as the woman laughed at her own joke.

"Do you know if he finished processing Chisolm yet?"

"Yes. He finished up about ten minutes ago. Did you want to put a call into Corrections to make arrangements for him to be transferred to their facility?"

"No. We're going to need a little bit of time with him beforehand."

"Fair enough. Just let me know when you need me to take care of that."

"Will do. And Barbara, thanks for staying late tonight."

"It's not every day our town sees this sort of thing. I wouldn't dream of missing out. It's like being given front row seats to a private screening." She returned to her desk, disappearing back behind the bulky cabinet.

Savage turned to Hatch. "Are you ready to have a little chat with our guest?"

"I thought you'd never ask."

"Barbara, we're going to head to Chisolm's cell and bring him into the interrogation room."

She appeared again from behind her file cabinet and tapped the headset she'd donned. "Just give me a call on the radio when you're ready for me to release the cell lock. And you do know you have a key to the cell doors on that big key chain by the back door."

"I know. Old habits from my days in Denver."

Savage led the way back toward the holding area.

Outside the door of cell two, Savage's eyes widened in horror as he peered in to inspect the status of their prisoner. "Barbara, open the cell door immediately! And call medics!"

A buzz and click announced the lock's release. Unlatched, Savage yanked the handle, slamming the massive door open with a loud bang as it came to an abrupt stop against the metal frame on the opposite end.

On the floor near the bolted bedpost was the sprawled body of Bill Chisolm. The large man's face was a bluish purple. His eyes bulged wide, the whites of which covered in red blotchy spots. Petechial hemorrhaging occurs for a variety of instances, but in this case it was the obvious sign of strangulation. Intense pressure in the veins cause the capillaries in the eye to leak, creating bloody Rorschach-like patterns in the sclera.

Chisolm's torn undershirt was fastened around his throat in a makeshift noose. The fabric, pulled tight, was almost invisible under the folds of skin cinched around it.

Hatch and Savage quickly set to work, trying to free the unmoving man from his constriction. Savage pulled a knife from a leather pouch on his belt, carefully cutting the shirt near the knot and releasing him from the binding. A hum and hiss came from the man's mouth as the trapped air released.

Savage ran his fingers into position along the carotid, desperately seeking a pulse. Hatch watched as he sat back, the answer written on his face. Bill Chisolm, the man who held information they desperately hoped to gather, was dead.

"Doesn't add up," Savage said. "Why would he kill himself?"

"Maybe there's more at stake than we realize. The arrest, his agreement to talk to us, might've left him in a bind. Literally."

Savage shook his head. "It doesn't make sense. Regardless of whether he cooperated with our investigation or not, his father is the richest man in the county. Probably the neighboring five counties combined. He'd have the best defense money could buy. And you know as well as I do, money can easily outweigh evidence."

"People do stupid things when facing a life sentence. I've seen that before, too."

Savage stood. "Let's pull the tape and see."

———

AT HIS DESK, the computer showed several live feeds from the scattered surveillance cameras around the sheriff's office. Exterior cameras covered the front and back of the building. There was a camera in the sally port, booking area, interview rooms, and the two cells. And out of all of them only one was turned off. Cell Two.

Hatch watched as Savage brought the administrative settings up and began manipulating the camera, digitally rewinding it to the point at which their suburban drove away from the station house. They took Cramer's car, not the Suburban. As soon as their vehicle was out of sight, Cramer appeared, exiting the back door. He was smoking and talking on his cell phone. The call took less than a minute to complete. After which, Cramer flicked the cigarette and disappeared back inside.

Savage adjusted the playback speed, increasing it until something changed. They watched Chisolm in his cell. He was unmoved, slumped in the same despondent position he'd been in when Hatch last saw him. A few minutes of nothing passed before Cramer appeared inside the cell. A verbal exchange took place.

"I can see they're talking. How come there's no audio?" Hatch asked.

"It's been intermittent, and by that, I mean off more than it's on. I put a work order in with the town. The technician is supposed to be coming out this week." He shook his head in frustration, realizing now under the current unforeseen circumstances, the repair should've been higher on the priority list.

They both turned their attention back to the screen and watched the silent movie play out as Cramer escorted the man from his cell. The two then entered into the booking area. For the next several minutes Chisolm was fingerprinted and photographed. It was a relatively uneventful exchange. Cramer returned the man to his cell and closed the door.

Cramer appeared as he walked through the booking area on his way back to the main office space. One minute and twenty seconds later, the feed to cell two went dark.

A toilet flushed and Don Cramer exited. Hatch looked up from the screen at the man, who didn't seem to notice them in Savage's office.

Savage was typing again, and then nudged Hatch with his elbow. She looked down as Savage pointed to the screen. The camera shutdown command had been sent from Cramer's computer terminal.

Hatch gestured at the man walking out of the bathroom. Speaking in a whisper, she said, "Speak of the devil."

"I think Deputy Cramer's got some serious explaining to do."

Savage stood. His large frame in motion caught Cramer's attention, and he turned in their direction. The portly deputy's face did little to belie his nervousness. He tried to smile, but it came out wrong.

Cramer walked over to his desk area and grabbed his coat off the back of his chair. He was in a hurry.

"Don, where are you headed off to in such a rush?"

"Just going to run my security checks. I've already finished up with Chisolm."

"About that."

Savage walked toward Cramer as Hatch moved along the wall. Instinctively, her hand drifted toward the snub-nosed .38 revolver still tucked in her waistband against the small of her back.

Cramer's eyes bounced from Savage to Hatch in increased rapidity, making him look like he was suffering from a manic episode.

"I think we need to have a talk. You've got time. Those security checks you're so worried about aren't going anywhere." Savage's hand neared the butt of his duty weapon, floating just above the tang's dovetail. His voice remained calm, but Hatch could see the focused intensity in the Sheriff's eyes.

Cramer started to absently shake his head no, taking a cautious step in the direction of the exit. "I've really got to get going."

"Funny. I've never seen you so desperate to do police work before."

"My mother's sick. I've got to go and look in on her."

"What is it Cramer? Security checks or your mother?"

He eyed the back door hard but didn't try to counter the failed argument.

"You keep looking toward the exit. That's not going to happen, Don. You need to stay here and talk to us."

"I didn't do it." Cramer dropped his coat to the floor. At the same time, he retrieved his gun from his holster and pointed it at Savage's head.

Hatch's revolver was moving, and a fraction of a second later, she had it leveled at Cramer. Savage was frozen with his left hand raised in submission and his right firmly locked on the butt of his holstered Glock.

"Hold on. Let's not make things any worse tonight. I know you're feeling desperate. Like there's no way out of this thing. But there is. You just need to lower your weapon so we can figure out what that is." Savage's calm while staring down the barrel of a gun impressed Hatch. More impressive was his ability to issue commands. Few possessed the poise it took to see beyond the tunnel vision of a situation like this.

"I'm walking out of here! You hear that?" Cramer's eyes watered, his voice screechy like a boy breaking through the invisible barrier of puberty.

Hatch cocked the revolver with a loud click. The effect, as intended, caused Cramer to become more unraveled. Panic caused people to tighten up. And that kind of tension made their reactions slightly slower. She planned to capitalize on this should the need arise. The revolver was now in single-action mode, requiring relatively no pressure to discharge the weapon and adding a millisecond of advantage should the situation dictate.

"Tell her to drop the damn gun!" His eyes pleaded with Savage.

"Not going to happen." Savage exhaled slowly. "I'll give you fair warning, she's one hell of a shot. From this distance, there's no way she'll miss. Do you know she killed two men tonight? And the only reason Bill Chisolm survived is because she decided he was worth more to us alive. Your life now rests in her hands. And the actions you take will help her make that decision."

"I'll still kill you!" Cramer's breath was a ragged wheeze. Control quickly slipped from the man's shaky grasp.

"Maybe. Maybe not. Either way, you pull that trigger and you won't be leaving here alive either. Are you willing to make that call? Are you willing to die here and now?"

Hatch worked to slow her heart rate. Even at a close distance, everything mattered. There could be no room for error.

"You're in a position to help yourself out. There is a way out of this thing, and it doesn't have to end in bloodshed."

"You want me to talk? I may as well put this gun to my head and pull the trigger right now. It's obvious you have no idea who you're dealing with. You never should have come to this town." Cramer, eyes wild, turned to look at Hatch. "And you. You should never have come back!"

"Didn't want to. But you assholes went and killed the wrong girl. And I'm not leaving until it's done."

Cramer clenched his jaw. She'd seen this facial expression. It was a determined commitment. Time had run out in this speed date version of a negotiation.

Hatch began to resign herself to the end game, hoping her shot would render Cramer's control of his trigger finger useless. She knew in taking the shot, chances of learning critical truths would die with him. The pad of her index finger resting on the half-moon of the revolver's trigger began to tense when something caught her attention out of the corner of her eye.

Cramer's head was knocked sideways as he discharged the gun in his hand. Standing over him with a heavy three-hole punch was none other than Barbara Wright.

Hatch closed the distance in two strides, landing a knee onto Cramer's head as she slammed into the man and controlled his wrist. His body went limp. There was no fight left in him. Barbara had made sure of that.

Hatch put her foot on the man's gun while she transitioned her knee from his head onto the center of his back, pinning him to the ground in his unconscious state. Looking back at Savage, she saw he was still standing in the same place he'd been. The calm poise dissolved as he cantered his head up at the ceiling where Cramer's round had gone.

"I never liked that little runt of a man anyway." Barbara gave a satisfied smile and shouldered the hole punch like a baseball player taking the plate.

Hatch laughed.

Savage walked over without saying a word and gave the older woman a hug while Hatch used Cramer's cuffs to secure his hands behind his back.

Hatch stood and placed her foot on Cramer's back. "We may not have Chisolm, but I think Cramer can fill in some of the blanks."

"That's if he talks."

"You do remember the conversation we had about what I used to do in the military?"

Savage nodded.

"Then, trust me. He'll talk."

26

"I TOLD YOU I'M NOT TALKING." CRAMER DIDN'T LOOK UP FROM THE spot on the table his gaze was fixed on. "Should've just killed me. I'm already as good as dead."

Savage leveled a hard gaze. "Is that what happened to Chisolm?"

Cramer shrugged and looked away.

"Listen, Don, it's no secret I'm no fan of you and most likely would've been firing you in the near future. But I see no point in you dying over whatever this is."

"I didn't kill Chisolm. He signed his death warrant when he agreed to speak to you. All I did was relay a message."

"Then why'd you cut the camera feed?"

Cramer winced as he gingerly rubbed the lump on the back of his head. "I didn't want that hole-punch-wielding lunatic to see and call the medics. I knew eventually you'd figure I'd killed the footage, but I hoped to be long gone by then."

"Or you'd hoped we'd be dead?"

Cramer gave a shrug of indifference. "You've been sheriff about a month. I've lived in this place my whole life. I can trace my family roots back since the town's beginnings. You waltz in here and think you understand things. That you can apply your big city mentality to us little country folk. In reality, you have no idea what's going on around here. And who's really in charge."

"I assume your uncle has some piece in this. Is that why you're really avoiding talking? You're scared he's going to be implicated?"

"He's just a pawn in the big game of chess that's been playing out here for years."

"This is about Nighthawk Engineering?"

Cramer sighed. "It's nothing new. Big company comes into a small town and before you know it, the whole economy is dependent. You dig too deep on this investigation and you're going to bury this entire town."

"Maybe that's exactly what this town needs." Savage's face hardened. "I've got a dead mother of two who'd probably agree with me."

"I had nothing to do with that. You're wasting your time on me because I don't know anything about what happened to her."

"I'd guess you know more than you realize."

Hatch sat quietly listening to the back and forth. The give and take moments in an interview were tedious things. Normally, she'd give hours or even days in some cases to this phase, but the events of the last few hours had exhausted her reserve of patience. She'd evaded a deadly encounter on two separate occasions tonight and the only person capable of providing some much-needed answers feared reprisal more than any protection the sheriff could provide.

Hatch interrupted. "Mind if Don and I have a private conversation?"

Savage seemed to understand the true meaning of the request. He stood without saying a word. Having almost been shot and killed by Cramer seemed to loosen his need for procedural protocol.

At the door, Savage turned. "I offer this advice. Think of Bill Chisolm's broken face and hand before you think of playing coy with her." He paused and looked up at the camera in the corner of the room. "And it's a shame how these cameras have been really glitchy tonight."

Savage left, shutting the door. Hatch waited for the sound of the lock to punctuate the awkward silence. She could almost taste Cramer's fear.

Hatch looked down at the man's hands. They were shackled to a steel hook bolted to the center of the table. The chain links gave Cramer just enough slack to bring his palms to the edge, but not beyond. She leaned in. "No more games. No more protecting the people you work for. And for every wrong answer you give. I'll break a finger."

"What? You can't—"

Without warning Hatch snatched the man's left hand. Finding purchase on the pinky, she locked her index finger to the outside and, using her thumb as a fulcrum, snapped the joint outward. The crack was loud, but Cramer's scream quickly drowned it out.

"I just did. Now you have nine more chances to get this right."

Tears filled his eyes. He cradled the damaged hand, looking at the deformed finger.

Hatch had already formed an assessment of Cramer during her limited interactions with him since becoming a member of the sheriff's office. He was weak and she'd selected this interrogation technique for its effectiveness. She had other measures at her disposal but wasn't sure Savage would approve. Hatch elected this minimally invasive technique.

"What's wrong with you?" He was still fixed on his broken pinky. "Who breaks somebody's hand?"

"I didn't get to your hand—yet. And by the way you reacted to that little bit, I sure hope we don't have to."

Cramer wiped his tears. The door to the interrogation room remained locked. And Savage, most likely listening in, wasn't intervening.

"Now that you understand my level of commitment to the truth, I hope you'll decide to cooperate."

His face was blotched with redness. The look of it reminded her of a child who'd skinned a knee and was trying not to cry. The grown man's chin quivered as he fought back tears. "What do you want to know?"

"Everything."

HATCH EXITED the interview room an hour later. Savage was in his office and stepped into the doorway. His eyes asked the question.

"He gave it up. Connected the dots. It appears Nighthawk Engineering isn't so green after all. In fact, they're the polar opposite. Not only were they forcing people out of their family homes, the mining has been tainting groundwater around the lake. The effect seems to be more pronounced in the young, like the boy from the hospital, or in the elderly."

"Doesn't shock me that the company is dirty. They've got mercenaries running their security team. Well, they did until you killed them."

Hatch furrowed her brow. "Fabio?"

"While you were having a conversation with recently fired Deputy Cramer, I ran the prints you took. Fabio is wanted by Interpol for a bombing in Uzbekistan. I did a little research and it seems Danzig Holdings was operating in that area at the time of the blast. The same name at the bottom of the buyouts is apparently the overarching company bankrolling Nighthawk Engineering's operation."

"Hawk's Landing might be a little understaffed to handle the implications in all of this."

"Couldn't agree more. That's why I put a call in to one of my contacts at the FBI. They're sending in support from the Denver office. Guys I personally trust. The EPA will be sending in a team as well to evaluate the extent of the contamination and assist in the cleanup."

"When will your bureau buddies arrive?"

"In the morning. I've talked to the Lieutenant from the state police who's overseeing the scene at Russell's place. I gave him the skinny on what went down and briefed him on what he's going to find when he runs the prints on the bodies. He said if everything checks out, you should have no problem getting cleared."

"That's good to know."

"He did say they're going to need a statement from you. I told them you'd provide it in the morning. I let him know we had a little hiccup here at the station tonight. Let's stuff Cramer back in a cell until morning. You can head home and get some well-deserved rest."

"I don't mind sticking around to help out."

Savage shook his head. "I think it's best if I can play keep away with you from the state police until we can get a handle on things. I don't want them paying a surprise visit and you getting forced into giving a formal statement until you've had a chance to put a couple hours of sleep between now and then."

Hatch understood. It was always good to give the mind time to recover from the trauma of a critical incident. She recovered quicker than most but figured a little sleep couldn't hurt. An involuntary yawn escaped her as if punctuating her thoughts on the matter.

"Plus, don't worry about me. I've got Barbara here to watch my back for a while. She's a dead eye with that hole punch."

"Don't you forget it," Barbara called out.

Hatch chuckled.

Savage tossed her a set of keys. She caught them in mid-air. "It's to Cramer's cruiser. He's not going to need it anymore."

"The last loner you gave me is shredded on Jed's lawn."

"Let's hope this one lasts you a bit longer. At least until morning." He smiled as he fished out his bag of licorice. "I think I've tripled my intake since you came to town." He tossed a handful in his mouth.

She patted his stomach. "Don't worry, looks like I'll be clearing out soon enough."

He stopped chewing and swallowed hard. "I hope not. I was just getting used to having you around."

Hatch attempted a smile as she pocketed the keys and put on her coat. She looked at the time. It was almost midnight.

The engine started and heat soon poured out from the vents, battling the icy air of the vehicle's interior. She sat in the quiet for a moment, pausing to recalibrate her mind after the events of the evening.

Four hours ago, she'd turned down Daphne's offer of a bedtime snuggle to meet Cole for dinner. The rest of the evening had spiraled drastically out of control. Now Hatch wanted nothing more than to get home and sneak into Daphne's bed, hoping whatever magic spell the child had would gift her another night of deep, uninterrupted sleep.

Dropping the car into drive, Hatch sped away into the darkness toward home.

As she drove, her mind replayed the conversation with Cramer. He spilled his guts on the inner workings of Nighthawk Engineering and why they were intimidating and buying out the citizens of Hawk's Landing. But Cramer didn't know who had actually killed her sister. And the fact she wasn't any closer to the answer bothered her.

All Cramer knew was she'd threatened to expose the company's illegal practices. But vehemently denied having any direct involvement in her death, nor did he know who carried it out. Hatch confirmed his honesty when she'd gone for another of the man's fingers. Cramer was resolute.

The FBI would be taking over the case in the morning, and the state police would be conducting the investigation into the shooting at Jed's place. Neither would give her the closure she sought.

She drove along the dark road, the headlights cutting a path through the night ahead. Hatch racked her mind for the answer. And was disappointed when nothing came.

Morning would come in a few hours and with it any chance of personally and properly avenging her sister's death would be lost to the bureaucracy of an official investigation.

IT WASN'T long before she began making her way up the windy red dirt driveway of her childhood home, bringing to close the madness of the night's events. Hatch saw the lights in the kitchen were on and thought it strange. Stranger still was the car parked at the top of the driveway. Cole Jensen's Jeep Wrangler Rubicon.

Hatch let out a grunt of annoyance. *What in the world was he doing here? And why would her mother be entertaining him so late at night?*

His persistence was bordering on stalker'ish behavior. But Hatch knew her mother had always thought the world of Cole. Even after devastating Hatch by cheating on her with her twin, her mother still tried to persuade Hatch to give him a second chance. Tonight would not be the night.

She wanted nothing more than to run a hot shower and then steal some sleep with her niece. Now she had to contend with Cole's relentless attempts at courtship. She planned to quickly dash any notion and then get some rest.

Hatch exited the car and walked by Cole's Jeep. She touched his hood out of an old habit she developed during her patrol days. It was still warm. She surmised he couldn't have been here long, less than twenty minutes, thirty at most. The cold air would've cooled the hood in that time. Hatch looked back toward the house. *Why would Cole show up at this hour of the night?*

She took her hand off the hood and started to head for the door when something caught her eye. She never really took a close look at Cole's Jeep before, aside from noticing the newness of it. But the oddity of seeing it here now caused her to give it further inspection. And what caught her eye made her blood boil and a chill streak down her spine.

The tires.

In particular—the treads.

Hatch bent down and ran her fingers over the ridges. Feeling the hard rubber, she recognized the pattern, an intricate network of grooves resembling a series of puzzle pieces.

Without looking at the photo she'd taken while at the location near where her sister's body was dumped, Hatch knew without a doubt it was a match.

She stood, looking at the house with a renewed sense of purpose. The man responsible for dumping her sister's body and most likely killing her was somewhere inside.

Hatch pulled the small revolver and made a crouched approach toward the front, hoping to get a read on the situation before coming up with an appropriate plan of action. What she saw inside unnerved her. Not an easy thing to accomplish.

Cole Jensen was standing with his back pressed against the wall. His left arm was wrapped tightly around both children. Jake's neck was in the crux of Cole's arm, nearest the elbow. Daphne was pulled toward his center and was being held in place by a tight grip on her shoulder. A handgun was pressed firmly against the soft skin of her temple. Hatch's mother sat frozen in a chair at the table. Her back was to Hatch, but she could see her mother's shoulders shaking uncontrollably.

Hatch hoped for a better alternative than going through the front door. But looking at the situation, any surprise could likely result in Cole shooting the children.

She took a minute to assess the situation and take in as much as she could before entering. Cole looked deranged. He resembled that famous image of Jack Nicholson in *The Shining* more than the handsome grown-up version of her high school love. His normally kempt hair was a mess. His face was slick with sweat and his chest heaved. Desperation permeated every fiber of his being.

Hatch had survived two standoffs tonight. Going for the hat trick, she stepped up onto the porch. The only difference was that, this time, she'd be facing it alone.

Cole must've heard her footsteps because he shifted, jerking the children tighter. Tears streamed down their delicate cheeks. Hatch fought to control the anger rising up inside her. She wanted nothing more than to walk through the door and empty all six chambers of the revolver into his head. That was a solution filled with dire consequences and was cast from her mind as soon as it entered.

She opened the door but did not enter. Instead, she remained outside, waiting and listening. All she heard was the rhythmic sobbing of her niece and nephew. She knew that once she crossed the threshold, nothing would ever be the same.

"Cole, I'm here now. You can let them go and deal with me."

"The hell I can! I know what you did to those other guys. No way I'm facing you one on one."

"Then what is it you want from me?"

"I want you to come in here and have a seat with your mother. There's lots to talk about."

Hatch could hear it in his voice. Cole was terrified. But on top of that he was slurring, which meant he had most likely used a little liquid courage to get him to this point. Or he was already drunk when he received the call to action. Either way, it was a disadvantage she hoped to exploit should the opportunity arise.

"Did you hear me? I said get your ass in here and have a seat!"

Hatch took two quick breaths, letting the oxygen clear her thoughts and bringing forth a controlled focus. She brought the gun up, entering the main hallway with the front sight post leading the way. She had a short wall, four feet long, before it opened up into the kitchen area and she'd be exposed to him.

She crossed the distance, keeping her elbows tight to her sides, providing a stable shoot and move platform. Hatch pivoted into the room and stopped. The front sight dancing along the forehead of her former high school sweetheart, turned cheater, turned murderer.

"Drop the gun, you crazy bitch!"

"No chance. And watch the language around the children."

Cole looked baffled at the comment.

"Rachel, please put the gun down. I don't want anyone to get hurt." Hatch's mother sniffled and choked on her words.

Hatch addressed her mother without taking her eyes off the man in front of her. "I put this gun down and we're all dead. Isn't that right, Cole?"

He didn't answer. He squeezed the children tighter, tucking himself lower. Daphne's head now reduced her ability to safely take a shot.

If Hatch could place a round in Cole's forehead, above the bridge of his nose and between the eyebrows, it would disable his ability to pull the trigger. There were a couple problems with her plan. She'd be firing at the target with two hostages and using a short-barreled weapon she'd never fired before. It was risky at best under the most optimal of scenarios. Her mind rapidly played out alternatives, running the numbers to achieve maximum survivability. The odds were not good.

"I never thought you for a killer. A cheater, yes. But a killer?" Hatch decided maybe she could buy a little time.

"Shut your mouth! You don't know what you're talking about."

"Nice Jeep. I never noticed the tires before."

Hatch watched as Cole tried to piece together her riddle. She noticed the grip on Daphne's shoulder lessen slightly and the white in his knuckles dissipated as he tried to understand her comment. "What—"

"The deputies made a critical mistake when they took for granted the location where Olivia was found. It's understandable. Most of them have never worked a real crime scene before. But I have. And I don't make mistakes. My sister drifted there. She was dumped elsewhere."

"Sit down." Cole spoke through his teeth. A tremor rippled along his body. He was becoming more unhinged.

"Maybe you're the one who should take a seat and listen."

Cole's eyes moved nervously around the room as if he half expected to see Hatch's reinforcements lurking in a dark corner.

"Your fancy new Jeep has some pretty unique tire treads. And the old boat launch you used to dump my sister's body left as good an impression as I've ever seen." She watched him. His breathing became more erratic with each passing second. "The sheriff knows. He's working up the arrest warrant as we speak. The feds and state police are also involved now thanks to the goons you sent to kill me. By the end of all this, you'll have lots of company in prison."

"I'm not going to prison. Do you hear me?"

"What's your plan? Kill me? Then what? Kill my family? Have you seriously gone mad?" Hatch regretted the last comment. No need to push the man beyond the point of reason.

"She was going to ruin everything. She was going to shut us down. Call in the EPA. People were going to lose their jobs. It would've crippled the town."

"So, you killed my sister to save the town? How noble of you."

"I didn't mean that—it wasn't supposed to go that way. I was just trying to scare some sense into her. Make her see how stupid she was. That these are people you don't mess around with. She wouldn't listen." Cole's fingers were now barely holding a piece of Daphne's nightgown. The grip loosening, Jake was now able to swivel his head and lock eyes with Hatch. She saw a strange determination replace his despondency. And in it, Hatch saw her opportunity.

Hatch was aware the decisions made over the next few minutes would decide the fate of everybody in the room.

"How much did my sister's life get you in return?"

"You don't understand."

"Explain."

"They told me to shake her up a bit. Scare the crap out of her. The needle was supposed to contain a sleeping aid. They told me it was benign."

"Why'd they pick you to do it? Why would a group of trained mercenaries ask for your help?"

Cole was quiet. His crazed panic giving way to sadness. His

voice cracked. "Because I could get her alone and away from her kids without drawing any suspicion."

Hatch felt the warmth burning her cheeks. "Just like you did with me?"

His silence was answer enough.

Movement caught her attention. Jake was mouthing something. It took her a second to realize what he was asking. Feign? He asked slowly. Hatch gave a barely imperceptible nod. Not that Cole would have noticed a more overt gesture. His eyes watered and his once ragged breath transitioned to long, drawn out sighs. Madness was quickly giving way to utter despair.

Hatch focused her aim, waiting for the opportunity.

Jake stomped hard on the man's foot. His bare foot crashing against Cole's shoe did little in the way of pain, but it served its simple purpose. A feigning blow. One that drew Cole's attention, lowering his head. At the same time Jake swung up with his arm. The plaster encased forearm gave the blow added weight as it struck the gunman's nose.

Cole's head snapped back. His body rose, an involuntary reaction to the strike. It wasn't much of a window of opportunity. But Hatch didn't need more than a crack.

The gunshot was deafening. The silence following somehow seemed louder. Jake lay atop Cole. Both unmoving. Daphne darted toward Hatch's mother. Hatch closed the distance as Jake rolled away. Her heart resumed its cadence as she evaluated the deadly accuracy of her shot.

The single entrance wound to Cole's forehead bisected the gap between his eyebrows. Hatch knew he was dead but kicked the gun out of his hand for good measure.

She felt a tug on the back of her jacket, snapping her out of her momentary tunnel vision. Hatch turned and saw Daphne looking up at her. The girl's face was twisted in anguish and she opened her arms wide.

Hatch stuffed the snub-nosed .38 into the back of her waistband as she took a knee, the warmth of the steel reminding her of its recent use. Hatch swallowed up the little girl in her arms. She felt Daphne's little ribcage vibrate her emotional release.

Jake came from the side, joining in. Hatch inhaled this moment. The embrace of her sister's children, washing away the violence she'd just committed. An absolution of sorts. And one she'd desperately needed.

"You really don't need to stay. We're fine now."

Savage folded his arms in protest. "I'd just feel a whole lot better if I waited here with you until the cavalry arrives in a few hours."

"Nobody knows we're here. Well, nobody except you and the motel clerk. And he doesn't even know our real names."

"I'm not caving. I'll stay in my squad car and keep an eye out."

"Suit yourself. But if you're going to stand guard, it might be more comfortable in here." Hatch opened the door to her motel room.

The kids were already asleep in the room next door with her mother. Littleton had kept watch while Savage finished up filling in the state police on the third, and hopefully last, crime scene of the night. The house was locked down by the crime scene techs and it wouldn't be cleared for a few hours. The state was bringing in a hazardous waste cleanup crew to remove the blood before the children returned.

"I guess it'd be warmer than sitting in the Suburban all night."

Hatch turned and entered the room. Savage followed.

Hatch removed the revolver from the small of her back and placed it on the nightstand between the two beds. Savage arranged his duty weapon in a similar fashion. Kicking off their shoes, neither bothered to undress before taking their respective beds.

"You know my bed's probably more comfortable if you want to try over here." Savage chuckled at his own joke.

Hatch didn't speak. She pulled off the covers and crossed the two-foot gap to the other queen bed where Savage lay. He slid over and patted the bed.

"Nothing's going to happen," Hatch said. "You know that, right?"

"Never crossed my mind. Just figured it'd be easier to watch over you if you were close by."

Hatch rolled her eyes and slid into bed next to him. She laid her head against his shoulder. At her height, few men fit naturally next to her. Savage proved to be a rare exception.

"You know. I could really use you around here. Plus, I've just had a full-time position come open."

She folded her hands over her stomach and shook her head. "I'm gone once the dust settles on this."

"It doesn't have to be this way. You could have a chance at starting over here."

Hatch sighed. "I've got unfinished business elsewhere."

Savage didn't argue the point any further.

Before drifting off, she wondered to herself if she could get used to this. Hatch fell asleep with the smell of licorice enveloping her.

27

For a month straight Hawk's Landing was inundated with law enforcement agents from just about every three-letter government agency in the country. The FBI led the charge on Chisolm and his company. The state police made quick work of their turnaround on the two shooting incidents involving Hatch. Both were ruled justified and because of her temporary status as a sheriff's deputy, were also indemnified from any civil suit should one arise. Regardless of the outcome, the past several weeks had proved draining.

Cole's DNA had been found on the needle used to kill her sister. The substance he claimed was supposedly a sleeping aid turned out to be something the lab referred to as Gray Death, an amalgamation of heroin, fentanyl, and carfentanil. The dosage was fatal. The confirmation added little beyond what she already knew, but gave Hatch a finality in feeling her sister's death was avenged.

Hatch sat in the kitchen waiting for the rumble of Savage's

Suburban to announce his arrival. She played with the tin star he'd given her, spinning it on the wooden table. The aromatic smell of her mother's coffee filled the air and Hatch took a sip.

It was early, but she heard the pitter-patter of little feet. Ever since that night with Cole, they slept less and got up early. Hatch made sure she gave each a big hug and kiss before leaving every day. The routine was starting to become normal, and that scared Hatch more than the people who'd tried to kill her.

The sound of the heavy Chevy's tires crushing their way up the dirt driveway caused Hatch to stand. Daphne and Jake entered the room, their bodies hurtling toward her.

As they crashed into her, Hatch absorbed their impacts with a broad smile. "You know I wouldn't head off without saying goodbye."

"Are you getting any bad guys today?" Jake's personality was different. No longer was he consumed by the grief of his mother's death. His heroics had brought out a new strength. And in the eyes of his little sister, he was now her protector.

"Just one more to go."

"And then what?" Daphne's eyes told her she already knew the answer to the question.

"We'll see."

Hatch ignored her mother's stare from the kitchen. She was well aware of her opinion, it having been voiced many times in the weeks since the shooting of Cole Jensen.

"Gotta go. I'll be back later."

Hatch kissed each child upon the head and then pried herself free. She exited as flurries began to swirl. The cold caressed her skin as she clipped the badge to her belt.

Hatch walked to the waiting vehicle. She entered and handed Savage a travel mug of her mother's coffee. The man seemed to be as addicted to it as he was the black licorice in his jacket pocket.

Savage accepted the mug. "You shouldn't have."

"I didn't want you getting the DTs today. Big day."

"Big day."

"Not every day you get to arrest a sheriff."

Tapping his badge, Savage grinned. "Former sheriff."

THE WARRANT BEING SERVED today was federal, and the FBI was actually executing it, but Savage and Hatch had requested to accompany the arresting team. All of the others who could be directly linked to any wrongdoing had been rounded up. Simon Chisolm was found at a bus station trying to take a Greyhound to Denver. Hatch participated in each related arrest, but former Sheriff Larry Jeffries was of special interest.

They didn't expect a shootout but, based on the details of the FBI's investigation into the man, it was assumed he was prepared for this day. Well, as prepared as anybody could be. But Jeffries was a lawman, crooked or not, and prison for cops held little promise. They were prepared for the worst-case scenario and went in a caravan of cars led by a small SWAT contingent out of the FBI's Denver field office.

Savage's was the last car in the procession and followed closely as they made their way up the long, ornate driveway leading to the retired sheriff's mansion.

The tactical element formed a four-man diamond and began their approach as Savage stopped his SUV. Hatch could see Jeffries sitting on the wrap-around front porch, smoking a cigarette.

As Hatch exited, she could hear the clear, calm commands of the tactical unit. It didn't look as though the former sheriff was planning a last stand. He complied, raising his hands into the air.

The cigarette dangled from his mouth. The smoke obscured his face.

Moments later, Jeffries was in custody. Savage looked at Hatch and shrugged. "That was pretty anticlimactic."

"I've just got one question for him."

Hatch began walking toward the handcuffed man being led by two operators in full tactical gear. Their AR-15s were slung to the side and each had a controlled grip under the older prisoner's elbows.

She waited as Jeffries was placed on the backseat of the transport vehicle. Secured, the two men stood back. Hatch put her hand on the door and gave them a pleasant smile. "Just got a quick question for him and then I'll be out of your hair."

The old man looked up at her inquisitively.

Hatch pulled out a report from the old file she'd located in the basement. "Why'd you dump the case?"

He squinted to read the paperwork she dangled in front of him. "I'll need my readers if I'm going to be able to see whatever you're holding. These eyes aren't what they used to be."

"Paul Hatch. Killed in '92. You were the investigator."

His eyes widened. "Why are you looking at a hunting accident from twenty-plus years ago?"

"Because he was my father."

Jeffries looked away. He began shaking his head slowly from side to side, each movement more pronounced than its predecessor. "I knew there'd come a day. For whatever it's worth, your father was a great man. What he did rescuing that family was one of the most amazing stories of heroism I've ever heard."

"Somebody bribed you. I need to know who." Hatch was suddenly leaning into the car, her face inches from his.

"I did it to protect you. To protect your family."

Hatch was confused. Her intensity shifted, and she backed off. "Protect us? By covering up the truth?"

"I'm not the one who can point you in the direction you're looking to go."

"Then tell me who can."

Jeffries cantered his head up. "Your mother."

Hatch's legs almost buckled under the weight of the man's words. She pushed back from the sedan, shutting the door as she righted herself.

She began walking back toward the Suburban. The loosely tucked police report fluttering under her arm. Savage hustled to keep up with her long strides.

"What was that all about?"

Hatch handed the file to Savage. "It's what I took that day in the basement. The case file documenting my father's death. Your predecessor wrote the report years back when he was on patrol. I was hoping he'd be able to tell me the truth."

"From the look on your face, I take it he didn't."

"No, but he told me where to look."

They got in the oversized SUV and Savage fired up the engine. "Where to?"

"Home."

HER MOTHER WAS in the kitchen, cleaning up breakfast. She startled at the sight of Hatch. "Rachel! You scared me half to death. I didn't hear you come in."

Hatch worked to compose the words.

"You're back so soon. Did everything go okay for you this morning?"

"Twenty-one years you've lied to me."

"I'm sorry. What are you talking about now?"

"I spoke with Larry Jeffries today. That's who we arrested this morning. But I didn't accompany the arrest team because of this case. I went because he was the deputy who investigated Dad's death."

Her mother dropped a dish. It crashed loudly on the floor, sending shards of porcelain out in all directions. "All these years. Do you know what finding his body in the woods did to me that day? Do you know the course it sent my life on?"

"I'm sor—"

"Save your sorry for somebody else. What I want now is answers."

"Your dad came out here to Colorado after Vietnam to get away from everything war puts on its soldiers. You know that part of it. What you don't know is what he did after leaving the war before he settled here." Tears began to stream down her face. "He worked for a private contractor, basically a mercenary group. He drifted after the war and told me it was all he really knew. But he eventually gave it up and came here to Hawk's Landing with the hope of starting a new life."

"Why was he killed?"

"Because the people he worked for didn't want to let him go. Because he breached a contract. He was a liability to them."

"Why did it take them so long to find him? Over twelve years and suddenly they come for him."

"He stayed off their radar. That was until he made national news rescuing that family lost in the woods. Your father was dead a week later."

Hatch spoke through gritted teeth. "Who did it?"

Her mother wiped at her eyes. With each tear she cleared, another took its place. "I don't know."

"You're going to have to do a lot better than that."

"Wait here a minute."

Her mother disappeared from the kitchen. Hatch heard her upstairs. A few minutes later, she returned carrying a small shoebox.

"What's this?"

"Mostly letters from your father." The waterworks had slowed. "He was quite a wordsmith, if you'd believe it."

"I'm not looking to walk down memory lane."

"I know." Her mother thumbed through the small pile, pulling out a weathered envelope. "Here."

Hatch looked at it. There was a stamped emblem with an address on the return section. Aside from that, there were no other markings. "What's this?"

"A few weeks after your father died, I received this. In it was ten-thousand dollars in cash and a note."

"What did it say?"

"Take care of your children."

Hatch exhaled slowly and looked at her mother. The woman whom she had battled with for most of her adolescence had protected her the only way she knew how. Strength came in different ways. And her mother's strength had been to silently shoulder the secret of her husband's death to protect the children they both loved.

Hatch stepped closer, porcelain crunching under her boots, and she pulled her mother in close. She held their embrace as her mother's body trembled.

"What are you going to do now?" Her mother asked as they separated.

"I'm going to set things right."

"How do you plan to do that?"

Hatch looked down at the address on the envelope before

folding it and stuffing it into her back pocket. "I'll start there. In Las Cruces."

"You might not find the answers you're looking for."

"I'm not looking for answers. It's vengeance I'm after."

28

Hatch sat across from Savage in his small office with the desk separating them. He fidgeted with a stack of papers. "Are you sure?"

"Never been more sure about anything in my life."

Savage looked hurt by the comment but cocked his head and smiled weakly.

"I've got to close some things out, or I'll never be able to settle."

"Make me a promise. If you do figure it all out, you'll think hard about coming back here and making a life for yourself?"

"Fair enough. You really think I'll ever find normal?"

"Well, you've been everywhere and nowhere, as you say. Maybe, Hawk's Landing is as normal a place as you and I will ever find."

Hatch smiled. She unclipped the badge from her waist and slid the metal piece across the desk. Savage looked down at it but refused to pick it up.

"You've got a job with this office anytime you want."

"Hopefully, someday I can take you up on it."

"It's an offer that never expires."

Hatch walked out of the sheriff's office. The landscape was now painted white. The snow covering would only be temporary. That's the thing with anything covered up: It's only a matter of time until the truth rises to the surface.

The powder crunched underfoot as she walked away.

She'd be leaving Hawk's Landing soon, but she couldn't help wondering if she'd ever return.

Read on for a sneak peek of *Downburst (Rachel Hatch book 2)*, or get your copy now:

Join the LT Ryan reader family & receive a free copy of the Rachel Hatch story, Fractured. Scan the QR code below to get started:

THE RACHEL HATCH SERIES

Drift

Downburst

Fever Burn

Smoke Signal

Firewalk

Whitewater

Aftershock

Whirlwind

Tsunami (Spring 2022)

Fastrope (Coming Soon)

RACHEL HATCH SHORT STORIES

Fractured

Proving Ground

The Gauntlet

DOWNBURST CHAPTER 1

He looked down at his watch for the second time in as many seconds, as if checking again was going to make him any less late than he already was. It was the bus driver's fault, but he couldn't use the excuse even if it was true. She never accepted anything but punctuality, and recently, he'd failed in that area more times than he cared to admit.

Juan picked up the pace. His backpack was loaded to capacity and the weight tugged down on his shoulders. His stomach rumbled and he thought about stopping to retrieve the granola bar from the bottom of the pack. Precious seconds would be lost to the effort. He decided against appeasing his belly's audible protest and continued on without sustenance. Maybe Miss Garcia would give him a little time to snack before they began today's session. Doubtful, but the thought of it, regardless of its probability, gave him hope.

Rounding the corner onto Serrano Drive, a cold gust of wind blew his hat off. Juan spun to grab it as the brim bounced off his fingertips. It was a valiant effort, but like most of his athletic endeavors, he came up short. Trotting back, he picked his hat up, cinching it down to prevent a repeat episode.

As he turned to begin his jog toward his tutor's house, he heard the pulsing bass of a subwoofer. The thumping shook him to his core, and Juan stopped dead in his tracks. He turned as the boxy front end of an older model Cadillac slowly eased around the corner of the street he'd just come from. The vehicle rolled to a stop alongside the curb.

The car's windows were heavily tinted and reflected the deep purple of the evening sky. It was impossible to see inside. The thumping continued, brake lights giving the plume of exhaust an eerie red hue, like the peel of a blood orange. He'd become all too familiar with the fruit when helping his father pack the crates at Gonzales's Grocery. His father's work had left their family with little in the aftermath of his death, so Juan picked up where he'd left off, stocking the store's shelves. At fifteen, he'd become the man of the family and what little money he earned went to putting food on the table for his three younger sisters. He knew his only chance to help his family would be to graduate high school. But with the hours spent at the store, his grades slipped, and now he spent his evenings with his teacher, Miss Garcia, who provided him with extra help.

The Cadillac idled. Juan's heart began jackhammering uncontrollably. His fingers trembled, the tips went numb. In his haste to get to his destination, he hadn't initially connected the dots. But he knew who was in the sedan and that knowledge paralyzed him with fear.

Juan sucked a cool gulp of air mixed with exhaust, turned and began running at a dead sprint. His thin legs carried the gangly lank of his frame. The load on his back slowed him down as he pushed the limits of his physicality.

The engine behind him roared, the sound momentarily drowning out the boom of the music. His feet couldn't move across the cracked cement of the sidewalk fast enough. He looked ahead and could see the black metal guide rail leading up the steps to Miss Garcia's home. It would be close.

Without looking back, he knew the car was gaining rapidly. Juan shed his extra weight, releasing the burdensome straps without breaking stride. The bag fell behind him. Books spilled out on the ground as the zipper split open on impact.

Just ten steps to go and he'd be inside the house. He wheezed under the exertion and regretted not taking a blast from his inhaler before getting off the bus.

Out of the corner of his left eye, he saw the car parallel to him. The rhythmic drumming reverberated in his rib cage, louder now because the back-passenger window was down. His peripheral vision picked up the long barrel of a gun.

Somebody from the car yelled, "You don't never mess around with an Outlaw's girl."

He'd walked Sophia home from school once. Juan knew she was Macho's sister, head of the local gang. She was nice, and they talked about life outside of Luna Vista. Nothing happened on the walk. He'd dreamed about her afterward and fantasized about running off with her and starting a new life. But he hadn't told her or anyone else. Running for his life, he wished now he had kissed Sophia or at least tried.

Two more steps and then the stairs. Optimism gave way to reality with the deafening roar of gunfire.

Juan was slammed sideways with the impact as he toppled over less than a foot from the first step leading up to Miss Garcia's. He smelled an acrid smoke and tasted the metallic burn from his lung's exertion. The sour bitterness of blood overwhelmed his senses, filling his mouth and choking him.

Another blast of wind lashed at him, again knocking his hat free. This time he made no effort to retrieve it. He couldn't. His motionless body yielded to the trauma.

The tires from the car squealed as it raced off down the street.

Juan heard the screen door open followed by a scream he could only assume was Miss Garcia's. He couldn't be certain because of the dark veil shrouding his view. A coldness wrapped him. He thought of his mother and sisters. What would they do without him to help out? Who would now stock the shelves?

It was a question he would never learn the answer to.

"Did you see him go down? Like he got hit by a Mack truck. Punk bitch never had a chance." The boy rested the Remington 870 pump-action shotgun across his legs, looking down at it with admiration. He stroked the long black barrel with his hand as if petting a lap dog. Although his face was hidden beneath the blue cloth of the bandana, it was obvious from the crinkled lines around his eyes that the boy who had just fired the gun was smiling.

Xavier Fuentes looked over at the gunman. Feeling his body shake, he worried the other boy would notice. Apparently, he didn't. He was focused on the shotgun.

"Yo, X. Hit this shit." The front passenger pinched a fat joint between his thumb and forefinger.

Embers glimmered at its burnt end, the smoke adding to the hazy layer already present in the car. Xavier took it. Putting it to his lips, he could feel the previous user's moist saliva. He pulled in hard, drawing a deep hit of the marijuana. The smoke burned his lungs as he held his breath. He was already high, higher than he could ever remember being, but it wasn't enough to block the image of the dying kid from his mind.

Releasing the aromatic smoke from his lungs, the heat of it tickled the back of his throat and caused him to cough. He handed the joint to his right, passing it off to Blaze, who pulled his face mask down before taking it. Blaze's real name was Juan Rivera, but it had been years since anybody had called him that. He'd been a grade above Xavier before dropping out of school in the eighth grade. The Outlaws had claimed him and, as was the practice, gave him a new name.

The front passenger, Psycho, was a few years older. A big, wild-eyed kid with long hair he kept in tight cornrows. He was the right-hand man to the gang's leader, Carlos "Macho" Ortiz. The two were inseparable, and Psycho would do violence to anyone who challenged Carlos. Thus, his name and reputation were forever intertwined.

Macho drove, putting distance between them and the dead boy. Sirens sounded in the distance. Xavier's hands shook and he tucked them under his thighs. He wasn't scared about the cops catching them. Even if there had been a witness, nobody in Luna Vista would speak to the police. Not unless they had a death wish. His hands shook. He'd just watched his best friend since third grade get gunned down.

He knew the shotgun in Blaze's hand would be given to him soon and a similar task would be asked of him. It was the way things were. A rite of passage in becoming an official member of the Outlaws.

Macho eyed him through the rearview mirror. "You ready for tomorrow, right? It's the first step in coming up."

Xavier tried to look tough. Puffing up his chest and sitting up straight, he gave a smile. He wondered if Macho bought the act.

Tomorrow night would be when he proved himself worthy. Everybody in the gang had to go through it. Some fared better than others, but nobody came out unscathed.

One thing was certain. Tomorrow night, regardless of the outcome, there would be blood.

DOWNBURST CHAPTER 2

She sat listening to the rising and falling buzz of the V8 engine. The air freshener clipped to the vent was supposed to make the older-model Camry smell like a new car. Instead, it barely masked the stench left behind by the previous renter, who'd clearly violated the rental company's non-smoking agreement. The end result smelled as though potpourri had been heated in a used ashtray. Hatch lowered the windows a crack, letting the cool breeze purge the air around her, and then turned off the car.

Sitting in silence, Hatch evaluated the exterior of the building. It stood out amid the bleak desert backdrop. One road, an arterial spurt from the main one, led to the dead-end where she now waited. She was parked just past the building, behind a utility shed. The nose of the Camry poked out a couple of inches, but the vehicle was positioned opposite any arriving traffic, making it difficult to spot unless looking for it. The muted beige of the car helped it blend with the bland, sandy surroundings.

There was little need to worry about visitors. The place looked long-since abandoned. Hatch wouldn't have been shocked to see a tumbleweed roll by while the leitmotif of *The Good, the Bad and the Ugly* rang out in the background. The lock had been cut on the fenced entrance leading in and it appeared local vagrants had long since ignored the Keep Out sign posted to it.

Spray paint adorned the boarded-up windows and walls, giving an unwelcoming vibe to any person who might have accidentally ventured out this way. To Hatch, these overt displays of dominance were a sign of weakness. Those boasting in colorful epitaphs proved to be more bark than bite. When or if she bumped into those responsible, she expected to validate her assumption.

Over an hour had passed since she first pulled up to the location, and she still hadn't seen a single person come or go from the building. Experience had taught her observation was an underutilized skill, and patience to do it for long durations even less so. One hour wasn't long for Hatch. During a sniper course, she'd once remained in position for three days waiting for the target to arrive. Three days of minimal movement and sleep, all in the hope of hitting a passing target that would present itself for less than thirty seconds. Hard to describe the release of pulling a trigger after seventy-two hours. In its crudest of terms, and the way she relayed it to one of her closest teammates, it was orgasmic. So, in comparison, sitting idle for an hour in a climate-controlled vehicle was a drop in the bucket.

She picked up the letter and traced the return address, which was for this exact location. A place that most likely looked very different twenty-one years ago. That or it was the most impressive attempt at urban camouflage she'd seen.

Hatch pulled the door handle. She was met with a resistant blast of sand-filled wind as she pushed the door open and stepped onto the packed earth. As the wind subsided, she heard a rhythmic drumming sound off in the distance. At first, the repetitious beat sounded like a Blackhawk, but after giving it more attention, she realized it was music. The source of which was an approaching car.

Shifting over to the utility shed's nearest wall, Hatch stepped out of view and waited. The noise amplified, announcing the arrival. A black Cadillac, the cause of the commotion, pulled up within a foot of the boarded double-door entrance of the main building. Hatch knew if they looked to the right, her car would be spotted. She'd worked up a non-violent contingency plan in which she'd pretend to be meeting a boyfriend out here for a private rendezvous. She always had an action plan, should the easy route fail. But she hoped it wouldn't come to that. Things worked out better for other people if they didn't choose option B.

She wasn't here to pick a fight. Today was about gathering intelligence. Nothing more. And by the looks of the four exiting the sedan, these were not the people she'd get it from. Their outer garments were all similar in color, dark navy blue from head to toe. One of them carried a shotgun. Hatch deduced these young men weren't an up-and-coming boy band looking for a quiet place to practice their routine.

Of the four, one stood out from the rest. He looked younger, less dangerous than the others. His face hadn't yet been hardened by crime. He stayed a few steps behind the three larger guys. His hands were stuffed in the pockets of his baggy jeans as he followed them into the building.

None of them paid any attention to the beige Camry or the woman standing along the wall of the utility shed. Hatch gave serious thought to making an uninvited visit into the gang's hangout, but quickly dismissed it, realizing the futility of such a move and the high probability of a negative outcome. Her fight was not with them.

The address listed this location as Las Cruces, but the official name for the town on the eastern outskirts of the city was Luna Vista. Hatch decided she'd need to do a little digging around the local area and see if she could find anyone who knew what this place used to be, and if anybody from those days was still around.

Loud music disturbed the still night again, similar to the car's, but this time the noise came from within the building. The sun dipped below the horizon, casting the sky into a dazzling wash of purple and pink. The mountains to the east darkened in contrast. On the other side of those high ridges lay the expansive White Sands of New Mexico, a vast, desolate area used by the US military. The proximity of it to the now abandoned address of her father's last connection to a private covert operations group made more sense in that context.

Hatch used the noise from the building to mask her departure. She got back into the Camry and started it, pausing for a ten count. No movement. Nobody exited. She shifted into reverse and backed out from her concealed position.

The Camry exited past the open fence and she accelerated toward the main road. Hatch turned right, heading toward the town of Luna Vista.

Neon battled for attention against a bright skyline. VACANCY glowed at the sign's base. The Moonbeam Motel was as good a place as any, and Hatch liked the fact the lot was empty except for a few scattered cars. Rooms were lined in a strip with the manager's office on the far left as she pulled the Camry in.

The motel was set back from the main road and was partially shrouded by a cluster of desert willows. A man wearing a lightweight buttoned-down short sleeve shirt was sweeping the walkway near the entrance to the main office. Dust kicked up with each stroke of the broom, surrounding the man like Pig Pen's cartoonish cloud.

As Hatch pulled into an empty parking spot, the man stopped mid-stroke and looked up. His skin, the dark color of chestnuts, was coated in a film of sweat. He wiped his forehead with the back of his hand and set the broom against the wall. Smiling broadly, he walked over to the office door and held it open for Hatch.

"Looking for a room?"

"I am."

The man tipped his head and outstretched his arm in a welcoming fashion. "Right this way."

Hatch walked through the open door and into the small office. A rectangular space heater on the floor at the base of the counter on the customer side pushed out a barely noticeable amount of heat. She looked down at it and hoped the rooms had more efficient units. Hatch had several exposures to hypothermia during her time in the military and was now more sensitive to the cold. She endured when necessary but preferred not to go into survival mode while staying in guest quarters.

The man must've noticed her examination of the heater because, as he walked around her to the other side of the counter, he said, "Don't worry. The rooms are equipped with a wall unit that will keep you nice and toasty."

"Good to know."

The man grabbed a small hand towel from his back pocket and wiped the remaining sweat from his face. Single threads caught and hung in his stubble. "How many nights will you be staying with us?"

"Not sure. Can I pay as I go?"

"Sure." He paused, giving hatch a measured look. "First time in Luna Vista?"

"Yes."

"Where are you visiting from?"

"Everywhere and nowhere."

"I don't understand."

"Sorry, just something I say." Hatch absently brushed back a piece of hair from her face, tucking it behind her ear. "I travel a lot."

"Oh, I see. I just saw the Colorado plates on the car and wondered. I've got family out that way. Beautiful country."

Hatch's recent experience in the Rocky Mountains left her bittersweet. She thought of her sister's kids, Daphne and Jake. Then her mind drifted to Dalton Savage and the offer he'd made. Giving her a chance at normal. An offer she'd turned down. Did she really have a choice? She looked at the man in front of her who expectantly waited for a response, obviously hoping for some type of connection.

"It's just a rental."

"Well, if you ever get a chance, I highly recommend you take some time and check it out. The mountains are amazing, much different from the range here."

Hatch nodded. She hoped when closure was reached, she would return. "I'll try to get out that way someday. Hopefully, sooner rather than later."

The man's smile faded, and he sighed. "You seem like a nice person, and I don't like to push paying customers away. By the number of cars in the lot, you can plainly see I could use the business."

"But...?"

"But this isn't the safest place to be." He lifted a crucifix attached to the simple chain around his neck and kissed it. "God knows I've done my best. But this area of town is extremely dangerous. Especially for outsiders."

"Doesn't seem so bad. I've seen worse."

"I'm just saying there are plenty of better places not too far away in Las Cruces. I can get you a map and show you, if you'd like?"

"I'd prefer to stay here."

The man shook his head and shrugged in resignation. He opened a drawer and pulled out a registration form. "Will you be paying cash or charge? But I should warn you, our credit card machine has been a little finicky lately."

"I prefer cash anyway. How much per night?"

"Forty. But if you'd like to book the room for the week, I can drop it to thirty-five a night."

Hatch pulled the cash from her wallet, handing the two twenties over to the man. "Forty will be fine. I doubt I'll be staying that long."

He took the money. Pulling out a small metal lockbox from the same drawer he'd gotten the form, the man took a small key and worked the lock open. He placed the cash inside and closed the lid, then looked up. "I have an incidentals form I'm going to need you to fill out. Just name and address stuff. Even though you're paying in cash, I am going to need a driver's license."

Hatch smiled, retrieving another twenty and placing it on the counter. "How about we leave that form blank?"

The man looked at the money and then up at Hatch. She was taller than him by a few inches. His eyes moved up and down, evaluating her. She was wearing a navy-blue fleece-lined windbreaker and khaki cargo pants. He began nodding, the motion indicating he had come to some satisfactory conclusion for her need for anonymity. Taking stock of her apparel coupled with the fact that she hadn't been phased by the man's reference to danger, he most likely assumed she was a federal agent.

Then the man did something she didn't expect. He pushed the twenty back toward her. "No need for that."

"Thanks." Hatch put the money away, impressed by the man, who obviously needed the cash, yet took the moral high ground and refused the subtle bribe. The simple gesture spoke volumes to his integrity.

He pulled a room key from a pegboard on the wall behind him and handed it over. "Room number three. Couple doors down from here. Can't miss it."

Hatch took the key and turned to leave. "Thanks."

"My name is Manuel. If you need anything, my family and I live in room number one. Don't hesitate to knock if I'm not at the front desk."

"I should be fine, but thank you." Hatch pushed the door open. The chime above rang out her departure as she walked to her accommodations.

The room was small, and the furniture a bit dated, but it was clean. Immaculate would have been a better word to describe it. A heavy scent of lemon emanated from the wood surfaces. The carpet, although worn bare in some spots, looked as if it had been cleaned by a professional-grade rug cleaner. Hatch had stayed in more luxurious places that paled in comparison to the effort put into the small strip of rooms.

She decided to shower and get a good night's sleep. Hatch wanted to get an early start.

DOWNBURST CHAPTER 3

Each footstep was light and quick. The cadence of breath in sync with every fifth heel strike of the sneaker. *Run as if your life depends on it.* She heard the words of her father as she picked up the pace. His philosophy was centered around pushing boundaries, both mental and physical. Ingrained at an early age and sharpened in recent years, Hatch lived up to his mantra. Here in a place somehow connected to his past, she pushed herself even harder.

No better way to find yourself than to get lost on a run. She didn't plot her morning's course, nor did she know how long or far she planned to go. Hatch took only the room key and some cash, tucking them into her waistline before heading out on the morning's trek.

It seemed like a good way to see the small town of Luna Vista. She had left the motel forty-seven minutes ago and her pace had been relentless. Even with the coldness of morning, she worked up a decent sweat as she opened her stride on a long stretch of road. The terrain was flat, but the elevation, three-quarters of a mile high, put a strain on her lungs. A slight touch of hypoxia gave her an endorphin rush, making each step feel lighter and more disconnected than when she ran at sea level. It was a euphoric experience.

The smell of bacon caught her attention as she passed a corner diner. The saltiness of the rendered pig fat caused her to slow to a stop. Hatch walked back to the diner and stood on the sidewalk looking in through the plate glass windows. Her legs tingled from exertion, but her stomach rumbled at the marvelous odors seeping out from the restaurant. The diner wasn't crowded. After taking a minute to stretch her thighs, Hatch entered.

Local diners were the hub of a small town, and she could think of no better place to start her fact-finding mission than inside the diner. There was a sign inviting patrons to seat themselves, but Hatch didn't want to take up a table, so she meandered over to the bar-styled counter. She took up a stool a few seats down from a plump gentleman in a heavy plaid coat, the orange and black of a hunter. He was reading the paper and slurping from a mug of coffee and didn't break from his routine with her arrival.

An older man with bits of white stubble coating his ruddy jowls approached. He wore a paper hat, covering a head spotted with buzzed hair the same color as his unshaven face. His brow furrowed as he approached.

"Get you somethin' to drink, Miss?"

"Coffee's fine. Maybe a glass of water, too."

The man in plaid folded his paper and Hatch could feel his stare fall on her. He then grabbed his coffee, announcing his return to the morning's routine with a loud slurp. A moment later, a mug filled to the brim was set in front of her. The aroma had a boldness to it which Hatch enjoyed. She took a sip of it before rehydrating with water.

She picked up a menu stuffed between a napkin holder and bottle of ketchup. The stubbled man behind the counter waited patiently for her decision. It didn't take long.

"I'll have the Luna Vista special."

The man cocked an eyebrow. "That's a pretty big plate and it comes with a side of pancakes too."

"Pretty sure I can handle it."

At that, the man's rough exterior softened. He smiled, drawing up his hound-dog-like cheeks. "One special, coming up."

She watched as the man who'd taken her order walked back to the grill. Hatch could see him still smiling as he cracked eggs and flipped the pancakes. He took great pleasure in building the pile of food for her. Must not be a menu item commonly ordered by the women of the town.

Hatch quietly enjoyed her coffee while she waited, taking the time to survey the other patrons by using the angled mirror above the cooking station. Only a handful of people were in the diner. There were murmured conversations amid the occasional clink and clatter of a dish or utensil. But at some point during her brief observation, each and every one of them took a moment to check her out. Growing up in a small town and having just recently revisited it, Hatch knew the distrust and guardedness with which outsiders were received.

And she felt it now.

"Enjoy." Two plates were set in front of her, one containing eggs, bacon, hash browns, and toast. The other held three of the biggest pancakes Hatch had ever seen. She smiled, understanding the man's shock at her decision to place the order.

"Thanks. Mind if I get a refill on the coffee? I'm going to need it to wash down these pancakes."

The man laughed as he turned to get the pot.

He held the pot over the mug, bringing the black liquid back to its brim. Before he walked away again, Hatch asked, "Have you been in business long?"

The man set the pot on the counter. A small droplet of water sizzled under the heat of the pot's base. "I've been working this counter since this hair was as black as that there coffee. Why you asking?"

"My father had travelled out this way a long time back. That's why I wanted to check it out."

"Most people don't travel to Luna Vista. You sure he didn't mean Las Cruces? Much more touristy."

"I'm sure. He worked here for a bit."

"You don't say. How long ago are we talking about?"

"About thirty plus years ago."

"Well, that's going back a while. I was here then. Not sure I'm going to remember, but I'm pretty good with names."

"Paul Hatch ring a bell?"

The man behind the counter scratched at his stubble. Giving a healthy pause, the answer came in the slow shake of his head. "Can't say it does."

The man in plaid stood abruptly. He tucked his paper under his arm and headed out the door.

Hatch said, "What do you know about that old abandoned warehouse on the outskirts of town?"

The man shrugged. "Not much to say about it. Been that way for years. There's been a couple businesses take up shop there over the years, but nothing seems to last here. I heard it's been taken over by a bunch of local punks and used as some kind of hangout."

"Can't the cops do anything about it?"

The man laughed and turned. Placing the pot back on the

burner, he said, "That man who just walked out is the chief of police. Why don't you ask him?"

Hatch turned. The man in plaid had already slipped from view. There was no need to chase after him. She'd know where to find him should the need arise.

She cut into the eggs and began the task of taking on her second challenge of the morning, the Luna Vista Special.

The cook smiled at her efforts. "There is somebody else who may be able to help you out. Wilbur Smith's been here since before me. He runs the gun shop across the street. Doesn't open up for a couple hours, but it might be worth talking to him."

"Thanks."

"I'm Harry, by the way."

She held up her mug in salutary fashion. "Rachel. But people just call me Hatch."

"Well, we serve lunch and dinner, also. So, don't be a stranger."

Hatch looked down at the mountain of food, giving a conciliatory smile. "I don't think I'll be hungry again for a long while."

"Can't say I didn't warn you."

Hatch set about devouring the meal. The long walk back would give her time to digest. She needed to shower off from the run and then pay the gun shop owner a visit.

The town of Luna Vista owed her some answers, and Hatch wasn't leaving until she had them.

Order Downburst now:

Join the LT Ryan reader family & receive a free copy of the Rachel Hatch story, *Fractured*. Scan the QR code below to get started:

ALSO BY LT RYAN

Find All of L.T. Ryan's Books Today!

The Jack Noble Series

The Recruit (free)

The First Deception (Prequel 1)

Noble Beginnings

A Deadly Distance

Ripple Effect (Bear Logan)

Thin Line

Noble Intentions

When Dead in Greece

Noble Retribution

Noble Betrayal

Never Go Home

Beyond Betrayal (Clarissa Abbot)

Noble Judgment

Never Cry Mercy

Deadline

End Game

Noble Ultimatum

Noble Legend

Noble Revenge (Coming Soon)

Bear Logan Series

Ripple Effect

Blowback

Take Down

Deep State

Bear & Mandy Logan Series

Close to Home

Under the Surface

The Last Stop

Over the Edge (Coming Soon)

Rachel Hatch Series

Drift

Downburst

Fever Burn

Smoke Signal

Firewalk

Whitewater

Aftershock

Whirlwind

Tsunami (2022)

Mitch Tanner Series

The Depth of Darkness

Into The Darkness

Deliver Us From Darkness

Cassie Quinn Series

Path of Bones

Whisper of Bones

Symphony of Bones

Etched in Shadow

Concealed in Shadow (2022)

Blake Brier Series

Unmasked

Unleashed

Uncharted

Drawpoint

Contrail

Detachment

Clear (Coming Soon)

Dalton Savage Series

Savage Grounds

Scorched Earth

Cold Sky (Coming Soon)

Maddie Castle Series

The Handler

Tracking Justice (Coming Soon)

Affliction Z Series

Affliction Z: Patient Zero

Affliction Z: Abandoned Hope

Affliction Z: Descended in Blood

Affliction Z : Fractured Part 1

Affliction Z: Fractured Part 2 (Fall 2021)

ABOUT THE AUTHOR

L.T. Ryan is a *USA Today* and international bestselling author. The new age of publishing offered L.T. the opportunity to blend his passions for creating, marketing, and technology to reach audiences with his popular Jack Noble series.

Living in central Virginia with his wife, the youngest of his three daughters, and their three dogs, L.T. enjoys staring out his window at the trees and mountains while he should be writing, as well as reading, hiking, running, and playing with gadgets. See what he's up to at http://ltryan.com.

Social Medial Links:

- Facebook (L.T. Ryan): https://www.facebook.com/LTRyanAuthor

- Facebook (Jack Noble Page): https://www.facebook.com/JackNobleBooks/

- Twitter: https://twitter.com/LTRyanWrites

- Goodreads: http://www.goodreads.com/author/show/6151659.L_T_Ryan

Printed in the USA
CPSIA information can be obtained
at www.ICGtesting.com
LVHW022349261223
767493LV00010B/774